The Beckoning World

Also by Douglas Bauer

THE BECKONING WORLD

A Novel

DOUGLAS BAUER

University of Iowa Press, Iowa City

University of Iowa Press, Iowa City 52242
Copyright © 2022 by Douglas Bauer
uipress.uiowa.edu
Printed in the United States of America

Design by Erin Kirk

Printed on acid-free paper

Library of Congress Cataloging-in-Publication Data
Names: Bauer, Douglas, author.
Title: The Beckoning World: A Novel / Douglas Bauer.
Description: Iowa City: University of Iowa Press, [2022]
Identifiers: LCCN 2021056908 (print) | LCCN 2021056909
    (ebook) | ISBN
9781609388478 (paperback) | ISBN 9781609388485 (ebook)
Subjects: GSAFD
Classification: LCC PS3552.A8358 B43 2022 (print) |
    LCC PS3552.A8358
    (ebook) | DDC 813/.54—dc23
LC record available at https://lccn.loc.gov/2021056908
LC ebook record available at https://lccn.loc.gov/2021056909

For Sue, more than ever

BOOK ONE

///

Earl and Emily

At which point I conceived a realm more real than life.
At which point there was at least some possibility.
Some possibility, in which I didn't believe, of being
   with her once more.

     —FORREST GANDER, "Beckoned"

PROLOGUE

October 15, 1918

The two soldiers left Macauley's general store with their sacks of black licorice and hard molasses candies and sat down on the bench just outside the door to watch the life of the village moving past. They were tall and lanky and fair-complexioned young men, and in their handsome, high-collared uniforms, they resembled one another very closely. One was nineteen, the other was twenty. The twenty-year-old bore a prominent scar, the feature that distinguished them, which ran beneath his lower lip like a plump white worm.

They lit cigarettes and smoked in a relaxed silence. They greeted the people passing by, tipping their caps to the women and nodding to the men, returning crisp salutes to those who crisply gave them. Their voices when they said hello were high-pitched and respectful. People were surprised, a few even startled, to come upon the two of them, these look-alike soldiers enjoying the ideal autumn sun. There was, in their handsomeness and the occasion of their being there, an aura of something like celebrity about them. And only later, as the shocking news spread, did people think to ask how they'd found their way from wherever they were camped on a Tuesday afternoon to that bench in front of Macauley's store.

As the soldiers sat there, a bird, a squawking blue jay, flew overhead and shat, hitting the small spot of bench between the two of them. They burst out laughing and began to argue about whether the bird had found or missed its target. Maybe it had been a sharpshooter taking morning target practice, aiming for that very spot and hitting it exactly. Or maybe it had flown all the way across the ocean, trained by the Huns to patrol America's skies, to look down for anyone in a uniform to shit on.

They sat a few minutes more, softly chuckling, pleased with their silliness, until the soldier with the scar said he was feeling light-headed. At the same time, he was having trouble getting his breath. He'd started smoking just a few days before, and he knew the cigarette was the reason for his dizziness and for the sense that his chest was suddenly closing. He flicked the cigarette away, *Goddamn weeds, why'd I start?* and ground it beneath his boot. He reached into his uniform's tunic pocket for his handkerchief and blew his nose and the cloth came away streaked luridly with blood. His friend helped him stand and asked an old woman who'd stopped to gawk at them for directions to a doctor. The house was fortunately close by, and when they got to the address they were told by the shy widow who helped the doctor run his office that he'd left an hour ago, a house call in the country.

As they sat waiting in the parlor, the soldier with the scar was growing very frightened and working not to show it, and after a while he turned to his friend and told him he should leave. That he'd be fine and they would both be in trouble if one of them didn't report back to their unit and explain what had happened.

His friend rose with some reluctance and said he was sure their lieutenant would tell him to return right away bearing orders for where to rejoin them the next day.

The soldier with the scar said he was sure of this too.

Left alone with the shy widow, who thought to bring him tea, he felt free to gasp desperately for breath, furious rhythms of breath, and after a while, from inside the first of the delusions he would suffer, he heard the gawking old lady who'd given them directions telling him he'd done right to send his friend away.

He died early that evening, lying on the office cot, bathed in sweat, the doctor, just returned, holding a wash pan under his chin to catch the coughed-up blood.

Word, of course, traveled swiftly through the town. Many more than had actually seen the young soldiers or been anywhere near them during their brief, sorrowful visit described passing the two of them, so memorably striking as they sat there on the bench.

As the news was repeated over and over, the soldiers became twins bearing an uncanny resemblance. To see them sitting next to one another outside Macauley's store was to have seen double. A few remembered noticing the prominent scar—*Have I got it right that he's the one't died?*—and eventually this detail was folded into the lore as having been some sort of childhood accident, which the twin who'd suffered it was probably glad for, if not at first, then in time, since the scar was the thing that had made him separate from his brother.

People said the fact that one had caught the influenza and the other had not felt even more haunting since the young men were identical. Someone said it was as if the scar were a mark made by God to help Him remember which one to give the influenza to. This appealed to a few as biblically compelling, some vengeful Old Testament episode, and they eagerly passed it on. But most, when hearing it, said *Hogwash* and *What rubbish*. The influenza wasn't the Lord's doing and even if people look exactly alike, He hardly needs any help keeping them straight since He made us all to start with.

When word of the soldier's death reached Earl, he thought immediately of the supper table talk a few nights before, when he'd learned of their visit. How innocent that conversation seemed to him now as he heard it in his head, how ignorant, the way they'd joked about the soldiers being there. And then, thinking of them being such a perfect pair, it inspired Earl to wonder, *Why the one and not the other?* And to imagine that the soldier who'd survived—wherever he'd disappeared to, wherever the unit was he needed to rejoin—must be asking that same thing. *Why him and not me too?* and it did not occur to Earl that the soldier who'd apparently been spared might be dead by now from the influenza too.

Thinking more, thinking harder, Earl began to see it as an instance of his belief in life's fated randomness. This is where his thoughts took him, it's as far as they extended. It was as if with his embrace of the life he'd made his way to, he now saw it as impregnable, its pleasures immune, and the fear that should have seized his heart when he heard the news did not.

What came to mind instead was the morning in Chicago, when he was seventeen, the day he rode the elevated train, and looking from his seat into the tenement he was passing, he saw the filthy little urchin, that half-naked dreamer who appeared to want the world, standing at his window and waving madly at the train, and Earl waving back as if waving to his twin.

CHAPTER ONE

His life, Earl Dunham's life in the mines, began when he was twelve in the camp town of Evans near the hamlet of Beacon in the subtly steep hills of southeastern Iowa. He sat for ten hours a day, his long legs bent at praying mantis angles, on a pine board bench with a dozen other boys, watching coal move past on a conveyor belt. Hunched over, his eyes squinting and alert, he reached into the unceasing flow of coal to remove the impurities, the pieces of slate, their edges as sharp as razor blades. Soon into the morning, his hands, like everyone else's, were bleeding from new cuts and from freshly opened old ones. The boys were forbidden from wearing gloves. The company believed gloves made it too difficult to grasp the shards of slate.

The air was granular, a weather of black dust as dense as hell's hot fog. The boys wore bandanas to cover their noses and their mouths. They looked like a gang of child outlaws in blackface. Their boss walked back and forth behind them. When he sensed their minds were wandering, he shouted, "*Hee*ya!" a herding call to livestock, and struck them in the back with a heavy stick. Their postures and their thoughts came instantly to attention. Some of the boys' backs showed ladder rungs of bruises climbing their spines. He was doing them a favor. Often, boys who grew distracted got their hands and arms caught in the conveyor.

It was 1909.

The mine was named Eureka.

Earl mostly avoided the boss's stick. He was able to keep his eyes on the belt of passing coal while his thoughts took him away to the vital places in his life—his bed, for instance, where he wished he still lay sleeping. Or his mother's every Sunday dinner of fatback and beans and cornbread. Or actually, any hour of Sunday, since Sunday was his day of light above the ground. Especially the Sundays in spring and summer and into early fall, when the men and boys played baseball virtually dawn to dark on the dirt lot behind the double row of run-down miners' cottages.

The coal pouring from the cars onto the belt was a deafening cascade. The conveyor's wheels and gears groaned and screeched, operatic sounds of great suffering complaint. Muffled in their masks, the boys stayed silent as they worked. There was no way their voices could be heard in the high chaos of noise, and really what was there to say about this world that they hadn't learned, hadn't felt, hadn't mumbled to themselves in the first hour of the first day they'd descended into it?

At fourteen, Earl left the pine-board bench to become a coal car driver. He stood at the front of the car, the reins in his hands, guiding the mules along the underground tracks. This work was not so grim, and his mind was naturally fanciful, younger than his age, and he liked to pretend he was steering a chariot in battle.

Two more years passed before he became a miner, laboring in the warrens of rooms carved out of the coal. He swung his pick into the walls, leaving the supporting pillars of coal. But the company wanted that coal too, and his challenge became a delicate felling of the pillars while he stayed poised to flee should the room start to collapse. He willed the task a death sport, as close to play as he could make it, a contest between his talent with the pick and the mine's eagerness to kill him.

He left the camp in Evans a year later to escape not the mines, but his father, Sean. They often ended up working side by side, and it seemed to Earl that at some point every morning, his father slipped in, stepping out of the dark, to stand next to him, a smirk on his face. In the closet-close space, his father's elbow or his hip frequently grazed Earl, and his father's touch in any form, in any way, revulsed him.

The rhythmic meanness of this life meant the two of them had something to quarrel about as they drank at the table after supper.

Earl got drunk quickly. He hadn't at his age learned to hold his liquor. He never would; age had little to do with it.

Slouched in a kitchen chair, he would look past the low doorway into the tiny sitting room where his mother, Dorothea, sat with her knitting in the weak lamplight, her eyes straining, her forehead scored with lines of concentration. She appeared oblivious, indifferent to the voices in the kitchen. To her, they were simply the routine after-supper sounds.

One night, as he and his father argued, it came suddenly to Earl why they fought so eagerly. It was because his father hated him, and he had grown to hate him in return. This was a straightforward insight, not a question he'd been pondering or an answer he'd been seeking. It simply presented itself to him, pure, like a bestowal. A feeling of lightness and reprieve moved through his drunkenness and reached his heart. And he saw then that his father hated the whole of life, but with an appetite that thrilled him, and that it thrilled him most when he was drunk, when his hatred was a love for every ugly second of it.

That night, his father was shouting on about Earl's ignorance in general, and in particular some pansy-ass thing he'd seen him do that day, swing his pick so recklessly at one point, by all rights the ceiling should've fallen, should've killed them all. "You and a slug switch brains, he'd fucking lose."

From inside his epiphany, Earl heard all this as noise in the far distance. He rose slowly from his chair and placed both hands on the table to steady himself. Much taller than his father, he loomed over him.

"Where you going?" Sean asked, affronted. In the kitchen's shadows, his wrinkled face looked flat as an iron's.

Earl said nothing. He left the kitchen, unsteady on his feet, needing to breathe some outside air. But at the door, he paused. His work shovel and his pick stood there, propped up against the wall next to his father's. He reached for the shovel and held it, testing its weight and balance in his hands. He looked to be imagining it for some new purpose, and he was. He was picturing himself coming back into the kitchen with the shovel and striking the bastard in the side of the head. His father had hit him routinely when he was younger, before he grew tall and strong and could easily fend him off. He'd hit Earl hard enough to knock him down, but not so hard he couldn't get up, a miner's touch for the strength with which to swing a pick.

And now Earl saw the shovel crushing his father's cheek and jawbone. He saw him dropping to the floor, blood seaming from his ear, his eyes rolled back in his head, their whites showing improbably pretty, like a pair of ivory buttons.

But as he imagined the blow, he could only hear it as a dull, flat thud, and he felt greatly let down by this soft-sounding violence. He needed the shovel to ring murderously as it struck, and the powerful depth of his disappointment frightened him. As he set the shovel down, he told himself what he must do.

He lay awake the following night until he heard his parents' snores through the wall. He rose, already dressed. He'd already packed as well, his few possessions stuffed into an old gunnysack. He tiptoed past their room to the kitchen. He'd written a note, saying he'd be untraceable. He said he'd send repayment soon for the money he was stealing from the sitting room cabinet. He placed the note on the table, opened the door, and stepped outside. The night was moonless and starless and the sky was pale with clouds.

He spent the rest of the night hiding in one of the storage huts next to the mineshaft. When he heard the first work whistle, his heart leapt to the fact that this would not be a day like all the days to which that sound had wakened him. He hurried from the hut and waited in high weeds next to the railroad tracks. When the Minneapolis and Saint Louis train arrived to fill its cars, he climbed into an empty boxcar.

He rode east with the coal. He had something like a thought that he and the coal were escaping together. He didn't know his rare good fortune at having the boxcar to himself, no hoboes, no criminals, no feral perverts. Just a family of emigrating rats, as he quickly came to see them, scurrying about but keeping considerately to their corner of the car, their eyes tiny, bright pins shining from scattered nests of straw. Otherwise, the grander world he sought was visible to him as a vertical stripe of blurred countryside, barely wider than a ribbon, made by the gap where the car's sliding doors didn't meet.

And it was world enough for Earl.

He spent three nights in Chicago in an Uptown boarding house on Wilson Avenue. He was two months shy of eighteen. His deep brown eyes were bovine with innocence. His thatch of sandy hair was thick and untamable. His very large ears lay fortunately close to his head. He looked like a river rascal out of Twain.

The weather was hot, the air so humid it had a thickness almost tactile, but his first night there he lay shivering with excitement. He came to the open window and looked down. He saw a group of men on the sidewalk below. They wore soot-powdered derbies and frayed straw boaters. He watched and listened as they laughed and argued and spat in several languages. He saw packs of boys, potato-faced hooligans, running wildly among the men like fierce pets off their leashes. He watched them racing about in the street, heard their cries of vicious joy, and what he saw was a permission to move crazily wherever impulse took you because life let you do it.

Early the next morning, he boarded an elevated train. He had no destination. Like a boy at an amusement park who'd discovered a thrilling new ride, he simply wanted to be on another train. It rattled through the city at a southeast meander. His car was sparsely filled at this early weekend hour.

He left his seat and made his way to the open platform at the front. The city's sky was pewter-colored and held its sulfurous smell, but Earl compared it to what he was used to breathing at this hour. To him, this air was crystalline and its scent was ambrosial.

"Smells like the stockyards this morning."

Earl turned to see another passenger stepping out onto the platform. He wore denim overalls and a stained wool cap.

"I've smelled worse," said Earl.

"I could make a joke at your expense," said the man. His smile was satisfied. "I could say, 'you mean there's days you smell worse than you do now?' I could say that, but I won't."

Earl was taking in the morning with too much pleasure to be bothered, and he said in response, "And you can see the sun." He closed his eyes and gave his face to it.

"The sun shines everywhere, praise the Lord," said the man.

"No, not everywhere," Earl said.

The tracks cut with the authority of a primary vein through the packed-in neighborhoods. The train slowed to a metal-shrieking crawl for sharp turns, passing so close to rooming house windows it seemed to Earl he could lean out and touch the people inside. An old man in his undershirt, his bones looking to Earl like brittle twigs, held a magnifying glass to the newspaper he'd spread out on the table. A boy, maybe four or five, maybe six years old, stood on a chair at the window, his eyes avid for the morning. He wore a filthy T-shirt, but he was otherwise buck naked, his hooded little penis curling like a comma, and when he waved eagerly at the train crawling past, Earl waved eagerly back. A woman looking ravaged as a Goya refugee stood at her stove stirring something in a pot. She wiped her brow with the back of her hand, and Earl imagined reaching in and moving the lock of hair off her forehead. Each world, framed by its window, drew him powerfully in. He saw the common squalor, but to him it looked exotic. Every room, every person in every window he passed, seemed to beckon him; to beckon him; to beckon him; to beckon him.

CHAPTER TWO

///

May 1914

Compelled as he was by the unruly festival of Chicago, Earl decided that to survive, he was going to have to resume the miner's life. He felt no real regret about this, for wherever he might go, whatever the mine, it would be a place in the world where his father wasn't.

He moved east and south, a nomad tracing the Midwest's bituminous seams. His pattern was to spend a few months in a camp, then head for another. It was easy to find work. Sometimes, after he'd settled in a new place, he indulged the fantasy that he was on the lam, and he liked the sense of mischief this gave him for a while.

He'd mailed repayment of the money he'd stolen, including with it a note addressed to his mother saying he was well. He gave no address. He asked nothing about his father, and the omission gave him pleasure.

It came to Earl in nightmares: The old man falling to the floor from the sadly soundless blow. The lines of blood tracing from his ear. The pretty ivory-button eyes.

Months became a year and a year became two and he was working in Riverton, on the Sangamon River, in the rich coal fields of central Illinois, when his life took its first extraordinary turn.

There'd been Sunday baseball games at every camp, and he played with the joy he'd always brought to them. He was a capable hitter; his years swinging a pick precisely at a pillar of coal had sharpened his eye. But what he loved to do was pitch, and he'd begun on his own, trying this grip and that, to find ways to make the ball dart and drop and veer. His only instruction came from the book *Pitching in a Pinch: Baseball from the Inside*, by the great Christy Mathewson. Earl had spotted a copy one day, lying by the side of the railroad tracks. When he'd reached down to pick it up, he felt powerfully a sense that he'd been meant to find it. He assumed someone had dropped it from the window of a train. Its pages were bleached and warped and stuck together, but enough of the text had survived. Before leaving school at twelve, he'd been an indifferent student, but here was a book more than worth the work of reading. There were entertaining anecdotes, lively baseball lore, and along with all that, Mathewson described how to throw his famous screwball, which he called the fade-away, as if it were a ghostly pitch that vanished just as it reached the batter. He warned of the strain it put on the elbow and advised not to throw it more than a few times in a game. It was advice, he confessed, he himself found hard to follow.

It was dusk on a cool and overcast spring Sunday, and a group of miners had just beaten the Riverton town team on the local field where the outfield gave to the vast quilt of open land with its rectangular patches of fields and earth and pastures. Not as many people as usual, no more than a hundred, had come to watch. Riverton normally played teams from nearby towns, Rochester, Buffalo, Dawson, half a dozen others. The players rode down the main street to the field in a horse-drawn wagon while the manager sounded a call to the game by blowing sourly on his dented trumpet. People left their houses and followed after the wagon as in a children's fable. But today, the other team had been made up of miners, and miners were viewed by everyone in Riverton who wasn't one as a sect of soiled albinos, emerging from their workdays weak-eyed as moles, coughing thick, tarry phlegm.

Earl had never pitched so well. His fastball climbed. His curveball broke abruptly. His spitter weaved its inebriate path toward the plate. He threw Mathewson's fade-away three or four times, and it cut sharply into the right-handed batters as they were starting their swings. The Riverton team had gotten three hits, none of them solid, and the players skulked away, small and surly in defeat.

Earl was leaving the field with his friend, Donnie, the miners' catcher, a toadishly built young man, when someone sitting alone in the bleachers behind the backstop waved and caught his eye. The man was short and fat, round as a buddha. He was dressed as if for August in a soiled, wrinkled, cream-colored linen suit. Picture a buddha as a derelict Dixie colonel sitting in the gloaming in the stands behind home plate on a Sunday in spring in Riverton, Illinois.

"I watched you pitch," the man said to Earl, as he and Donnie approached. "The swings those farmers took, they looked like the last-place team in the epileptic league." He stood and made his way down, light-footed on the bleachers. "Saul Weintraub," he said, offering Earl his hand. His clean-shaven face was large and round. His eyes and mouth and nose were bunched closely in the middle of it, so there was a lot of large, round face left empty. His skin was smooth and pink; in the way of many fat men, his age was hard to guess.

He turned to Donnie. "You played well yourself, son. I recall only three passed balls."

"Two," Donnie said.

"You're right, of course, that there were two. Arithmetic! It's why I nearly failed first grade." His smile stretched extremely, dividing his large globe of a face in half. He said to Donnie, "It can't be easy catching pitches that move as much as his." He nodded at Earl as he said this, then looked again at Donnie. "Would you mind if I spoke a few words to your friend?"

It took Donnie a moment to realize he was being asked to leave. He looked at Earl, they both shrugged, then Earl winked at Donnie, a kind of fatherly reassurance, and said, "I'll catch up with you." He and Weintraub watched him walk away into the fading daylight.

"It was three," Weintraub said quietly to Earl, "as I'm sure you know. One in the fourth, two in the sixth, and no harm done with the bases empty."

"What's on your mind?" Earl asked. "What's this about?"

Weintraub swept his arm toward the bleachers. "Step into my office," he said. "Earl—may I call you Earl? I asked two ladies sitting near me if they knew your name. I determined they were miners' wives. Sad little creatures. Old before their time. My heavens, they should devote more time and care to their appearance. Teeth, for instance, would help them both immensely."

They were now sitting side by side on the bleachers. Earl leaned back, resting on his elbows, his long legs stretched out in front of him. Weintraub, beside him, was perched rotundly.

"In my mind," Weintraub continued, "I called them Mrs. Forlorn and Mrs. Dejected. When I meet people, I like to award them names that reflect my first impression of them. It's a way I entertain myself on my travels, and it serves to keep my vocabulary active. But you were naturally wondering why I wished to speak to you."

Earl said, "And I still am."

"Of course you are!" Weintraub said. "It's about the things you made the baseball do today."

"You waited just to tell me that?"

"Not just, not just," Weintraub said, "though that's certainly central, isn't it?"

"I don't know. Is it?" Earl said.

Weintraub turned to look at Earl more directly. "Let me ask you, if I might, how you've ended up here in Riverton. I have to say, as a town it looks to occupy a distressingly low rung on the ladder of cultural amenities."

"It's got a coal mine," Earl said, "and I mine coal." The afternoon was getting cooler, and he reached for the flannel shirt he'd brought and slipped it on. As he did, he gave Weintraub an amused, head-to-toe assessment. "I'll ask you the same question. You don't look like you mine coal. Your white suit there would get awfully dirty."

"No, I don't, and yes, it would," Weintraub said. He smiled once more, this time wanly. "Actually, my being in Riverton is a happy accident." He cleared his throat and his voice got softer. "Well, not 'happy,' not at all, I spoke in error in that regard. I was returning this afternoon from my aunt Bessie's funeral in Springfield. I loved my aunt dearly, and my heart was heavy as a stone as I was motoring along, when I happened to look over and see your game in progress.

The sight of it instantly brightened my mood." Now his first voice, its liveliness, returned. "There are a few things in this life I'm gluttonous for, and one of them is watching a baseball game." He absently patted his belly as he said this. "I would journey to watch the lepers play the lame if I knew the place and time."

Earl was sucking on the stem of a furry headed weed he'd plucked from the grass beside the bleachers. He had no idea what to make of this man. His appearance, his manner, his very words. He was a portly elf, speaking, affably, a language that Earl felt he could only understand odd phrases of.

Weintraub began to ask more questions. He asked Earl his age. He asked him if—and Earl's being so young, he certainly hoped not—if he had a wife. Or a wife and, God forbid, a mewling little tyke or two. He asked him how devoted he was to a life of mining coal. He said that, speaking in all ignorance, he'd be hard pressed to fathom such a loyalty.

Then he changed his conversational direction and asked Earl where he'd learned to throw his breaking pitches. Earl said he'd taught himself and then, giving credit where it was due, he mentioned Christy Mathewson's book. "You ever heard of it?"

Weintraub nodded. "More than that, like you I've read it, and, not to disappoint, but I've been told many of the stories Mr. Mathewson shares are, shall we say, tall tales. Very tall." He raised his hand high above his head to show just how tall they were. "But as for the way to throw a screwball—his 'fade-away,' he calls it, as you know—and why you shouldn't very often, there he likely writes the truth. I've heard stories of old men, old screwballers, their arms hanging from their shoulders like salamis in a butcher's window, and twisted so badly the backs of their hands brush against their thighs. Although, who knows, all that may be apocryphal."

Earl was telling himself he should be at the least annoyed by all the questions, all this prying into his life, and normally he would have been. He was sure he would have been. But he was feeling something he couldn't quite admit to. He caught the tummler's twinkle in Weintraub's eye, and whatever was behind it, Earl sensed it was genuine. And maybe most important, he was flattered by the little fat man being curious about him—the reasons almost didn't matter—because, to this point in Earl's life, no one had been.

Saul Weintraub pulled a blue bandana from his suit pants' front pocket, and in the cooling twilight he wiped sweat from the back of his neck. He took some time to do this, as if he felt the need to freshen up before continuing.

"A few months ago, I was hired as a scout by the Chicago Cubs. That's Chicago, as in Chicago. Cubs, as in Cubs. My brother-in-law, my sister Winnifred's husband, is well connected in South Side real estate and is himself a White Sox fan, but he knows the Cubs' general manager, I can't recall right now just how." Weintraub smiled again. "Are you following so far?"

"It's not exactly complicated," Earl said. "'So far.'" He'd meant to offer this lightly, but that's not how it sounded, for the moment he'd heard Weintraub say he was a scout, Earl's heart was a commotion, his mind urgent with the effort to keep his thoughts from going where they'd already gone, no way to stop them. So his voice was edgy, jumpy, and sounded falsely like anger.

Weintraub nodded. "That was patronizing of me, asking if you followed. I apologize. What I mean to say is I've loved baseball all my life, I emerged from my dear mama's womb shouting 'Batter up!' and I cherish the game's nuances. Harold, my brother-in-law, knows this very well, and when the Cubs' general manager happened to mention that he'd been looking for someone to scout parts of the Midwest, Harold said, 'I have your man.' To make a long story short and as fate would have it, I've secured the occupation of my dreams."

At some point the furry headed weed had fallen from Earl's mouth and he was wishing, like an infant, that he still had it to suck on. "Well, good for you," he said. "Why are you telling me all this?" The adrenaline moving in him was nothing else but hope, dangerously exposed, a hope for something he'd had no idea was a life, a world, a man might wish were his, and he *was* getting angry now, feeling the need to protect himself from his hope and knowing very well he couldn't.

"Oh," Weintraub said. Earl saw his look of surprise. "Well, I suppose I wanted to establish my credentials. I assumed it was plain what I was leading up to."

"Make it plainer," Earl said.

"Fair enough," Weintraub said. "I'm tempted to sign you to a minor league contract right here, on the spot." He smiled his equatorial smile. "I always have some contracts with me in case I happen on a game featuring a coal miner pitcher who's learned how to throw a screwball from reading *Pitching in a Pinch*." His laugh was a cadent, eyes-closed, *eek! eek!* sound. He opened them to look at Earl as if inviting him to join in, but Earl's face gave him nothing. Even this pause for silly laughter felt to him like a delay, like a cruel tease. "So. But," Weintraub continued, "tempted as I am, I'll need to watch you pitch at least a second time." He nodded more firmly. "Now tell me, how does all that sound?"

This, then, was how the world worked. You're playing a game on a Sunday afternoon, pitching better than you can remember for no particular reason you can point to, and a portly Jewish baseball scout on his way home from his beloved aunt's funeral happens by and pulls over to watch the ball jump out of your hand as if you and it were joined in a sublime conspiracy. *As fate would have it.* Saul Weintraub's phrase from a moment ago.

Such was the essence of Earl's thoughts and close to what he'd felt the morning he rode the El: that he was peeking in on life from a moving train, life in all its desperate appeal. But if everything was decided by what you couldn't control—the ball doing its own dance, the little fat man motoring past by wild coincidence—weren't you always, in the end, looking in on it, your life? Reaching vainly out to touch it? Living at the mercy of it?

A part of him, too, was still disbelieving.

"There's always a pick-up game on Sunday if we don't find another town to play."

"I'll be there," Weintraub said. "As I said, I'd happily watch—"

"The lepers play the lame," Earl said, and for the first time in speaking to Weintraub his smile was unguarded.

Weintraub extended his hand and Earl shook it.

Now Weintraub stood and stretched and stepped away from the bleachers. He offered Earl a ride to wherever he was going. Earl shook his head. The camp was a short walk, and he wanted the time and the air.

But more than that, he needed just to sit there in the quiet, the sky tinted now with lavender evening, and let in the pleasure he'd been fighting to keep out. He sat, poised as a held breath, while a wildness moved inside him. And with it, still, the doubt that remained. For Weintraub was as different as Earl could have imagined from his idea of a baseball scout—some leather-skinned cracker, a plug of tobacco swelling his cheek, a hitch in his walk from the injury that had ended his career. "How many others have you signed?" he asked. "Am I your first?"

"As the lecher asked the damsel?" Weintraub said, and laughed again. *Eek, eek!* Then his face grew serious. "I understand your concern. That's likely why I took such pains to tell you the story of my good fortune. I mean, if my brother-in-law weren't friends with . . . and so on and so forth. But as I said, I've loved this game all my life. I've studied it with a devotee's passion." Earl heard another tone coming into Weintraub's voice—solemn, jester free. "So let me just assure you, despite what my corpulence might suggest, I know baseball talent when I see it, and this afternoon I saw it." They looked evenly at each other until Earl nodded.

"Good," Weintraub said, and he gave the bleachers a quick tap with his knuckles.

Earl watched him moving away toward his automobile, his fat man's walk a tick-tock gait.

"I am *not* in a dream," Earl said out loud, reasoning that nobody in a dream says he's not in one, and saying he wasn't was his way of making sure.

"Mr. Weintraub!" he called.

Weintraub stopped and turned around. "Changed your mind about my driving you somewhere?"

"No, I'm fine," Earl said. "I was wondering. What's my name?"

"You mean it isn't Earl?" Weintraub called. "You're asking me to guess?"

"No, no. Like Mrs. Forlorn and Mrs. Dejected. What's mine?"

There was a silence. With so little daylight left, it was difficult for Earl to make him out from this distance. "You're a hard one," Earl heard finally, Weintraub's voice coming to him virtually disembodied. "You don't give away much." Another longer silence, and Earl surprised himself with his patience as he waited. "I'll call you Mr. Cocksure. Yes. That would seem to fit. It's how you appeared to be on the mound today. Cocksure. It's a marvelous vocabulary word, don't you agree?"

On the bleachers, Earl frowned. He'd never heard the word. He considered its syllables. Surely, he thought, that could not be what it meant. The town library was open for two hours on Sunday afternoons. He would go next week before the game and look up the definition.

He heard, behind the drape of darker evening, Weintraub's Model-T rattling to life.

The night before he left to play for the Waterloo Loons in the Class B Three-I League, Earl sat on a hilltop outside the mining camp with Donnie. They were far enough from the town and the mines so that the air, which had stayed chilly, didn't hold its usual stench—a smell like rodents dying in the walls. They'd been celebrating since their shift had ended, and because Earl got drunk so easily, that's what he was, and Donnie was too. Earl couldn't remember why they'd decided to take a walk, but he was glad they had. This was his favorite spot in Riverton, so it must have been his idea. In daylight from up here, you could see the ribbon of river, gilded with light, as it flowed toward Beardstown, where it joined the Illinois.

They were sitting with their legs crossed, which emphasized Donnie's toad shape. Earl narrowed his eyes to try to focus on Donnie, who'd gone silent. Donnie was normally a garrulous drunk, but this was not a normal hour. His friend was leaving in the morning for a life vastly better than his own. Earl understood and he sympathized, but the world was just too fine and his spirit was impervious. Even drunk, he felt the air on his skin perfectly. It was fainter than a breeze, just a light caress. That's how fine the world was.

They heard a coyote howl from somewhere in the near distance.

Breaking his silence, Donnie said, "It's like a kid I knew growing up."

"What?" Earl asked.

"That coyote," Donnie said.

"I meant *where*," Earl said. "I know I said *what*, but what that meant was where."

Donnie said, annoyed, "Out there somewhere. You didn't hear it?"

"Where *you* grew up," Earl said. "You never told me where you grew up."

"Indiana," Donnie said. "Kokomo." He pronounced it with effort, needing time between the syllables.

"You never told me," Earl repeated.

"You never asked," Donnie said.

Earl thought. "That's true," he said. "I apologize."

"Some kid in town, wasn't right in the head. What's their name, the family? . . . Can't remember, I'm too drunk. He'd walk around at night making sounds like that."

Cooperatively, the coyote howled.

"Like that?" Earl asked.

"Just," Donnie said.

Earl asked, "Why'd they let him out?"

"He's a coyote," Donnie said. "He's a fucking wild animal. Nobody let him out."

"Jesus," Earl said. "The *kid*."

"He lives outdoors. He howls at night. That's what coyotes do."

"The *kid*," Earl repeated. "They shouldn't let him out."

"Oh," Donnie said. He waited for a hiccup to pass, then another, even stronger, that made his chest jump. "Actually, come to think, he was the smart one in the family."

Earl laughed, which started Donnie, and they were quickly helpless inside their laughter, Donnie snorting, Earl making high, pig-squealing sounds. They fell onto their sides, pushed themselves upright, and fell back again. A full minute passed as they fed each other's fits while a bright affection passed between them and their drunkenness let them feel it unembarrassed. When the laughter had played itself out, they lay on their backs, exhausted from it.

"Ah, Christ," Donnie said. He gave a long, savoring exhale.

Earl looked up at the stars. The sky was dense with them. He saw it as a ceiling of coal with countless pinpricks of light somehow shining through. Through the coal to light. *Perfect*, was Earl's drunken thought.

The coyote called again, causing a weak trading of giggles that trailed off quickly. Earl closed his eyes to wait and listen. When the coyote cried once more, he heard its haunting tremolo. To him, it sounded wise, sounded savvy, sounded shrewd.

CHAPTER THREE

May 12, 1916   *Waterloo, Iowa*

The first time Earl visited the Good Day luncheonette on Washington Street, he and several teammates entered as a ruckus, antic and oblivious. Anyone watching them stumble through the door, still in their uniforms and filled with exuberance, would have guessed they were celebrating a game they'd just won. Except that the Rock Island team's train had broken down twenty miles from Waterloo, and Earl and the others had all the stoked-up energy they'd have used up if they'd played.

They headed for a long communal table, there were nine or ten of them, shouting friendly insults and shoving one another. Earl led the way. The luncheonette opened at five-thirty and closed at three. It was nearly half past two, and the room was otherwise empty of customers. Though it was new to Earl, it felt oddly familiar and inviting, despite the rough plank floor, the low tin ceiling, every surface gray and old and worn, the air rank with tobacco smoke and greasy, fried food smells.

The two waitresses had been cleaning the tabletops with soapy rags, their bent-over postures like Millet gleaners in the field. They'd stopped and watched, exchanging disappointed looks as the ballplayers entered. They were both young and strong and healthy, but at this hour their feet hurt and their backs were tired. One of them, Irma, was working next to the dirty front window. The second waitress, standing next to the table Earl chose, was Emily Marchand.

She watched the players arranging themselves around the table, and her attention was drawn to Earl at the near end. Even as he was sitting down, smiling and nodding, an energy like ardor came off him, which made the others' slack and stuporous in comparison.

Gretel, the plump cook, had come out into the room. She'd heard the voices shouting over one another and the chair legs scraping the wide-plank floor, and now she announced, "The stew's all that's left."

There was a flurry of talk at the table about a sudden hankering for stew. It simply had to be stew. No one had better try to talk them out of stew.

A few minutes later, Irma started down one side of the table, Emily down the other. From where he sat at one end, Earl was watching her closely. She was a petite young woman with rich chestnut hair, which she wore attractively in a full bun. Her round face was solemn, its powder of freckles helping to soften the solemnity. She moved from one player to the next, placing bowls of the stew in front of them. She was trying not to show she heard their whispered appraisals, but she couldn't keep a lightness from enlivening her face.

Earl saw her change of expression, he read it rightly as amusement, and it caused his heart to lift with a kind of thrilled relief. When Emily set his bowl in front of him, he lowered his nose to it and inhaled theatrically. "Wonderful," he said. He looked up at her and smiled. "What kind of stew is this?"

"Brown," Emily said. "We call it 'brown.'"

"Lucky me," he said. "Brown's my favorite flavor."

Emily's smile was quick. "Then you should eat here every day."

He returned three or four times over the next few weeks, always with other players, and Emily came to conclude that he flirted indiscriminately. On his second visit, he rose at the end of his meal and walked over to Gretel, who'd left the kitchen for a few minutes to sit and smoke her pipe. Without a word, he took the spatula she held from habit like a greasy wand and bent from the waist to kiss the back of her hand. Gretel, deeply charmed, made a sound as if she had the croup. Earl looked out of the corner of his eye to see who might be watching. Emily was, but so was Irma, the other waitress, and a couple of Earl's teammates, grinning idiotically. Earl smiled in Emily's direction, which pleased her, and then she quickly felt foolish for having thought his little show was meant for her.

Six weeks before she met Earl in the Good Day, Emily had informed her father, Frank, that she felt it was time she learned something of the world, and he could get her started by helping her find work away from the family farm, which sat three miles south of the village of Hinton. Four miles farther south was the town of Sioux City. She had recently turned nineteen.

"'Something of the world'?" her father asked. "What's that mean exactly?"

He was sitting at their kitchen table. Three tall east-facing windows looked across a sloping lawn to a cornfield, and the room was filled on sunny mornings with an outdoors brightness. The kitchen wallpaper was a pattern of climbing roses, and he liked to make the bad joke— all his jokes were bad, which was why he liked to make them—that this morning light kept them blooming fatly.

Emily turned from the woodstove to bring her father's breakfast to him. Her mother, Lottie, had as always risen first and eaten and was outside in the barnyard, well into morning chores. She was a quick-moving woman, elfin-sized. She stayed out of disagreements between her husband and her daughter until they asked for her opinion, which unfailingly they did.

Emily said, "I don't know what it means *exactly*." She set his plate in front of him. "I'm hoping to find out what I want to learn about the world by going out into it." Her voice was low and unruffled.

Her father took a bite of eggs. Like his wife, he was barely more than five feet tall and very thin. Given his size, the amount of weight he could lift and the immensity of the loads he could push and pull and carry as he went about his farm work were legendary in Hinton. Only his wife called him by his name. From the time he was a boy, he'd been known to everyone as Rooster because he walked like one. When she was a little girl, Emily had assumed his high-stepping fowl's gait was an entertainment meant for her.

At the table, he took a sip of coffee. He adored his daughter and admired her intelligence, which was to say he was a little fearful of it. He'd had no hint this was what she'd been feeling.

"But we already let you finish school," he said.

Emily wasn't insulted by her father's remark. She understood it was innocent, well-intentioned even, and she'd been prepared for him to say something of the sort. She adored him as much as he adored her and felt she knew him so well she could anticipate almost anything he might do or say. She thought she could tell when he was thinking to roll a cigarette. She believed she could sense when he was feeling pain from his worsening arthritis, no matter how well he worked to mask it.

All her young life she'd loved the sense of his attention protectively enfolding her. But over the past months, she'd started to fear she might be coming to rely on it. She wasn't sure why she was feeling this way. Maybe it had to do with her recent birthday. But more likely, more deeply, she'd been sensing as she moved through her days that if she paused to take note of whatever she was doing at that instant, it was as if she were *recalling* it, recalling having lived it. Not that she was wishing to summon her past, but that her *present* seemed her past. And if this was how it felt to live her life at nineteen, what would it be like in ten, in twenty years, when she'd have so much *more* of a past that felt like her present? This was the very language she couldn't get out of her head, and she heard its awkwardness as a symptom of her ignorance.

Feeding more wood to the stove before frying her eggs, she said, with her back turned to her father, "I don't think what I learned in school has much to do with anything I want to find out now."

"Hmm," Rooster said. He stabbed at his eggs and drank more coffee. He was a quickly certain and warmly biased little man, and *his* interest in the world was aggressively parochial. He knew the long life of the farm—it had been his parents'. He knew the many ways of weather that determined his days; he knew the nuanced narratives of the seasons. The work, the life, the husbandry, the homely wisdom—all of it came to him as naturally as breath. Everything else was his deep feelings for his wife and his daughter.

He watched Emily moving in the kitchen from the stove to the sink pump and back, and in his mind he again heard her saying she didn't know exactly what she wished to learn about the world. He told himself that her mother had taught her to cook and had tried in vain to teach her to sew. He told himself that he'd advised her years ago to picture green, sweet-smelling places if she was spreading manure or slopping the hogs. Wasn't *that* the world, at least until she married? That, plus her girlfriends from her school days, and the books she loved to read?

"Where're you going to go to find out about the world?"

At the stove, the skillet sizzling, her back still turned to him, she said, "Somewhere, I don't know. That's why I'm asking you to help."

"You could learn about it from right here. You could step outside and walk across the pasture and climb the ridge and see the world for quite a distance in four directions and ask all kinds of questions about what was going on in it. You could get to be a regular philosopher is what you could get to be."

She carried her plate of eggs and bacon to the table and sat down. She frowned at him as if to say, *Surely you can do better than that*, and then her face broke nearly, but not quite, into a smile. It was a quite particular look, and one so familiar to Rooster that he saw it right away for what it was—her signal that said, *Shall we begin?* There might as well have been a sound that went with it—a bell ringing, a loud switch clicking on. It was the joy of the contest! Days of argument during which he would remain firm in his position, and so would she while she waited for his resolve to erode. It was their long-familiar pattern, and Rooster understood she'd come to count on it, for he knew how much *he* did.

He pushed his chair away from the table.

"Where are you going? We were talking," she said.

"I'll be back," he said, as he got up and headed for the door.

Outside, he walked the length of the porch and leaned against a post and looked up at the scrim of morning clouds. He was forty-one years old, and lately, for the past six months or so, he'd been feeling like an old man more days than not. The arthritis in his hands and back had arrived suddenly and announced its stay, moving steadily deeper into his bones and joints. This morning, for no reason, he'd waked feeling a quite tolerable discomfort.

Still looking at the sky, the thin clouds making an anemic sun behind them, he reached for the buttons on his overalls and undid them. He set his stance, flexed his knees, and aimed, and his arcing stream glistened in the chilly morning light. He liked to say—it annoyed Emily no end to hear it—that pissing for distance was the one thing in this world men could do that women couldn't. Another of his dumb jokes, yes, but this was one he saw real truth in.

Finished, he leaned again against the porch post. He looked up once more to watch the sky, the listless sun. From the barn where Lottie had started the milking came a low, extended moo, and Rooster heard the sound as the whole farm collectively pondering what to do and what to say and how to steer through this latest with his Emily.

At the table, she'd listened to him walking to the edge of the porch. She knew what he was up to, and it seemed to her a low way to distract her so he could win points in their brand-new argument. When he came back into the kitchen, Emily turned in her chair to face him. "Daddy, I've told you before, I really wish you'd—"

"Let's this time skip the song and dance."

"What song and dance?" Emily asked, and damned if he could tell from the look on her face and the sound of her voice whether she was pretending not to know what he meant.

He said he was offering a compromise. He would write to Patricia in Waterloo to ask if Emily could visit until the end of summer. That should be far enough away for long enough so she could get all she wanted to learn about the world. In any case, it would have to do. "For the *summer*," Rooster repeated, emphasizing.

"Aunt Patricia?" Emily said. She didn't know her father's older sister well. The distance to Waterloo meant they didn't often visit back and forth. But she liked her, felt in fact a bit awestruck in her company and, growing up, had thought the story of how she'd met her husband, Melvin, a kind of fairy tale.

Rooster said, "She's always had a million big ideas about the way the world should work. Maybe she can show you some. Maybe she can find you something to do—a maid or helping out in a shop. Something, I don't know."

He paused. "You said just now, you 'really wish'? What? You really wish I'd what?"

Emily didn't know how to answer. Really, what did it matter if her father stood at the end of the porch and relieved himself in that ridiculous way he somehow found amusing?

And so, in the spring of 1916, she journeyed east, two hundred miles, to Waterloo. Her Uncle Melvin, as it happened, knew the owner of the Good Day. She'd been working there for a month, feeling, all in all, quite pleased with the sense of being on her own in the world, the afternoon Earl and his teammates came stumbling in like boisterous boys at recess and sat down at the long table and raucously ate stew.

He started coming to the luncheonette for breakfast by himself, and one morning in late June, he paused as he was leaving, his hand on the doorknob, turned to Emily and said, "I'm pitching tomorrow. It'll start before you close here, but you could see some innings if you came right after." He told her what trolley would take her directly to the park.

She knew almost nothing about the game of baseball, she wasn't sure what an inning was, but she had to think she knew what it meant that he was inviting her to come, and when she looked at his face, she was stopped by his smile. Not by its usual uncomplicated dazzle, but the opposite. It looked shy, tentative. Yes, he was still being flirtatious, but now, she sensed, accidentally so. For in this smile she read a nervousness, which she took to mean he was feeling uncertain, that he was earnest and sincere. Uncertainty. Earnestness. Sincerity. These were qualities she hadn't imagined men his age possessed. So here was something she'd learned about the world, and looking at Earl, she felt a jolt of happiness. Which was how she would remember it all her life—a happy jolt. She'd be unable to think of a word, a phrase, that sounded wiser, more sophisticated when she recalled it to herself.

Their conversations up to now had been a mutual circling, comically cautious, sharing details that risked little. He'd told her he lived in a boarding house, in a room next to a man he never saw, whose weak, consumptive coughing he could hear through the wall at night.

She'd told him she was living with her aunt and uncle, and that the two of them had been romantically fated to meet, both visitors from Iowa standing by chance next to one another at an exhibit, a Kinetoscope showing an old man sneezing, at the Chicago World's Fair of 1893.

She hadn't told him she was here just for the summer. She didn't want to admit this to herself, and she feared if he knew he would think, *Well, then, why bother?*

He hadn't told her of his being discovered by a portly herald, a fated meeting as he saw it, who'd sat perched on the bleachers in Riverton like something conjured. He'd been practicing the story in his head, his description of Saul Weintraub as rumpled and joyous and mythic and wise, thinking as he did that he would bet the world's last nickel she knew what "cocksure" meant.

The crowds were small for weekday games. By the end of June, Emily had been to three, and at two of them she was the only woman there, arriving midway through and sitting in a section of the stands protected by a roof to keep the summer sun from her fair skin.

She'd seen right away that Earl was very good at pitching. She wasn't surprised. Why would he have asked her to come if he weren't? She watched as players swung and failed, swung and failed, swung and failed, and walked away shaking their heads and studying their bats as if they'd chosen the wrong tool and that explained it. She watched as the ball, off the bat, bounced obediently to an infielder like a pet being called. And she watched when it rose lazily into the air, or arced and fell untouched to the green, green outfield earth.

From her shaded spot in the stands, she observed an impatience, an *eagerness*, building in Earl when he pitched. His hurrying from the dugout to start an inning; the subtle liveliness of his gestures and his forward-leaning posture as he stood on the mound. And what she saw, she decided, was a man inhabiting the moment he was living entirely, and barely able to wait for the even richer next one. She viewed each pitch as a complete narrative, and she began to feel drawn in to a depth that surprised her. She was sensing his exuberance and sensing hers rising with it and taking for herself a share of what his body was expressing.

Until the most recent game she'd watched, a few days earlier.

Earl was pitching well, he'd given up two runs, and when he struck out the last batter in the top of the eighth, her eyes followed him happily as he left the mound. And then she noticed something—the way his limbs were moving with a looseness, a kind of dexterous ambling she hadn't seen before. She'd thought of him as perfectly well coordinated, his long legs striding deliberately. But here he was, walking to the dugout with a peculiar grace, moving beautifully, *balletically*. She knew it had everything to do with how he was pitching, but for the first time she sensed she couldn't find her way to where he was; that she was watching a stranger.

She studied Earl intently through the final inning, waiting for him to return, his familiar gestures, his usual bearing, but it didn't quite happen. He seemed to her someone who was portraying Earl, playing a slightly grander version of who he was. She felt disoriented, nearly dizzy as she sat there.

Afterward, they walked to the trolley with perhaps a dozen others, the last of the afternoon's small crowd to leave the park. "Thanks for coming," he said to her, in the light tone she'd heard from him each time they'd done this.

"You're welcome," she said, "you did very well," and when he smiled, he seemed to her some distance from the smile, still in the world where he'd moved with that silken confidence. He was in *both* lives— yes, that was it—attentive to her in one without having left the other. She felt at the same time embraced and abandoned, and she knew how outlandish, how unfair to him this was.

At the stop, they watched the trolley approaching. He would walk the mile or so to his boarding house as he liked to do after games, but she and a few others moved to board. He gave her his hand with a playful elaborateness, and she stepped up into the car. He looked at her as she turned back to him. His eyes were squinting into the low, orange sun behind her. The trolley started with a lurch, and from where she stood she leaned out and saw him waving, the tall, slender man with a puckish grin, wearing baseball flannels, his cleated shoes tied together and slung over his shoulder. Her wave in return was absentminded, for she was already thinking of tomorrow morning, when he would walk into the Good Day with a slight hesitation, a sweet self-consciousness in his step, and be simply Earl again.

In her room that night, she looked into her mirror. She pressed her fingertips to her image in the glass and was briefly surprised that she didn't feel their touch on her cheek. She was wondering what to call it, this roil of emotion, the fear she'd felt when Earl seemed to be both himself and someone else. What she was feeling was not what she'd imagined any part, any glimpse of love should feel like. And yet, she thought, still looking at her reflection, what else could it be but her horribly selfish rendition of it? She was waiting for the feelings she'd felt before today, for their return. The certainty of his desire for her, and that hers for him always knew who he would be. And this was how she spent a sleepless night.

When Earl entered the Good Day early the next morning, he saw her standing with Gretel at the Dutch door to the kitchen. She appeared to him, as always, beautiful and solemn and fine-boned as a fairy, particularly next to Gretel.

He opened his arms and said, "I'm here and I'm hungry," as he moved to the spot he favored by the large, dirty windows that gave onto Washington Street. The room was more than half-filled, including the long table he and his teammates had chosen that first day. Looking around, he pictured, as he often did, the bunch of them tumbling in like a slapstick troupe, and he thought once again, *The world! The way it works!* He watched Emily start across the room toward him and noticed that she looked a bit wan this morning, wan and waiflike.

"Everything all right?" he asked.

"Fine," she said, her face softening slightly, but as if it required an effort.

He'd finished his pancakes and bacon and his third cup of coffee, and he hadn't yet solved her disposition this morning. She'd been friendly enough, but her smile had continued to look somehow applied.

She was clearing his table when he said, "I wanted to tell you, I won't be in for a while."

"Oh?"

"We're playing in Davenport, then Rock Island. Six games before we're back."

Standing opposite him, the wobbly table between them, holding the long, damp cloth she used to wipe the tabletops, with the light little more than a rumor through the filthy windows, she came to a decision. *All right. I'm going to say it.* "I'm sorry," she said, "I'm *disappointed* you'll be gone so long." She looked at him full face, both bold and blushing.

"Well! I'll miss you too," Earl said.

Her smile changed, became nearly hers again and close to sly. "I didn't say I'd *miss* you."

"Sure you did," he said. Of course, he'd been aware of his own growing feelings, and now he was feeling them brightly. "I've been thinking to ask you something. If you'd like to go dancing." It had been on his mind for more than a week, after seeing an advertisement in the Waterloo *Courier* for a new ballroom on the outskirts of town.

"Dancing?"

"We could go tonight. I don't leave till tomorrow."

Emily looked around the room. No customers were signaling, no new ones had entered. She dropped her cloth on the table, pulled out a chair, and sat down next to Earl, and it felt to him for all the world as if the two of them were sitting at their breakfast table.

His voice had sounded casual, making her wonder. "You've never mentioned you liked to dance."

"Tonight'll be my first time."

"So what gave you the idea?"

He tilted his head slightly as he thought of how to answer. "It seemed the kind of . . . it seemed the *perfect* thing to ask a lady, if the lady was a lady you were trying to impress."

Once again, she scanned this dreary room she felt such odd affection for, with its stamped tin ceiling and its grim gray surfaces and the mange-spattered house cat sleeping in the corner. Turning now to look at him, she felt herself wanting to reach and press her fingertips to his cheeks and to his very large ears, sleek as wings in her extremely biased opinion. "Well, speaking as a lady," she said, "that's what it seems like to me too."

Earl began the night an extremely awkward dancer. The difference in his and Emily's heights was great, but that wasn't the problem. He couldn't get a feel for where to put his arm around her and how to hold her hand. But that wasn't really the problem either. Emily's beauty was the problem. He'd been struck by it, of course, the first moment he saw her. But it was one thing to see her in daylight, in the Good Day, in the grandstands at the ballpark. But seeing her here, this evening, in her best royal blue silk shirtwaist (she'd brought it with her, packed it thinking it was what she'd wear to church, and she had), lit by the burnishing light of the ballroom's wall lamps—this was so distracting to him for the first hour and more that he took the music into his body clumsily and sent it out the same way.

"You doing all right?" Emily asked. She felt the tension in his body, and she was touched by how gamely he was laboring to please her.

"Of course," he said. "Are you?" And at some point in the evening, it came to him that he should think of dancing as a kind of sport, though not a contest, and he began to move with something closer to confidence, still counting the steps in his head, still distracted by her beauty in the amber light, until he found himself giving over to the fantasy that he would at any moment lower his face into the softness of her deep chestnut hair, its luster some ultimate refinement of light, removing her combs and watching it come free, and with it her royal blue silk shirtwaist falling away, and her layers of undergarments slipping from her shoulders until she was naked in his arms, her hair a radiant cloak that grazed the base of her spine. No nakedness had ever been so entire, not in myth or marvel, not some shameless Eve's at the instant she realized she was.

CHAPTER FOUR

July 10, 1916

Rooster and Lottie stepped down from the eastbound train, following four other passengers also getting off in Waterloo. They stood and looked around, blinded for a moment by the sudden sunlight. The small brick station sat in a flat and dusty yard. Behind them, the train was sounding its huffs and long sighs of arrival. Lottie shifted their empty picnic basket from one arm to the other. Rooster put their suitcase down and flexed his hand. He was grateful for the hot sun on his painfully stiff back. He took off his hat to wipe his brow with the frayed sleeve of his suit jacket. His sweat was a wet dust that would leave a permanent dark smear near the cuff.

"Ah," Rooster said, spotting Emily, who'd emerged from the shade of the station's overhanging roof. She was coming toward them, extending her arms, and they met in an embrace. Their kisses were quick pecks in the way of wary diplomats. Emily asked about their journey.

"Mother packed us a fine meal," Rooster said.

Lottie said, "We played canasta with a couple from Sioux City."

Rooster said, "Foolish bidder, the husband. Thought he was a big shot. We cleaned their clock."

Lottie's quick smile confirmed it.

Emily laughed and a warmth filled her. As she'd thought about their coming, her nervousness had kept her from admitting to herself how much she'd missed them.

Over these spring and summer months, Emily and Lottie had written back and forth daily. Lottie's letters were filled with the minutiae of weather and the social calls she'd paid and received and the gossip of Hinton, such as it was.

And Emily's were as bland. She enjoyed Sunday strolls in the park with Aunt Patricia while they talked about the books they'd been reading together—a new *Anne of Green Gables* and a Charlotte Perkins Gilman novel. She enjoyed her waitressing job at the luncheonette, where customers brought home the fact that everyone was different. She enjoyed Uncle Melvin's descriptions of his workday as a postal clerk, though it seemed from his accounts that the postal service employed the slothful and dim-witted, which wasn't meant to reflect necessarily on Uncle Melvin.

So when she wrote that she wanted to stay on in Waterloo, she wasn't sure how long, Lottie wondered whether there'd been something in Emily's letters she had missed. Why, she asked in her reply, didn't Emily want to come home?

Expecting the question, Emily sat down at her aunt's oak desk, breathed deeply, and began. She'd met a thoughtful, light-spirited, handsome young man. She paused, her pen hovering over the inkwell. She didn't want to sound like a foolish, lovestruck girl, although, being a foolish, lovestruck girl, she was tempted to describe his deep brown eyes and his rapscallion smile. Instead, she offered phrases she'd been composing in her mind. Their tone was oddly eulogistic. *He invites the day like an adventure. . . . He has a warm and witty way. . . . He sees the spirit of a game in everything.*

At the railroad station, Emily led her mother and father toward the stop where they'd wait for the trolley to Patricia's house. Lottie remarked as they passed the red brick depot with its many-gabled roof that it looked in the high sun like a gingerbread cottage and then, without pausing, as if it just logically followed, she said, "Your young man—Earl, is it?—he isn't with you."

Emily's breath skipped. She'd been worried that her father might blurt out a question. But here was her mother, quaint as an artifact in her farm-wife bonnet, going straight to the emotions yammering away in Emily. It was her mother's gift, Emily was reminded; her sensibility was like a divining rod.

"Yes, it's Earl, and, no, he couldn't come." Emily mustered a small smile. "Aunt Patricia has invited him to supper tonight. She likes Earl very much. Uncle Melvin does too, of course. He thinks it's funny that Earl's first name is so close to their last. Add a 'y' and he's 'Early.' That's what Uncle Melvin says."

Rooster shook his head, thinking that sounded exactly dumb enough to be something Melvin might say. It took a person maybe half a minute in his company to know the man's brain was a piece of gristle.

Reaching the trolley stop, they stood with several others. Emily began to hum absently.

A horse-drawn confectionary wagon passed on the street that paralleled the tracks. The mare was old, white-whiskered, and alarmingly swaybacked, but her gait was sprightly, as Rooster noted, feeling envious.

Then he said, "You never told us what this Earl does for work?"

Emily had been peering down the tracks for the approach of the trolley and still looking away she said, "He's a baseball player." She shut her eyes and squeezed them as if she were bracing for a loud sound.

Rooster cocked his head, but before he could speak, Emily turned to face him and Lottie. "He's on the Waterloo team. It's called the Loons, which is very unfortunate, don't you think? I mean, the *Loons*? He's their best pitcher. It's a Class B professional league, though I'm not sure how that compares to other leagues. I mean I'm not sure how far down the alphabet they go. I keep forgetting to ask him."

Rooster was making a real effort to follow his daughter, nodding faintly as he listened. He'd always thought baseball an idiotic waste of time. He hadn't known the joy of physical games as a boy—the grace and muscle, the fluid sinew of excelling. He'd never been especially agile; his reflexes were not particularly quick. He'd only been mysteriously, incredibly strong, and what his young body could and couldn't do had set for him an understanding of the uses a man should put it to. He might take pride in knowing he was laboring well, might even compete with himself to labor better, but none of that was anything you could call enjoyment. Enjoyment meant pleasure and pleasure meant play and play wasn't work. Wasn't it that simple? It had always been for Rooster.

"Most of the time," he heard Emily saying now, "the batters can't hit the baseball when Earl throws it, and when they do it usually doesn't go very far. He's not pitching today. He's probably the best pitcher in the league. Did I already say that? It's a Class B league, though I'm not sure what that means. Did I already say that too?"

She paused finally for a breath, and Rooster felt relieved, as if they'd all just *survived* something, a sudden blast of extreme weather.

Lottie, standing next to him, nodded her bonneted head. There was a stillness in the air after Emily's mad Gatling chatter and speaking into it she said, "Did you hear that, Frank? Emily's friend, Earl, has discovered how to make his livelihood playing a game."

Rooster quickly turned to her, and as he did, he saw her winking at their daughter. "He must be very clever, dear," Lottie said to Emily.

A new wooden porch, built high off the ground, ran along the front of the dance hall, and it was here, sheltered beneath it, that Earl and Emily had found themselves the night before. They'd been sitting on one of the long porch's benches, the dance ended, everyone gone home, the hall door locked, Earl listening to Emily fretting about her parents' arrival, when the skies opened and the rain came down in fast flat splats.

"Under the porch!" Earl called, and they'd scurried for cover, laughing, hurrying down the steps and crawling underneath it. So recently built, it hadn't had time to kill the grass. Its floor made a protective overhang for them, and they sat comfortably side by side, facing one another, their legs extended in opposite directions.

Earl took off his suit jacket. It was the first suit he'd owned. He'd bought it the week before, hoping to impress Emily's parents. Its cream-colored linen was the same material as the suit Saul Weintraub was wearing the day he'd changed Earl's life. It had been soiled and wrinkled, but even so, Earl had admired and remembered it. Now he offered his jacket to Emily as a towel. She patted her face and neck with one of its sleeves and gave it back.

As quickly as it started, the downpour had become a sprinkle. Emily's hair was wet and disheveled, her shirtwaist was soaked and clung to her, and glimpsing both these gifts—her hair come loose, her clinging shirtwaist—Earl thought, *Thank you, rain.* He held the moment purely, this late-summer night under a porch with Emily Marchand, who was wondrously wet, with the light rain sounding on the planks overhead like the scampering of tiny agile animals.

There *was* a lot to thank the rain for. He felt his luck and quietly laughed.

"You're laughing," Emily said. "It's mean of you, to laugh at me."

"Never at you," Earl said. "But I wish you wouldn't worry."

"I wish I wouldn't too. But—"

"Besides, you're forgetting."

"What?"

"That they haven't met me yet."

She worked to smile, and managed to.

Since sending her letter, she'd been feeling more and more nostalgic for the quibbling and cajoling, the private lyrics of affection she shared with her father. But now she was fearing a disagreement, where they didn't know their parts by heart, one that mattered in a way unlike any they'd had. Sitting beside Earl, brooding about it all, she began to run her fingers absently through her hair to straighten its wet tangles.

Earl was watching her. Given how much of his life he'd spent beneath the ground, he thought he knew the varieties of darkness entirely. But what Emily was doing, the slow, caressing gesture of her fingers through her hair, made this darkness under the porch something new and nearly luminous. He reached, his fingers joining hers. She started, he felt it like a current, then she moved her hand away as if saying to him, *Here.* She leaned toward him slightly and closed her eyes. He continued, a light, ineffectual combing, being careful not to tug, and she sat still, letting him attend to her. She opened her eyes and lifted her chin. Earl's fingers touched the base of her throat. He could feel her heart there, and he could feel his own with hers, though his was beating everywhere in him, so he imagined hers was too, in her. He drew his fingertips along her collarbone and felt her fineness beneath the green silk shirtwaist. He said, "Here's what you should say, to make sure they'll let you stay."

"What? Tell me."

He said, "I need to kiss you," as if *that* were his answer. They kissed, their mouths moving, drawing in what they were wanting and giving it back, and Emily's breath of pleasure was a word she spoke to Earl. He edged closer, his thigh, his hip touching hers. He moved to kiss her again, and she put her hand to his lips, her fingers asking him to kiss them, then pressing them to her own lips and smiling from the taste of his.

She whispered, "What's your idea?"

"My idea?"

"What I should tell them."

"Ah," he said. His hands were resting lightly on her shoulders feeling the dampness of her hair, and he moved them down, tracing silk, to touch her breasts. She caught her breath and said his name. He said, "You should tell them you can't be living in one town and your husband in another." His fingers made slow circles, finding her nipples.

Emily didn't speak; she closed her eyes again and sat up straighter to offer him more. She put her hands on his to help him cup her breasts, then took his hands away and lay back on the ground. She whispered again. "Lie down with me."

They lay close, their bodies not quite touching, Emily placed his hand on her breast again, guiding him, and Earl heard the light rustling of her skirts as she barely moved her legs over the grass like a girl making an angel in the snow. For a fevered instant, he imagined she was asking for his hand there, between her legs, but she took it from her breast—he felt the quick grief of what was gone, the touch of silk, the softness beneath it—and pressed it to her cheek.

Lying beside her, alive and confused, Earl was feeling he could live his whole life in confusion, smiling every blessed minute of the day, if this were what confusion felt like. When he turned his head to Emily to whisper something of the sort, she said, "I'll be so happy when I'm your wife." She took his hand from her cheek and pressed hers against his.

He said, "You're saying yes?"

She said she was. She said, didn't he know that's what she *had* been saying.

He said, "I want to hear you *say* it."

She said, "Yes."

He looked at her closely. He saw her happiness.

Her bliss felt to her complete, the same as his, and it would shock her to her core to learn the next night that it hadn't been everything she was feeling.

CHAPTER FIVE

July 10, 1916

Earl and Rooster sat in the white wicker rocking chairs on the porch of the Earlys' modest frame house. As they rocked, Rooster's high-topped brogans with their big blunt toes grazed the floor to make a sound like a soft-shoe slide. The moonlight and starlight gave the sky an artful cast. More houses, plain and well-kept like the Earlys', looked across at one another for the length of the wide dirt street. All but two had put their lamps out; it was just past ten o'clock.

As he'd thought about tonight, so eager for this hour and this talk, Earl had imagined Emily's father and himself, the two of them comparing what they each loved most about Emily. But sitting with him now, he wondered how in the world he could have thought they'd do that. He obviously couldn't speak to him of how her low, sultry laugh thrilled him, sent a feeling through him that started in his groin; or the way the stillness of her face was awakened when she smiled; or the shocking softness of her skin where he had touched her, and his knowing that those places he hadn't touched yet would feel still softer.

Somewhere out there in the night, two dogs were trading coon-hound conversation. Hearing them, Earl envied their boasts and rejoinders, so sure of themselves, and he remembered the cries of the intelligent coyote on his last night in Riverton.

Earlier, as they were all sitting down to supper, Emily had stayed standing and announced that she would serve. She reached for the tureen of beef and noodles sitting on the table beside Patricia. In Emily's arms, it looked as big as a washbasin. Earl caught her eye, and the private pleasure in her face told him she was hoping to remind him of the day she set his bowl of brown stew in front of him.

Melvin was saying something about the war in Europe. He was an exceedingly ordinary-looking man, his body soft and shapeless. His only feature was a trig mustache. His voice was resonant, richly amplified, but Earl was paying no attention, lost in his and Emily's hour beneath the dance hall porch the night before. His eyes followed her as she held the bowl in her arms, her small breasts pushing against her blue shirtwaist, and the thrill of touching them through silk returned to him.

He saw Patricia make a grotesque, mocking face at whatever Melvin had been saying and flap her hand in a shooing gesture, as if ordering his opinion to the dunce's corner.

Earl and Rooster had been talking on the porch for nearly an hour. Now Rooster was detailing his canasta bidding strategy. It was held back, apparently emotionless, relying on opponents to make inevitable blunders. There was a lesson about life in that, Rooster said: hold your cards, bide your time, wait for it to come to you.

Impatient as he was, Earl heard this as a cue. He'd been biding his time, he'd been waiting for it to come to him, though he wasn't really sure, in Rooster's world, just what "it" was, and he turned in his rocker to say, "Mr. Marchand, I like Emily very much."

Rooster continued his slow rocking. "You'd be a fool if it were otherwise." If his tone wasn't hostile, it wasn't especially cordial either.

"Yes," Earl said. "And I can say she likes me too . . . also."

Rooster was looking out toward the empty street. "From what she wrote her mother, that would seem the case."

Speaking to Rooster's profile, Earl took a very deep breath, then said, "But what's important here is, I *love* her. So I hope you'll think it's all right if we were planning to get married." He took another breath, as deep. "Since we are."

Rooster stood up and repositioned his chair to face Earl directly. He sat down again and resumed his slow rocking. Though moonlit and starlit, the night was dark enough to veil his face. He said, "I was twelve years old and so was Mother—so was Lottie—when we first noticed one another. It was seven years passed when we got married, so there was all that time growing up to find out what the one didn't like about the other."

He turned to peer through the large porch window into the darkened kitchen as if he were checking to make sure the coast was clear. He turned back to look at Earl. "Maybe Emily's told you the story of her aunt and uncle, which she's always talked about like it was Snow White gets the prince. At least that's how she used to. How they met and said hidee and the next week they was married, because, Patricia writes to us in a letter, his voice is pretty and he's got a handsome mustache. Well, he's still got the voice and he's still got the mustache." He opened his arthritic hands to Earl as if he were serving him the lesson in that on a tray, then rested them in his lap.

Earl said, "We met at the start of summer, Mr. Marchand. That's two months, plus a little more. It's not seven years, I know, but it's not 'the next week' either, and—"

"I think Emily's the finest thing abiding on this earth. But what I'm saying, being that we're humans, there's plenty wrong with all of us. You, me, Emily, the exception being Mother. And it's them, the things that's *wrong*, a person's got to like about the other."

There was now a kind of pedagogy in the sureness of Rooster's voice.

For reasons he didn't really understand, maybe just the relief of announcing their intentions, Earl's heart was feeling light, enough to bring a bit of mischief into their talk. "So what's wrong with me, Mr. Marchand?"

"How's that?"

"You said there were some things wrong with all of us, including you and me. I'm curious about me."

Rooster said, "You're asking you in particular? How the hell could I know? I just met you, and you're on your best behavior." He stopped his rocking again and placed his elbows on the arms of the chair and scooted forward to say, "Explain to me about the baseball."

Earl frowned. He'd been expecting this in some fashion, but he felt thrown by Rooster's tone. *Explain to me about the baseball.* It was skepticism, it was doubt, a shade of doubt that Earl heard. For him, the nearest thing to feeling doubt about playing baseball for a living was his amazement that he got to. "Well, my record at this point is ten and three." He paused, uncertain if he needed to explain. "That means I've won—"

"I know what it means," Rooster said. "Emily already told us you're the best pitcher in the league."

"She might be a little prejudiced."

"I factored that in," Rooster said.

Earl smiled and nodded. "And since I'm asking for your blessing, it's only fair you know what I'm earning. And what I hope to in the future."

Rooster raised his hand to say Earl didn't need to bother. But Earl waved it away, and Rooster was glad he did; he wanted very much to hear what Earl would say.

Earl began to speak in a hurry, saying he was earning a hundred and fifty-eight dollars a month this season, which didn't sound like very much, because it *wasn't* very much, but he had no doubt he'd be promoted to a higher league next year, where he'd make twice or three times that. He said more promotions would come, he didn't doubt that either, and, looking to the future, a few years from now, a major league pitcher might get paid, oh, seven thousand, eight thousand dollars a year.

"And," Earl said, slowing, nearly finished and wanting the emphasis, "a very good one can earn even more than that." He paused. "I think that's what I can be, Mr. Marchand. A very good one."

Some moments passed before Rooster said, "I see," then leaned forward in his rocker as if to whisper a secret to Earl. But he merely held his seated posture, and it unsettled Earl to have Rooster's face so close until he sat back in his chair again.

Rooster wasn't angry at Earl for assuming he'd believe what he'd been told just now, the sums of money Earl expected to earn, the prosperous life he saw for himself and Emily. Instead, he was genuinely alarmed. In the dark, on the porch, he'd leaned close enough just now to see in Earl's eyes that *he* believed it, every goddamn word of the nonsense he'd been speaking, which someone must have fed him, probably whoever it was that signed Earl up and got himself a fat commission.

"Mr. Marchand?"

Rooster looked at Earl.

"Do we have your blessing?"

And with everything going on in Rooster's mind right then, a knife blade of pain, arthritic pain, sliced into his hands and scraped their bones, and his sharp intake of breath was a sound like a gust.

His thoughts and the pain had arrived together; that's how it had seemed. So he hadn't been able to think through what he was about to say. But even so, he knew this much: that the work he could offer took all you had, and often, certain seasons, you were at it from first light to dark. But mostly in the infinite outdoors, the air sweet, almost a taste—not almost, a *taste*—and the midwestern skies holding every kind of drama, and the days of enormous, cloudless calm the most dramatic of them all.

He said, "I'm coming to like you, Earl." And it was true. As they'd all risen from the supper table, he'd watched Earl walk to Emily and bend down to whisper something in her ear. He'd watched his daughter smile, and Rooster felt he'd seen something creaturely, a nuzzling, in their exchange, which he approved of. "I could even see me liking the things that's wrong with you, whatever they turn out to be." He smiled weakly. "Though I can't expect you'd ever like what all's wrong with me. So, yes," he said, "I do give you my blessing. But which comes attached to this proposition."

As he'd been listening to Rooster, Earl was also hearing sounds coming from inside, a floor creaking, a door shutting. He assumed it was Emily moving nervously from room to room as she waited to hear how this talk had gone. "A proposition?" Earl said.

CHAPTER SIX

"I can't believe it," Earl said for the fourth or fifth time. "He said it and I heard it and I still can't believe it."

Emily sat on the sagging, brown damask couch in the Earlys' drab little parlor, watching him pacing back and forth in front of her. The flame from a candle on the table in the middle of the room made a shimmering smudge of light. Lottie and the Earlys were asleep, and Rooster had bid him a very awkward good night, so Earl, forced to whisper, was speaking in fierce hisses. He was crestfallen and not a little manic, and watching him, Emily thought, *Of* course *he is.* She was miserable for him. She was making moist *tssk* sounds of commiseration with her tongue against the back of her teeth.

"'A baseball player's wife,'" Earl said, quoting more from Rooster that he still could not believe. "'That's not the wife I raised her to be.'"

Emily offered her most heartfelt *tssk!* so far, a wet smack of a sound. She was startled, insulted, that her father would speak this way about her. What he'd "raised her to be," as if she were a head of livestock. She thought, *What was the wife you* were *raising me to be?*

And yet, sitting there listening to Earl, she realized that—even more than her misery for him, more than insulted by her father and startled by his words—what she was feeling most was enormous relief. And she was startled in turn to recognize *that*; she was doubly startled.

"He said, a ballplayer, there's no guarantee. And I said, 'Of course there isn't,' but what *was* in life? Guaranteed?"

"What did he say then?"

"I could hurt myself playing and that would be the end of that."

"And what did you say?"

"I don't even remember. It was all such nonsense."

He stopped and looked over his shoulder as if for Rooster's nonsense sneaking up behind him. He sat down heavily beside Emily and reached to take her hand.

"Squeeze," she said. He did, and she said, "Squeeze harder."

He frowned, *why?* but gripped her hand more strongly, then relaxed his hold. "I don't want to hurt you."

She shook her head, and they sat quietly like that, holding hands and looking into the flickering light of the candle on the table. She kept hearing what Earl had just said, that he didn't want to hurt her. Watching the pale flame, her hand warm and damp in Earl's, she was liking less and less what her feelings were revealing. For she was hearing Rooster's words, his demands and his proposal, as the granting of a wish she hadn't realized she'd made.

Earl sighed deeply, and she marveled at how expressive a single sigh could be. All of someone's feelings could be in it. At least as she heard Earl's.

"He didn't believe me when I said what I might earn. He didn't say he didn't, but the look on his face . . ." Earl shook his head.

Emily lifted their entwined hands and kissed the back of his. She was searching for words that would make some sense to Earl, and all she was finding was what she couldn't imagine how to say.

Earl said, "Can you see me a farmer?" He gave a bitter laugh at the absurdity. "Can you imagine that for a second?" She knew these weren't questions; he wasn't waiting for her answer. She kissed the back of his long, slender hand again and placed it carefully, arranging it, on his thigh. How frightening this was, this blankness of not knowing— not knowing what would happen when she'd said what she must try to say. Or was it her fear that she *did* know; what she knew and what she didn't, the greater fear of them together.

"Yes," she said. "I can." Her normally low voice was high and strained.

Earl turned to her slightly. "You can what?"

"I can . . . imagine it. That life."

"*What?*"

"I *can* imagine what Daddy's offering you. Offering *us*. No, *you*. No, you *and* me. Us."

"Wait." Earl gave his head a quick, strong shake to clear it. "You're saying that's what *you* want too?"

She turned to look at him directly. If she couldn't find a way to say what she was feeling, at least she had to let him see that in her face, see what it was showing—that her heart was at war with itself, that with her great relief was her great guilt for feeling it.

"Why didn't you . . . ? You never said anything. Why didn't you tell me this?"

Her breaths were her words, Earl let the silence happen, and with each one she felt relief, then guilt, and then they somehow merged. "Because . . . I didn't realize—"

"Why didn't you tell me how you felt?"

"I didn't *know* how I felt."

Earl was on his feet again, pacing, and speaking loudly now. "Come on, Emily. Please. How could you not know what you were feeling?"

"Because I *didn't*. And I don't . . ." Her voice faded, trailed off.

Earl's step as he paced was heavy, almost stomping, and the teacups on the sideboard trembled in their saucers. Emily imagined he was trying to make them fall to the floor, but the furthest thing from her thoughts was to ask him to step quietly because everyone was sleeping.

He stopped and looked down at her. She'd bowed her head. "So . . ." He kneaded his forehead. "So you're saying it's either or?" His voice was aghast with a sudden recognition. "I come and be a farmer with your father—either that, or else? I can't believe you're saying that. Are you? Saying that? Look at me, Emily. Tell me that's what you're saying."

Her head stayed lowered, and when she finally raised it she said, "I'm not *saying* . . . *any*thing. I'm trying to find words. I know you're upset, just let me—"

"Up*set?*"

"More than upset, much more, and you—"

"Jesus Christ, Emily. You and your words. You don't need *words* to say what you're saying. You're saying it just fine. You've never said anything better."

"Tell me, then. What I'm saying. Tell me what you hear me saying." She was sincere. It was a plea.

He could see her tears in the candlelight, and she knew he could, but again she felt obliged to let him see her face. A few nights ago, she'd lain awake imagining her father's objections to Earl, and now she was realizing that they'd been hers. Not to Earl—of course not him, not that—but to the life she imagined he was leading them to. She whispered, "It's complicated."

"No, it isn't. It's a *choice*. A hard one, I guess, for you, but not complicated."

"I'm sorry. But it is."

"Agghh!" he said, "I've heard enough." He spun around and took a step to leave and caught his toe on the oval rag rug and the small room shook a little. The teacups stayed, but the candle toppled from the holder, and the flame went out as it rolled off the table and fell to the floor. Earl bent down to pick it up. He'd wanted to leave in a show of graceful fury, it was the least this night owed him, and here he'd been as clumsy as his first hours on the dance floor. Which is what Emily thought of when she watched him stumble, those perfect hours, and she felt an instant of guilt-sick love.

"Earl, please!" she called, but he was moving to the door. She stood and started toward him. "Please come back!" She didn't care now if she woke the house. She wanted to. Anything to interfere, anything that might make him pause.

At the door, he stopped and turned to look at her. The hallway lamps made a ghoulish light, and she was taken by the expression on his face. His hurt, the frenzy of it.

He didn't slam the door, but it rattled in its frame. Melvin Early had been promising for months to fix its loose hinge. In the quiet, the rattling seemed to Emily to go on and on and on.

In his bed at the boarding house, staring up at the ceiling, Earl heard the insomniac pacing of the old man overhead and the tubercular coughing of the mysterious one next door, so continuous and rhythmic that he had come to think of it as just sadly noisy breathing. The pacing and the coughing fashioned a duet.

Sick to his stomach as he lay there, Earl surrendered to the notion that he'd been set up, and that Emily was complicit. Rooster stating the terms, then handing him to her sitting primly in the parlor, pretending she was unable to find the words, and when had that ever happened—Emily Marchand unable to find words?

On the porch, he'd asked Rooster why it had to be the farm. If he wanted his blessing, why did it have to be *that* work, *his* company, and the question had stopped Rooster.

"Well," he managed, "of course it *don't* have to be," but what he'd come up with, he'd said, was how he saw that Earl could save his bacon, save himself from disappointment, with a life, with work that was more guaranteed. "Which I'm ready to show you all of it. And then, too, you'd have Emily into the bargain. Well, not into the bargain. She'd be the *main* thing of course."

Earl sat up in bed, feeling he was going to throw up his supper. The empty chamber pot was in the commode in the far corner. He stood and walked toward it. In tears, he bent to the pot, looking strangely like a supplicant.

CHAPTER SEVEN

July 11, 1916

On the mound the next day, he searched the stands. The dark skies threatening rain had kept the crowd away. She'd have been easy to spot if she were there. He knew she wouldn't be, but he couldn't believe she wasn't. Distracted, he took no note of the first batter walking to the plate.

"Hey! Pitcher!" Earl saw the umpire approaching. His face was cranky. He'd apparently been shouting as he started to the mound, a short, slight man in his blue suit, his chest protector looking like a great fat bib. He pointed to the ball in Earl's hand. "How this works, it's pretty simple: first, you throw it, then we see if they can hit it."

His sleepless exhaustion. His queasy stomach. After four innings, the score was 8–2.

The hitter's lip curled softly as he stepped in to start the fifth and Earl saw it as meaning the bastard was eager for the pitch. He wound up and threw and hit the batter in the ribs, sending up a squeal, and the two of them ran toward each other, grabbing uniforms and holding tight, spinning this way and that like violent waltzers, until they let go and started throwing punches and Earl caught one in the eye.

"What in heaven's name?" Emily asked. She reached up to touch the eye, then caught herself. "Does it hurt as much as it looks?"

"I'd guess more," Earl said. "Obviously I can't see how it looks." He made his voice as cold as possible. He wanted to make her feel stupid, to hear how ridiculous her question was.

His eye was already swollen nearly shut, and he had to move his head back and forth to see the full sweep of the world. He'd left the field still dressed in his flannels, his cleats tied together and hanging from his shoulder as always. He'd stopped and panned the view when he heard her calling to him, and there she was, twenty feet away and walking toward him.

They were standing on a dirt pathway leading to the street through an opening in a sagging, white-washed fence that rimmed the park. She was wearing a new hat, ochre-colored silk with a wide, feathered brim. She was carrying a lemon-yellow umbrella of her aunt's against the rain that hadn't come.

He was loath to describe for her his woeful pitching, his throwing at the batter to release his rage, his feeling lost—a dizzy, disoriented depth of loss. "There was a fight," he said. "Somebody lost his head and things got out of hand. What are you doing here?"

She hesitated. "I was worried it might go badly." She saw his awful-looking eye as the proof of what she'd feared.

"That's not what I asked."

Again she hesitated. "I think it is. You're asking why I didn't come."

She heard Earl make a dumb, dismissive sound.

Last night, lying awake, she'd asked herself over and over what it was she'd felt in that moment he'd asked her to marry him as they'd huddled in the lovely dark beneath the dance hall porch. Had her fear been there then, which meant she'd had it all along? How was it possible she hadn't known it, hadn't felt it waiting for the moment to appear? The closest she'd come to an answer, which didn't feel to her nearly close enough, was that her love for Earl was the same love, in her fear and in her joy; it was there in both of them; it was in each and all of her emotions.

He asked, "You didn't think I might pitch just fine?" His anger was bringing him a kind of comfort, and he felt it as the thing, the one thing he could count on.

She said, not answering his question, "I thought you'd hate it if you saw me in the stands. Then I thought I'd be letting you down to stay away. Then—"

"It's a little late to worry about letting me down."

She looked at the ground again, noticing his shoes, ankle high and badly scuffed and clownishly misshapen with years of wear. She'd seen him wearing them countless times, but now something about them moved her, their age, their having lost their shape, his wearing them anyway, which seemed like an act of devotion. She was about to burst into tears with the thought that Earl was a man who was loyal to his old shoes.

"I didn't know it was what I wanted until you told me what Daddy said to you. It was like I was hearing *me* saying it to you. The thing I didn't know I'd been thinking. Myself." She closed her eyes and shook her head. What a hash she'd made of that. It had been so much easier speaking her thoughts to herself through the night and all morning, with Earl not standing there in front of her to hear what she'd get wrong. She inhaled deeply and let her breath out, and her lips made a sound like old playing cards being softly shuffled. She was starting to perspire, and her new hat pinched her head.

"What difference does it make?" Earl said. "You still want what you want."

"It makes all the difference. To *me* it does. I can imagine you've been thinking we, that Daddy and I had it all planned."

"So you know what I'm thinking, you know what I'm asking. You've got me all figured out, don't you." He felt unnerved by how much it seemed she did.

"Maybe I have you more figured out than I do myself."

"What does that mean?"

She feared that if she said, *It means I love you*, he would make an ugly, disgusted face. "I'm not sure what it means," she said. She wanted to look down again at his sweet old shoes, but she couldn't risk the tears.

"What'd you tell *them*?"

"Just . . . that you were very angry. Which they already knew."

Talking to Rooster and Lottie, she'd been fragile with fatigue, with the shock of Earl's absence the moment he'd left the house, the rattling of the door in its frame like a cell door clanging shut and locking her in with her life before she'd known him. Her voice straining, she'd told them that her months away had given her what she'd hoped for. She'd left the farm to learn some things about the world. And she'd discovered that a life with Earl was that world, one she felt certain would be filled with many things to learn, *too* many for one lifetime, and how wonderful, that thought—to have too many things to learn.

Now Earl looked down at her with his good eye and said, "So it *is* either or, just like I said. I come and work with your father, or that's it."

Once more, she felt called out, as she had last night. She said, "I don't know." She shook her head. "All I seem able to say is 'I don't know.'"

"You sure as hell knew last *night*."

The first drops found the flat crown of Emily's new hat before she could open her umbrella.

"Here," she said, offering it to him.

He held up his hand, declining. He wanted the rain. He wanted to imagine it rinsing this day away. She kept the umbrella closed. She wanted to imagine the same thing.

"Go home," he said, and she thought he was dismissing her, telling her to leave and catch the trolley back to her aunt's house. He saw her confusion. "Go back with your parents and think about it. Maybe then you'll know, since you're saying you don't." As he heard his voice, it sounded not quite as cold, though his feelings were the same, and he felt unprotected without the full sound of his anger.

She squinted up at him through the hastening drops. "And you'll think about it too?" She was determined to hold his look for as long as he'd let her. She wanted badly to touch his eye. Swollen nearly shut, it looked sadly like a clam.

He began to move his head slightly back and forth again, causing her to leave and come back into his vision. He could see her, then he couldn't, then he could, and so on, could, then couldn't. He was seeing his futures—with her, without her.

Watching him through the rain, coming harder now, she thought he was shaking his head, saying, *No, he wouldn't think about it,* and she felt her heart coming loose and flying furiously about.

CHAPTER EIGHT

The rest of July and the first days of August 1916

Emily was gone, and Earl felt himself adrift, his life a calamity, woeful days, and his spirits' bleak surrender.

With his eye turned the purple-and-yellow of a ghastly sunset, he lost the first game he pitched after she had left, giving up six runs without really noticing. He won his second, 6–4, lost his third, 4–3, but now his pitches were beginning to show some signs of renewed life, his body increasingly able to perform for the time nine innings took. As for the other twenty-two hours of his day, he continued to feel his heartsickness in the pit of his stomach, and it absolutely took his appetite.

He slept poorly, some nights barely. He lay in his bed listening to his neighbors, the insomniac pacing overhead, the consumptive coughing weakly on the other side of the wall, and as he listened, feeling he had joined them, that it was now a *trio* of pathetic invalids, he repeated to himself, until it grew to be a mantra, that before she'd come into his life, he had the world he'd dreamed of without having known it was a world a man *could* dream. If he could live with, live through, this heartbreak, however long he had to bear it, then when it had quieted, wouldn't that world still be there, the one he'd had before he met her? Of course it would. If his pitches could find their life again, then so could he find his.

Even so, he continued to sleep badly, waking to a gloom that had itself already waked and was waiting by his bed for him to open his eyes. And he imagined that Emily was waking just then too, which meant that in a way he was imagining himself at *her* bedside.

He sat in the boarding house kitchen drinking coffee, and in his mind he watched her leaving the kitchen on the farm and moving outdoors, to clotheslines and milking stalls and chicken coops and pastures. As his day continued, he saw hers growing darker, an emotional eclipse moving swiftly across it, until he realized he was doing it again, turning her into the cruelly treated girl in the fairy tale. Why was it so tempting to cast her this way, held against her will, with raw red hands and a chimney-soot-streaked face and sweat-damp strands of her chestnut hair come loose and falling in her eyes?

He saw himself reaching into her life and his hand moving her hair off her forehead, as he'd fantasized doing for the woman stirring gruel on her stove in the window in Chicago.

As he'd stood with Emily in the rain that last afternoon, he'd asked her not to write until she'd heard from him when the season ended.

"Very well," Emily had said. Greatly disappointed, it gave her voice a priggish tone.

Dear Emily, he wrote in late July, *I trust this letter finds you in good health. I extend my greetings to your mother and your father. Our season will be done by the time you receive these thoughts from me, so I'll be free to visit you if you are in agreement. That is to say, I would like to see you so that I can* talk *with you, and I would like to hear what you have been thinking during this period of time. Although I suppose I know that already, in that I expect what you want hasn't changed. I will wait to have your reply before I make arrangements to come. Not wishing to presume, I am,*

> *Yours sincerely,*
> *Earl*

What he'd been feeling more and more was the need for her advice. He'd divided himself in two—there was how he felt living his life and how he felt when he played baseball—and he'd done something of the same in thinking about Emily. She wanted keenly to be with him, but in her familiar world. And yet she could choose against herself if she thought it better for him. Unsettled as he was, leading up to when he wrote her, a part of him actually believed she'd find it possible to do this.

CHAPTER NINE

Earl rose from his chair to signal Emily as she came through the doors of the Rutland Hotel, a woebegone four-story brick building at the intersection of Iowa and Fourth Streets, where he'd reserved a room. She was wearing the royal blue shirtwaist he remembered she'd worn the first night they'd danced in the ballroom in Waterloo. Seeing she'd chosen it, he felt for an instant a sense of reassurance, and he resented the thought—that he needed a signal from her in order to feel it.

He watched her walking briskly toward him through the long dim lobby, past the unmanned cigar counter stocked with no cigars, past an enormous grandfather clock and a large brass spittoon and a tall dead fern standing sad and valiant in its pot. The last time he'd seen her, she'd stood with him, holding a closed umbrella and starting to get drenched in a late-arriving rain. And he'd been carrying that memory, that picture of her looking pale and wet and lost. But here she was, her beauty all afresh. Through the summer, their charmed summer, it had often happened, his being abruptly taken with her beauty, even if she'd simply turned away for a moment and then back to him.

As she approached, she looked somehow changed, he *sensed* a change in her, while at the same time she looked lovely in just the same way and in every detail he'd worked the month to forget.

When she reached him, they greeted one another awkwardly as she offered him her hand. They sat down in overstuffed chairs that showed a remarkably similar pattern of stains.

She said, "I trust your trip was comfortable."

On the train from Waterloo, when he looked out the window, he'd heard the landscape, nearly harvest-ready and nagging as a shrew, asking him if he'd made up his mind. "It was fine," Earl said.

She said, "The Illinois Central is usually quite reliable."

Her words—*I trust . . . Usually quite reliable*—they were as rigid as her posture in the chair. It made him think that, however she'd been faring, she was as nervous now as he was, and with everything he felt, he had the impulse to calm her. Here they'd barely said hello, and he was already caught in some emotional middle, looking for signs that she was who she'd been, wanting to draw her close while feeling, threaded through it all, how badly she had hurt him.

He said, "It's the Land'o Corn Limited."

"What?"

"The name of the train."

"Oh," Emily said. "I'd forgotten that, if I knew."

Earl said, "It's the Illinois Central line, but the train's called the Land'o Corn Limited," and his thought was that he couldn't possibly be sounding more stupid.

He looked around the empty lobby. Its air smelled of mold. Its dimness had the quality of a sepia veneer. He cleared his throat. "It just occurred to me. How'd you get here, from the farm?"

"I drove!" she said.

"You drove?"

"Daddy's taught me." And she was suddenly lively with this to talk about. She said her father had shown her how to set the spark and throttle. "He says I've got a safecracker's touch. Plus, he showed me how to stand so I'm strong enough to turn the crank." She said they'd started in the pasture so she wouldn't run into anything. "I'm always looking for an excuse to drive somewhere. You should see the stares I get! 'Is that a *woman*?'" Now he watched her blush as she hurried to add, "I didn't mean I thought of coming to see you as an excuse."

He said, "I didn't think you did."

"Good," she said. "Because I didn't."

They sat, cautious as litigants, and looked around at everything but one another.

Emily had vowed that no matter how this went, she wouldn't tell him how unhappy she'd been. She knew she had no right to, and who would want to hear it? Certainly *she* wouldn't, listening to herself whining on. But as she sat there in her overstuffed chair with its very ugly stains and heard the air's beating stillness, she felt herself wanting, despite her vow, to describe for him what her life had been. *I walk around dropping things and bumping into things. I forget to eat. I feel like I'm watching myself from somewhere outside my body.* Wanting badly to tell him, she sat looking down at the dark folds of her skirt and picking at lint that wasn't there. She was wondering hard. Wondering, and yet not really surprised that she felt only Earl knew how to hear her speak of her days without him. She knew she'd made him miserable, but she'd made herself miserable too. The same person had caused them both the same misery, so in that sad sense, weren't they joined, meaning he alone would understand?

Momma asks me if I'm ill, but of course she knows what's going on, the way she always does.

I lie awake and I berate myself because I haven't been brave enough to follow you.

She sensed that a rush of these words, these self-pitying words, were about to leave her lips if she didn't say something else right now. "You wrote that you wanted to come so we could talk."

Earl was flustered. He'd been trying and failing to get some guiding sense of her, and it seemed to him his best chance was first to listen to *her* talk. "You go ahead."

She nodded, hesitating. "I've been trying to think things through every which way."

Earl said, "Aren't there only *two* ways? Me here, this life, or not?"

He watched her face, but her expression, that deep stillness, told him nothing. He remembered the first time he'd seen her, waiting tables in the Good Day, when her smile had erased her solemn face and he'd felt an outsized relief. *She's not sad!* he'd thought. *And she's lovely!*

She shut her eyes and held them closed for some seconds. This somehow moved him, stirred him, and he felt his wanting her, right there, sitting across from him in her special occasion dress in the ugly high-backed chair. And yet, with that, still furious at all her saying no had caused him these past weeks.

She said, "That night, when you were so angry, telling me what Daddy said, I realized how much I'd been thinking about our future."

Earl said, "And what's wrong with that?"

"Nothing. Nothing's wrong with that, except I hadn't known how frightened I was."

"So I gathered. So you said that night in so many words." His voice was sharp. "But you know what, Emily? It would help me, I'm serious, it really would, if I knew just what it is you're so damned frightened of."

Again she was studying the folds of her skirt. "Earl." Her voice was soft after his sharpness; she was trying to keep a pleading out of it. "You *do* know. Surely you know."

He shrugged. "I guess I'm just a dunce. I guess I'm your Uncle Melvin."

"The uncertainty," she said. "I'm afraid of the uncertainty."

"About what?"

"About *every*thing. About where we'd be living year to year. And how often you'd be gone. And what work you'd find when your season was finished if you couldn't say for sure where we'd be for the next one." She lifted her eyes to him. Whatever his resentment, his face looked attentive, and she saw in it that sincerity she'd loved right away and hadn't known young men his age could feel. And she was reading it now saying something in particular, that he was realizing suddenly what he truly hadn't known—or hadn't let himself know. That the life she was describing, as against the one he saw, they were, yes, on the surface the same life, but beneath it they had nothing in common.

She shifted in her chair. "I've been thinking these weeks, about us being married, and that we'd settle, at some point, into a . . . day-to-dayness. A sameness. I don't know how long it would be before that happened, but I'm sure it would."

Earl said, "Why would that be so bad?"

"It wouldn't! That's what I'm saying. I've loved thinking of us that way." She thought she saw his face change, close slightly. "What are *you* thinking?"

That he'd been hurt and angry, and that much of him still was. But that wasn't thinking, it was feeling. As for thinking, his thought was that she'd read his face exactly. He was thinking how far her uncertainty was from the life he saw ahead for them, the life she said she feared. "Just, everything. All of it," he said in answer to her asking.

She looked at him again and risked a small smile, and seeing it, Earl felt his heart lift, pure reflex. It was defenseless, his love; he couldn't keep it from behaving. He said, "You know how much you're asking me to give up?"

She slowly nodded. "I watched you play. And I listened to you talk about—"

"Pretty much everything. That's how much."

He saw her wince. He'd stung her, and he knew he'd wanted to. He felt certain he was justified, but it came to him too that he was beginning to grow weary of that feeling: he had no wish to go through life feeling that some woundedness he was nursing was justified.

He saw her shaking her head strongly. She said, "This will sound completely selfish. Never mind 'sounds,' it *is* completely selfish, I hate myself for it, and besides selfish, it's arrogant, but—"

"Emily. You know a million words. Please. Just choose a few."

She shifted again, her body tight with tension, and she had the urge to stand, but that would look ridiculous, like she was speechifying. "I just keep coming back to thinking how much better a wife I can be to you. Better here than there." She waited, then added, sounding suddenly shy, "And a better mother too, I dearly hope."

So much was alive in Earl now. Desire, anger, that rascal delight of wanting her as she sat there in her chair, a wish to comfort her, the anger coming around again.

They let a long silence happen. The grandfather clock near the varnished double doors was making its pendulum sound, the metric noise of time, and Emily was thinking of what she hadn't been able to say just now: That he might give so much to baseball he could not give them enough. She couldn't say, even to herself, give *me* enough. But how many times over the past month had she felt deeply ashamed to remember the day she'd watched from the grandstands and sensed in the way his body moved that there'd be times when he was someone who wouldn't need her?

Finally, she said, "Don't hear this as advice. How could I give you *advice* about any of this? But it's to maybe help you think about it. Help *both* of us. At least that's how it sounds to me when I—"

"Please. Really. Just go ahead."

She nodded. "If you decide you . . . *can't*, my heart will break. Snap! I'll feel something that deep. That awful." She paused. "But I think, I *have* to think, I'd start to heal. I can't imagine how long it would take or all the ways I might be changed." She paused again. "And so would you, heal. *Your* heart would. Which I guess means—doesn't it—that I'm assuming it would need to."

"Yes," Earl said. "I guess that's what it means." He'd been trying to give these words a bit of mockery, but he felt instead the pull of what she'd said. That she had faith in the strength of both their hearts. That they would heal, their hearts would; much the worse for wear, scarred and halting, they would heal. From the same kind of hurt, in the same determined way, and he felt, not yet fully wanting to, allied with her in this business of their hearts.

They both started as the heavy office door behind the registration desk banged open. Emily turned and peered around the side of her high-backed chair, and Earl leaned forward in his to see a hotel clerk emerge and maneuver a large Victrola around the desk into the lobby. He was dressed in a dark-blue uniform with fake brass buttons and epaulettes that lay like long tongues on his shoulders. He looked like a Gilbert and Sullivan commandant. He carried the Victrola past Earl and Emily to a walnut table in the middle of the room. He set the Victrola down and adjusted its giant lily horn. He stepped forward— his little head was shaped like a squirrel's—and loudly announced, as if he were speaking to a crowded lobby, "Beginning today, the Rutland is proud to feature Victrola recordings during the luncheon hour from noon to one o'clock, compliments of the management."

Earl and Emily looked at each other, and they were tremendously relieved they could smile together at something ridiculous and safe. Earl whispered, "When word of this gets out, they'll be turning them away by the tens."

The clerk began cranking the Victrola, then swung the playing arm over, and as he lowered the needle he said, again loudly, "'They Didn't Believe Me.' The most popular song in all of America in 1915." And after some bars of introduction, a tenor voice began to sing the tune.

Returning to the registration desk, the clerk passed Emily and Earl again, nodding formally, while the tenor sang that the woman he loved had chosen him from all those in the world she could have had. And when he told his friends, as he was certainly going to tell them, they wouldn't believe him.

Earl looked at Emily and saw that she'd turned her eyes toward the tall dead fern near the varnished front doors. He slowly took her in, from head to toe, her lustrous hair to her soft black boots. He imagined her thinking that she'd said all she could, and now he was making his decision, that her looking away was as near as she could get to leaving him alone to think things through. He could believe she might be staring at that God-awful fern for the rest of time unless he said something to her.

There'd been days when his confusion had made him weak, as with an illness, and there'd been days when his anger had given him an almost bestial strength. He'd traveled here across the top of Iowa on the Land'o Corn Limited of the usually quite reliable Illinois Central line, listening to the hectoring landscape and banking on his belief that she would tell him, judicial as Solomon, what she thought was best for him no matter what it meant for her. But she hadn't done that. She couldn't begin to give him advice.

"Emily?"

She turned away from the fern to look at him. He saw that she was composed.

He reached for her hands, then stood, and she rose with him from her chair. He led her to the middle of the lobby, and she moved into his arms.

They began to dance to the sounds of the Victrola. They were silent, dancing nearly in place, a gestural to and fro, and the lobby became all at once even dimmer as, outside, clouds moved across the sun and blocked its light from coming in through the tall front windows.

Earl welcomed this, the lobby in an even denser shade; it made it intimate; it made it feel like theirs, for all its shabbiness, like a room he wished to claim.

They danced, and she asked him to hold her more tightly, and in his head Earl heard, *It's the things that's wrong a person's got to like about the other.* If that wasn't quite what Emily was telling him, he sensed that it lived right next to what she'd said, and maybe this was what he'd come to hear from her. Her admission of what, in a life with him, she couldn't do. In hearing it like this, Earl felt all at once that, as with their equal hearts, their confusions too were equal, and they were equally desperate to move beyond confusion's sadness. And maybe, most crucial, there was *this* equation: his anger and her despair for having caused it. Maybe he'd needed to know that *they* were equal.

All of this, again, was what he *felt*; too new, as before, too unshaped to be thoughts.

They danced, taking their pantomime steps, and with the music he was hearing all the nights he'd asked himself why, once his pain had begun to ease, he couldn't have the life he'd had before he met her. And now he heard the answer in his head: *because you met her.*

He said, "I imagined you there, on the farm." He'd just been thinking how he had, but the words slipped out; they'd felt vulnerable, unguarded, and he hadn't meant to say them.

Emily sensed she should say nothing in response, and later today, driving home, she will have a kind of vision. That in her life of loving Earl, there would be times when she must wait with her feelings. Wait until she knew just how to offer them, not falsely, certainly not that, but with a patience she must learn.

"I saw you in my mind, living your day." A swiftness of feeling was pulling Earl along; its strength was startling to him.

Emily looked up at him, and he could read her face for once. It was curious and thrilled.

He didn't tell her he'd imagined her the cruelly mistreated girl. He didn't tell her he'd imagined reaching into the frame of her life and lifting her hair away from her damp and soot-streaked forehead. He said, "I saw every detail of the place."

"And how could you do *that*? You've never seen it."

He was reaching for a fancifulness. He sensed that's what they needed now. "I just know it."

"Prove it," Emily said.

"Well. I pictured a barn on your farm. Is there a barn?"

"Why, yes, there is."

"And fields. I saw fields, where you grow things. Are there fields by any chance?"

"There are."

"I saw a house, with a kitchen, and in the kitchen, a stove."

"That's amazing," Emily said.

"I'm a wizard," Earl said.

The song had finished some time ago, the lobby sounding with the static of the needle plowing the end grooves. They'd come to a stop, still holding one another. The clerk at last appeared and bent down to change the recording. He lifted the arm, the static ended, the lobby going silent, and in the silence Earl could hear their breathing. Which meant their hearts. He could hear their equal hearts.

CHAPTER TEN

September 5, 1916   *The farm south of Hinton, Iowa*

"It ain't that he mopes exactly," Rooster said to Lottie. They were lying in bed on this unseasonably frigid night, but even so the windows were raised to receive the country air. The upstairs bedrooms, this one, and Earl and Emily's down the hall, looked west to the dirt road and to the gently climbing pasture where Emily had learned to drive the Model-T.

He hadn't yet talked to Lottie in any detail about his days working alongside Earl. He'd been wanting to report some good news, some encouraging sign, whatever it might be. As was typical, she'd been waiting patiently to hear. "But if I say something, just an innocent remark, 'Sun feels good today, don't it,' what I'm likely to get back is a damn silence so loud it makes me want to plug my ears."

"He doesn't answer you?" Lottie asked. "But that's rude. I've never seen a hint of rudeness in Earl."

"Not that," Rooster said. "It's like he's listening to somebody else saying something he thinks is a lot more interesting than what I am, and he gives a nod to this other fellow, 'Hold on,' and *then* he answers me. Some days is worse than others. Today was the worst yet."

Their wedding had been quickly planned and small, inspiring the predictable rumors in the village. Lottie's white gown, lace trimming its neck and sleeves, fit Emily perfectly. The years it lay neatly folded in an attic trunk had turned its silk, unevenly, a beautiful, creamy shade. Her best friend from high school, Maude MacKenzie, had been her maid of honor. Rooster, wearing his frayed gray suit with the sweat stain on the cuff, had stood with Earl in his off-white linen.

The question of Earl's family had been raised when Rooster and Lottie asked about their coming. Emily too had paused to hear what Earl would say. She'd asked about them early on, in Waterloo, and he'd spoken vaguely, his phrases drifting.

He'd answered Lottie and Rooster vaguely as well, saying there were feelings he'd had to get away from. He'd said that what he meant was his father's violent anger and his mother's indifference to what it was and what it did, which he'd come to understand was an emotion of its own, and one he'd also needed to get away from. Briefly, he'd been tempted to describe the old man's drunken rants. But as he'd heard them in his head, their mad gabble, he'd known he couldn't do them justice. And from this distance of years, they had a black hilarity about them.

As Earl and Rooster had moved together through the first, long learning days, Earl was attentive to the physical work and quickly capable. Rooster assumed that he was working hard at letting go of what he'd given up to have what he'd wanted even more, a life with Emily. It only stood to reason that he'd be doing that.

But Rooster was also feeling spurned, like a rejected suitor. It seemed to him that Earl was saying, with his being here and yet not here as they labored, that the working life he'd been asked into didn't measure up. And like all rejected suitors, Rooster was tempted to self-pity.

In their bed, Rooster and Lottie lay on their backs, arms folded identically across their chests. With their coupled pose, they looked like children playing husband and wife. "Maybe what you're saying to him needs to be more interesting," Lottie said. Her face was in darkness, and Rooster normally wouldn't have needed to see it to know she was having fun with him. He made indignant, harrumphing sounds, and she had to tell him to calm down.

The cold air moved the bedroom window's lace curtains. The house creaked faintly of its own accord, now and then, here and there, like a ghostly wooden ship.

"Frank?"

"What?" He waited. "What?"

"That night at your sister's. When you talked to him. Have you ever said to Earl that what you did was . . . hard?"

"Hard?"

"If you never have, I think you should."

"Well, for one thing, it *wasn't*. *Tricky*, yes, deciding just how to put it, but not 'hard.'"

Lottie sat up in bed and reached behind her for her straw-stuffed pillow. She plumped it up, placed it against the headboard, and scooched back against it. She said, "I meant hard like in hard-hearted."

Rooster quickly sat up too and turned to Lottie in the dark. "You're saying I'm hard-hearted?"

"Not as a rule, of course not," Lottie said. "I'm saying what you did that night was."

"What I am. What I did. Don't get fancy with your logic on me, Lottie." He was scrambling out of bed as he said this and now stood in his long johns, his toes curling up off the cold linoleum floor, his feet so gnarled with corns and bunions they looked primeval. He'd had it up to his Adam's apple with Earl today, and he'd turned to his wife for some comforting talk before sleep, and what had she given him but it was all his fault because his heart was hard. He set his fists on his hips, an oddly effeminate pose the likes of which Lottie had never seen in their long shared life. If they'd been playing charades, she'd have guessed, *Huffy? In a snit?*

"Listen," she said calmly. She straightened out the heavy quilt where he'd thrown it off and pulled it snugly to her chest. She said she'd known him as a boy, then a young man, and every day of his life since, right up to tonight and this very moment they were talking. Thirty years. "I think that makes me qualified to say you are *not* a hard man, Frank. Not mean, not cruel. Call it what you want, that's not your nature." She said, to further make her point, that it was easy to think of some around here who were. "Take a man like Pinky Ingram, for instance, just off the top of my head. I remember coming out of Sunday School once when we were kids; he tripped me on the church steps, and he was real disappointed when all I did was fall and cut my knee."

Rooster folded his arms against the frigid air. "We're agreed that Pinky Ingram was a son of a bitch growing up, and he still is, even worse. What's he got to do with anything?" He'd absently begun to tap the small brass ball atop the bedpost. He was upset, roiled, and his feet were going numb on the cold linoleum. The rag rug was on Lottie's side of the bed.

She said, "What I'm saying is you are naturally *decent*, and that particularly stands out when you think of some who aren't." She stopped for a moment. "But."

"'But'?" He unconsciously shifted his posture to receive what was coming.

Lottie said, "Saying to Earl he couldn't try for his dream if he wanted your blessing. Making it a stipulation. I have to say it, Frank, that was a hard thing you did." She spoke with her quiet matter-of-factness, no need to raise her voice, which she never did anyway except to call to him when he was working at the edge of a field near the house. (On the worst day of their lives, three years from now, she will shout his name and Earl's in this way, from the front porch out to where they're harvesting corn, her voice piercing the air, raw as a crow's in keening her distress.)

"'Stipulation,'" Rooster said. "Christ on a crutch, Lottie. The boy was talking nonsense. The fortune he'd be making? I did it for his own good as much as anything."

"I'm sure you thought you did. I'm sure you still do."

"Turns out, it's what Emily wanted too."

"All the more reason to stay out of it, let them work things out between them."

He looked around the dark bedroom, not for anything he might find there. He tapped the brass ball on the bedpost again. "Why didn't you light into me right then, at the time?"

Lottie had to think about this. She held the neck of her flannel nightgown and drew it tighter. "I should have. You're right. I suppose

I thought, why say anything after it was done. But that's no excuse." She shook her head with disappointment in herself. "Come on now and get back into bed. Your feet must be like ice."

He lay sleepless, his toes primevally thawing, remembering the day at recess when Pinky Ingram extended his hand to shake and, caught off guard, he'd offered his, and Pinky grabbed his wrist and pulled him close and kneed him fiercely in the nuts.

For the next few days, he and Earl worked in a conjoined, distracted silence, Mutt and Jeff as deaf mutes left to run a farm. And all the while Rooster was hearing Lottie's words in his head like a song that wouldn't quit.

September weather had returned, feeling almost balmy, but the barn was cool after the run of chilly days, so neither man was sweating as they sat resting side by side on bales in the hayloft. It was close to noon, and they'd just finished their morning of mucking out the barn. The sun shone in at crazy angles through places where the siding was loose or missing. Dust motes swarmed in these slanting bands of light.

Rooster said, breaking a silence, "You know how a man can tell if he's too crippled up?"

Earl looked at him and frowned. "Too crippled up for what?"

Rooster said, "Those cold days we had, my joints wasn't ready, and even now I'm sitting here, I can hold a shovel, barely, but it would be too hard if I wanted to pick my nose."

Earl looked at him again, a sideways glance that held a smile. "Are you asking me for a favor?"

Rooster laughed, a cackle he directed up past the lines of mote-crazed light, past the wooden crossbeams where half a dozen pigeons roosted, to the barn's peaked ceiling. "No, no favor. But think about it. Ain't that the perfect definition of a man who's too crippled up?" And from this highly unlikely start, he leaned forward on his hay bale, his forearms on his thighs and, looking straight ahead, not at Earl, said, "I need to get something off my chest, so hear me out."

Earl nodded, intrigued. A confession of some sort.

"The night you and me had our confab at my sister's, it's my belief I was thinking what would be the right outcome. You two wanted to get married, and here was the best way to do that. You'd have each other and be all set, was my thinking." He continued to look straight ahead as he talked. "That was the first thing I thought. But how I figure it now, there was something else."

He cleared his throat and waited, the pause inviting Earl to ask him what that something else was. He turned and saw that Earl was looking up to where he'd sent his cackling laugh, seeming to be fixed on the crisscrossing shafts of light.

All right, be *that way*, Rooster thought, and fought back a pout. He said, "So, while I was listening to you tell me about your baseball days that night, the arthritis just came out of nowhere and got me in both hands. Whoo! Nearly took my head off. It's like it was saying, 'Feel that, Frank? So how're you expecting the hard things'll get done when you're stiff and hurting like this pretty much nonstop?'" He paused again and raised his eyes, looking up, looking ceilingward himself; the two of them looking up, intent on the dancing motes. Then: "What I'm saying, it was the co*in*cidence. The pain shooting through me— that's why the silliness just now about being too crippled up—and I'm hearing you say you want to marry Emily, and it came to me—nothing clear-cut, it just sort of came to me—'Could this maybe be an answer to everything?'"

He turned once more to Earl and met his large brown eyes, now looking directly at him. They were narrowed, intense, and Rooster was unnerved by their frowning focus. It might have been saying, *Tell me more*. Earl might have been thinking, *I am looking at a fool*. Rooster couldn't tell.

Earl said, "There was a lot going on that night, wasn't there," and before Rooster could think how to answer, Earl got up and walked away, to the edge of the loft, some thirty feet from where he'd sat.

There was an improbable elegance to his posture as he stood there, a solitary figure outlined against the barn's dimness, not slouching, not military straight, the long length of his body a fluid line; it made him look powerful to Rooster and even taller than usual. He'd never thought of Earl's height as imposing, but he did now. Staring at Earl's back, he decided the only thing to do was keep talking, following the path he'd plotted until he reached the essential words, the ones waiting for him farther on. "I *still* think it's for the best, your coming, being here." His voice was quieter. "And not just for me, selfish me getting the obvious benefits. Best for you, too. And of course for Emily." He paused, wishing Earl would turn the hell around so he could say the next thing to his face, then thought, no, it was easier, if also maybe a touch gutless, talking to his back. "Time will tell, I know that. But however it proves right or wrong," he loudly cleared his throat, "either way, *I* was wrong. To make it a . . . stipulation."

He said he was wrong. But Earl hadn't heard him. Listening to Rooster describe his so-called reasons—he'd had Earl's best interests at heart; the *coincidence* of the pain arriving when it had—Earl hadn't been able to decide which one pissed him off more, sounded more like an excuse, so he'd stood up and walked away.

And adding to it, here was the night on the Earlys' porch returning. Rooster's pained and doubtful squint as Earl said what he might earn. Rooster saying his proposition was a way for Earl to save himself from a life of disappointment—save his *bacon* was what he'd said. Then their parting for the night in the hallway, and the etiquette of *that* well beyond them both, Rooster turning tongue-tied and formal, Earl frantic, nearly tearful, and working fiercely not to show Rooster any of it.

What he was feeling now was new, *this* instant's anger, but with it also was the return of that night's. And yet all of it together was somehow helping him think, and as he stood there, he was thinking he saw perfectly well what Rooster's reason had been: He didn't want to lose his daughter. He didn't want her to leave, and the way to keep her here was to have Earl be here too. It was that simple—and devious—and it was that complexly tangled.

Rooster continued to watch Earl. He'd done what he could, said what he could say. He would give himself that much; he'd be able to say so to Lottie. He'd said he was wrong, and as he'd heard himself saying it, he realized he meant it. He was thinking, wondering, how he might admit that to Earl so it wouldn't sound as if he'd been *surprised* to find how much he meant it. But Earl, his back still turned, hadn't given him so much as a grunt or a nod.

He reached into the bib pocket of his overalls and found his tobacco pouch. Working his stiff, joint-swollen fingers like tongs, he managed to reach in and withdraw a loose nest of strands and shape a wad to tuck in against his cheek. His mouth made rabbity twitches to draw juice enough to spit.

Looking down from where he stood at the lip of the loft, Earl saw a Bernard, one of the farm's several barn cats. They were all named Bernard here; it was the custom going back to when Rooster was a boy, however it had started. Earl watched this one, long and skinny, white with black patches, as it moved sinuously along the edges where the dirt floor met the walls. The pigeons in the eaves, the surveilling cats below, Rooster teaching him the maintenance of the vast in-between. It struck Earl as the farm's hierarchy, as the order of a natural world, with him in the middle of it all, standing at that moment beneath the roosting pigeons.

He turned and looked back through the chilly, held-in air, the smell of hay and cow dung in it, to the empty bale and Rooster sitting next to it on his. He started back, the thirty feet, walking now with more intent, and finally he heard it. *I was wrong.* As a son, it was what he'd wanted most to hear, until one morning, waking bruised and sore, he'd realized he never would, and after that he'd shut himself off from ever expecting anything resembling it. And this, along with everything he'd been thinking while Rooster was talking, had made him deaf to the words. For some seconds he just stood there, hearing them; hearing them.

When Earl reached him and sat down on the bale, Rooster nodded. He leaned sideways and sent a stream of tobacco juice some distance. Sitting next to him again, Earl saw Rooster looking old, weary, a worn-down country gnome; arthritis and admission, the two of them together, had taken it out of him.

Earl had been carrying his anger as he walked back to sit beside him. He'd been set to give it to him, and he still had ahold of it as he sat there. But now, within its heat, there was a warmth starting. This would take months to reconcile fully, but more and more aware of it, Earl would sense he couldn't stop his feelings, couldn't quiet their ambition, until he'd pause at some point, his heart ready at last, to ask himself why he should.

Earl said while looking at him, "I didn't want to lose her either."

He was sitting by the window in their bedroom in a chair too small for him. Its floral-patterned needlepoint cushion was one of Emily's primitive attempts, which she'd brought home from her sewing circle and presented to them all with a good laugh at herself. She'd never taken to the thimble and the needle and had once told her mother she'd rather wear a horse blanket on the hottest day of August and call it the latest style, rather that than having to sew a dress.

Now, in their bed across the room from where Earl sat in her chair, the sounds of her sleeping were her breaths pausing briefly, then resuming. She was snoring in stanzas, very lightly.

Looking out the window, he saw the shapes of the world in the moonlight. The line of trees that made a windbreak between fields. The row of fence posts running alongside the dirt road. The road itself like a brushstroke of moon across the night.

In the too small chair, looking out at the country night, the landscape lifting and folding, he thought again of seeing Rooster's startled face when he'd heard him say, *I didn't want to lose her either*. Earl could swear he saw Rooster blushing then, and he'd liked the sense of having startled him, of holding up a mirror and showing Rooster something of himself he hadn't thought of. He'd felt a surge of confidence, the thing that had always come naturally to him until he'd arrived here and begun this life. It had felt fine to know a moment of that confidence again.

"My sweet Earl." It's what Emily had said when they'd finished supper tonight. She'd come up to him as he left the long kitchen table and reached up to hold his face in her hands. "My sweet Earl," she'd said, then kissed him, and Earl took it to mean she'd somehow intuited what there was to know about his and Rooster's talk. He'd told her nothing really. It had seemed to Earl like something between him and Rooster, not secret, but private, and a real distinction there.

He turned from the window to watch her sleeping, quietly now.

She'd said it, too, the first night he'd lain with her in that bed in this room.

She'd said, "My sweet Earl."

He'd arrived that afternoon. He'd unpacked and Rooster had given him the tour and he'd sat through the polite talk at supper and after, until Lottie and Rooster had gone up to bed, and the house, dark and quiet, had seemed just theirs for the moment, his and Emily's.

They'd tiptoed into this room, still *her* room that night; he'd been given a cot in Lottie's sewing room downstairs. Emily shut the door and turned to him to whisper something, and he'd put his fingers to her lips to stop her. For Earl, all there was to say was wordless, was their wanting one another.

She'd looked up at him and smiled and mouthed, *Hello.*

He'd taken her hand to guide her to the quilt-covered bed, then reached down and lifted her up and held her in his arms. She'd put hers around his neck and kissed it softly, then again. She might have been a child being put to bed. She might have been a lovely invalid. She might have been a wedding-night bride. She'd whispered, "I was waiting for you."

He laid her down on the quilt and lay down beside her. "How long?"

"Oh, years. Many years. I'm much older than I look."

They'd kissed, their lips pressing, that giving of desire and asking for it back, gift and greed, as before. She reached for his hand, took his finger in her mouth and held it, slowly sucking, and his wanting her stayed there with how wonderful her lips felt.

He'd reached and felt through fabric for her breasts. As she had the night beneath the ballroom porch, she closed her eyes and arched her back to offer herself more, to help his touch go deeper. His hands moved beneath her skirts. She'd begun to raise and lower her hips, and he saw this as her showing him how she'd made love to him when she was alone in this bed, waiting. She'd opened her legs and his hand found her, and she moved against it, their breaths quickening, until he took it away, wanting both hands to undress her. Their breathing grew sharper, sounding falsely like work sounds, there were so many buttons, there were so many layers, until they were naked, his body long and rope-muscled, his face and neck and forearms brown against the milk-whiteness of the rest of him, her body small and delicate. He'd raised himself up and over her and sat back on his knees. She hoarsely whispered, her sound was not a word, then closed her eyes and opened them again as he guided himself into her. Looking at each other, their faces disbelieving, becoming children's, and she flinched with the pain.

Afterward, they'd lain side by side, her hand resting on his chest. All they'd done was still not done inside them. They were breathing together, but the rhythms of their breaths and thoughts were separate.

Over the months he'd mined in Riverton, Earl had fucked two whores in the brothel near the camp. One was a short, fat, pockmarked girl whose sense of humor was between her legs. She'd had *Pleased to* tattooed on the inside of her right thigh and *meet ya!* on the inside of her left. Otherwise, she was unsmiling; she made the mood memorial. The other whore was a large, big-boned woman who smelled of sickly sweet perfume and lye and who took hold of his penis when they were done and he was getting hard again and tapped down its life with the flicking of her finger the way you settle the mercury in a thermometer.

Lying next to Emily, he'd remembered those grim episodes, comical now, the dumb machinery of the sex, and he'd silently laughed a single laugh, really just an audible smile, at the idea that they had anything in common with Emily, with this appetite and lightness.

He'd leaned close to kiss her. "Where are you?" he'd asked.

She'd been adrift in her body, feeling it find its way back to what it was when she wasn't making love to him. She'd felt bewitched, startled by the sharpness of the pain, surprised by how well she knew how to give and ask for pleasure. She touched herself and felt the wet spot of blood on the sheet. She was very sore, feeling raw, feeling that and the lushness together.

She'd taken his hand and kissed his palm and said, "You are my sweet Earl."

CHAPTER ELEVEN

November 29, 1916

"Take a walk with me," Emily said to Earl after supper, the dishes, the pots and skillet, washed and dried and put away.

They started down the narrow path from the house toward the road. The night was brightly moonlit. She took his gloved hand in hers.

"Look, it's full," Emily said, pointing at the moon.

Earl looked too. "I'd say . . . a waxing gibbous. I'd say still a night away."

It was a game they played—whether it was or wasn't full—when a big round moon surprised them. Emily always claimed it was, and this one, who could argue? There it hung, low in the eastern sky, exactly fat and white as milk; the face, its simpleton expression, clearly drawn. "Mmm, yes," she said. "It is a waxing gibbous."

"What? You're agreeing?"

"I love the words. Waxing gibbous. You're not the only one who should get to say them."

They reached the road and doubled back, heading north, passing the dark farmhouse. Just the parlor was lit, by a lamp and the fire Lottie had made after supper. She built them expertly. The kindling caught quickly; the sprigs of flame appeared.

Past the house and the acreage, the fields on both sides of the road had been picked. Earl's first harvest, and he thought of them, the fields, as having been ransacked, pillaged, lying stunned now and recovering.

He'd begun to live his new life still more alertly, to bring a vigilance to it, and to who he was in it. And within it all—more often now it was only faintly felt—were his thoughts of the life he hadn't chosen. Missing what he'd had, yes, but more than that, feeling what he was sure he *would* have had. He'd waked this morning with that notion, moving vivid and molecular through his first thoughts of the day.

So there were times when he was seeing the world as if through a window, from a great confounding distance. It was like, but not the same as, years before when it seemed to him he was looking *in* on his life. Then, he'd been curious to observe it, feeling even entertained by the thought that that's what he was doing. But here it left him frustrated when he felt it playing out just beyond him in a place he couldn't always find the entrance to, and then a low feeling filled him, a blue lassitude.

They walked along in silence. These moments when he grew suddenly quiet, this depth of quiet, they were new to Emily in knowing him, and it worried her to think they were new to him as well. She'd loved her sense, in Waterloo, that he gave the world his personality, and the world—how could it resist? What could it do but give itself back to him? She'd thought of his days as comprised of this rich exchange.

The night was noiseless too, and the fat moon lit the silence. The road's dirt surface was firmly set, not yet frozen, so their footsteps barely made a sound. The direction of the breeze was keeping the smell of barnyards away.

Emily squeezed Earl's hand, her mitten in his glove, and said, "I have an idea."

"I thought you did," he said.

"And why—"

"It's been, what? a week? You're overdue."

Emily took one of her deep breaths with the lips-fluttering exhale. "I heard them talking in Macauley's today about a good, it sounds like a *very* good baseball league, and apparently Sioux City has a team."

"It's a semiprofessional league," Earl said.

His voice was flat, matter of fact. Not consciously, he let go of her hand.

Emily said, "You knew about it?"

"I did," he said. "I do." He said he'd read about the team, a summary of its season, in the newspaper shortly after he'd arrived.

"Oh," she said. She was taken aback. It seemed strange, *very* strange, that he hadn't mentioned it. She'd assumed she'd at least be giving him news, that whatever he would feel and what he'd say would come from there: her gift of news. "They were talking mostly about one player. 'Lester,' they said his name was. Lester Someone. Apparently, he's a wonderful batter and a good outfielder too."

Earl merely shrugged.

They'd slowed their step, this too unconsciously, as if they weren't sure of the road now, though the moon continued to light it just as brightly.

Hearing the codgers talking in the grocery, Emily had imagined them speaking about Earl, that they were saying *his* name, their voices rasping with old age, but lively in recalling pitches they'd seen him throw, smiling at the memory of their magic. She'd overheard such talk about him now and then in Waterloo, at tables in the Good Day, and listening in Macauley's she'd remembered the first game she'd gone to and how she'd felt the eagerness he'd given off, a kind of avarice for the instant, and for the one coming after, as he stood on the mound. Felt it reaching all the way up to where she sat.

He'd seemed a boy and she a girl. Not then, not at the time, but as she saw them now, thinking back.

She said, " 'Semiprofessional.' So they get paid, at least a little."

Earl nodded.

"What about how good they are . . . compared?"

"Semigood," he said, straining for a joke, because he felt his anger flushing up. Its suddenness surprised him, and its strength did even more. Of course, he knew what she was thinking, where this was heading, but he was going to make her say it. "Compared to what?"

"Compared to, you know, where you played, before."

He brought them abruptly to a stop. He looked down into her eyes, and she up into his before she turned away. She'd tied a dark scarf around her head to keep her ears warm. It made her face in profile look separate from the night, an ivory cameo set against the milky dark.

He said, "So you're thinking, if I played it would somehow be the same? I'd be, what, just as satisfied?"

She looked again into his eyes. "That's not what I was thinking."

"Because, let me just say it. It would not be the same. Not even close. I can't believe I'd have to tell you that."

"You *don't* have to tell me that. I *know* it wouldn't be the same."

"Do you? Do you really?"

"Yes!"

"Then why bring it up?"

"Because—"

"Because?"

"Because it sounded like something that might make you happy." She was managing to keep her voice steady. Thinking it through on her drive home from the grocery, she'd feared this might be how he'd react, and now her distress was calling her a fool, asking her why in the world, if she'd thought that, she had risked it.

He began to walk a tight circle in the road, his head down, as if he were searching for something he'd dropped and counting on the light of the moon to help him find it. Then he stopped and looked again at her.

Before he could speak, she said, repeating, "I thought it might make you happy."

"Unh-uh, I don't think so," Earl said. "I think you thought it might make *you* happy."

"Well of course I did. If you were, it would make me happy too."

He flipped his hand at her to push her words away. "You know that's not what I'm saying."

"What I know is, like I said, if you were happy, so would I be. That's what I know, Earl."

"Ahhh, *God*!" And she flinched from the sharpness of his cry. "Good *Christ*, Emily!" She imagined she heard this reverberating in the night, though the world here was wide open, just the sky, the sky for miles, nothing to catch the sound of his anger and throw it back.

He spun around and started up the road, and, speechless, she let him go into the bright night and the silence. She watched, and then she couldn't see him.

She was lit theatrically, standing inside a slender, even brighter column of moonlight shining through a gap in the leafless branches of a maple at the edge of the field where Earl had stopped them. Her heart was racing; she'd made this mistake and her heart was urgent, racing.

She stood right where she was, noticing now that it had gotten colder, and it came to her that the only chance she had to save something of the night was not to budge, not move an inch, so that when he came back he'd see she hadn't. Signaling what to him? Apology. Showing him what? Her devotion. She stood there, tracing this ridiculous thinking, knowing it was, but seizing it anyway. She heard the silence as a voice, and it was clearly on Earl's side. Its sound was a judgment. She felt outnumbered.

Ten minutes passed, a long time to wait in moonlight, making yourself a statue, your face getting very cold, your ears too, despite the scarf, holding tightly to a foolishness—that you should stay right where you were so as to make amends.

She heard his footsteps, light scuffings, and fast-moving; sounding near and nearer, and there he was in front of her.

"Earl—

"I'm cold, I'm going back. You coming?" And he continued, brushing past her, heading down the road toward the farmhouse.

She hurried to catch up with him, and when she had, he said, "You're just like your father." As he'd been walking, furious, up the road, he'd heard it sounding in his ears, *like father, like daughter*, thinking how often he'd said it to himself with amusement, with affection.

"What do you mean?"

"'Here, son.'" Earl's words as Rooster's were top-heavy with their sarcasm. "'Here's a life for you. Come and have it and we'll all be happy.'"

She was struggling to keep up, and it was clear he didn't care, wasn't slowing down for her. He continued, as loudly, now as Emily. "'Here, Earl! Here's a team just up the road! If you play for *it*—'"

"Earl, no!"

"'—it won't take too much time, I won't feel guilty anymore, and we'll all be happy.'"

"No! Not *fair*!" She was behind him again, rushing to keep a pace she couldn't. But now he stopped and turned around as she came up to him. They stood face-to-face, and she said nothing, waiting.

He said, "Except *he* said he was wrong. That's the difference. He said he was wrong."

She was weeping. And she was thinking, blinks of thought were what they were, that she *had* told him she knew how selfish she was being. Wasn't that a way of saying she was wrong? But her heart was in her throat, and it was telling her it wasn't, not close enough.

He saw her tears. Her face was flushed, with her upset and with her trying to stay with him and with the cold. His feelings were as livid, but he was done with speaking them. If he heard still more words, they would be the same words even if they weren't and that would make him even angrier.

There was at last a sound in the night that wasn't theirs, an owl somewhere close by, its *hooo* like a lute's note.

Her tears made sense to her, and that made her glad to have them. She said, "That day," and he knew the day she meant. "I said, that day, I couldn't give you advice. Do you wish I'd said you shouldn't? That I thought you shouldn't come?"

He shook his head and looked up at the night yet again. At stars this time, the cloudless sky so dense with them, but their brightness washed out, pale, losing to the moon's.

Emily asked, "If I'd said that, something like that, would you have heard me? What would you have thought?"

"I don't know." His resentment, spoken low, and then a silence, tutorial and grave.

Until she said, "I never could have said it. I wanted this too much."

The moon was loyal, still attendant, waiting for them in their bedroom, streaming through the window, and in its brightness Earl hurried them roughly to nakedness. They pressed against each other, he spread her legs, and she pushed against his cupped palm, watching him intently and saying with her body that however she'd been wrong, she wasn't wrong to want this. They fucked, their faces set and sly, and he made a witless, carnal sound as he moved inside her; on another night, they'd have smiled at hearing this, his pleasure dumbly spoken.

Finished, they lay holding one another tightly, a kind of contest, competing against themselves, against each other, to claim what they each wanted badly to claim, neither of them sure what all that was and right then neither caring. They simply needed to hold on, not be the first to let go, until, gradually, they began to.

When he heard her steady breathing, Earl turned to her; her body was an outline beneath the blue-and-white quilt. He got up and went to the window and pulled the curtains closed, then bent down to where their clothes were strewn together on the floor.

"Where are you going?" Her voice surprised him. It was small and sounded lonely.

"I thought you were asleep."

"No."

"Downstairs," he said, as he began to dress in the dark.

They were whispering, though they and the night were wide awake.

"I'll come and sit with you."

"I want to be by myself. Go to sleep."

"I won't be able to."

"Think of something," Earl said.

"I love you, Earl."

"I know you do."

He tiptoed out and down the hall, past Lottie and Rooster's bedroom, to the stairs.

In the parlor, he sat in front of what was left of Lottie's fire. It had died in the orderly way it had burned through the evening, its well-behaved flames furling and unfurling. But he'd revived its embers; they pulsed redly in the grate. He held Rooster's bottle of corn liquor in one hand, his filled glass in the other. His aim was to get quite drunk, to numb all his feelings except for one, the self-pity; he wanted purely to feel that.

He lifted his glass and drank and closed his eyes against the liquor sliding rawly down his throat.

His mind was pacing.

He knew her past. He knew she'd gotten what she wanted from the day she was born. She'd admitted this to him, with embarrassment and wonder. But he'd believed she understood that her life now was far more complicated than the easy history of her father, poised to spoil her, saying, *yes*.

Until tonight, that's what he'd believed.

He drank Rooster's awful liquor.

He was thinking, maybe she *had* been foolish enough to believe it could be the same.

He was thinking, maybe she knew very well it couldn't be, which was why she'd felt it was safe to suggest.

He was thinking, as he had been since he arrived and read about the league, that he couldn't imagine pitching against teams of amateurs. And he was thinking, as he hadn't, not in the way he was thinking it now, that he couldn't imagine never pitching again.

He drank and watched the embers, grateful that Emily had known to stay upstairs and let him be alone, until he'd gotten to his mood and well beyond it, and then a doubt, one he'd had no idea he carried, came forward wholly formed out of the drunken dark. What if he'd chosen this life not because, on that day they'd talked in the hotel lobby, he'd watched her risk a smile and felt it lift his heart? What if his choice had little, maybe nothing, maybe not a damn thing finally, to do with the pact he felt their hearts had made? With their strength, their scarred resilience, with her faith in how they'd both heal if they got broken. What if he'd made his choice instead so that he'd never have to know if he was good enough?

It was a fear that found him just this once, set loose by Rooster's liquor and on the embers of his anger.

A Saturday morning in late April, he will drive to Sioux City, to the ballpark where the team is holding tryouts. He'll wear a sweatshirt and loose, heavy twill pants, no cap, his scuffed cleats slung over his shoulder as always, looking like a rube who's wandered in off the street, hoping, whatever the reason for this gathering, there'll be sandwiches and coffee.

He'll wait for his turn, then throw his warm-up pitches. He's wild at first. He's been throwing for a week at the side of the barn, but still his pitches have been in hibernation, they're eager, glad for spring, and the ball has too much life coming out of his hand. He'll gradually settle in, stay just wild enough to keep the batters uncomfortable. He'll face a dozen of them, and a few will make contact. Low, looping fouls. Slow ground balls. He'll wonder if one of the hitters is Lester Someone.

But when the season starts, he'll find the play better than he thought it would be, and sometimes a hitter who's quick and canny with his bat will take him back to his season when all of it mattered, every pitch, every moment, mattered absolutely.

For Emily, there'll be a game, only one, when her old fear returns. Sitting in the stands in early summer with her father, they're watching Earl, his arm moving liquidly through and finishing like a whip-snap. And as she watches, she will realize, astonished, appalled, that she's wishing he would lose just enough of how good he is right then to make him struggle, only for this game, but that when he gets it back he won't get quite all of it. Disgusted, she'll force herself to watch him still more closely, and through the next innings she'll see nothing in the way he stands and moves and walks that makes him anyone but Earl. And she'll think, thrilled and relieved, that Earl and that man she didn't know, the one who moved with grace and surety, there's no distinction, no separation of their gifts; they're the same man for her now, and whether they are for the rest of the world, that doesn't matter.

In the parlor, the fire was cold, and now Earl was remembering something else she'd said that day. That she was sure she could be a better a wife to him here. And that *was* what she had given him—her certainty about their life. What it was already and what she was sure it would be. It was all through her, this bright insistence, this conviction. It was in the rhythm of her footfall and the timbre of her voice. In the Stephen Foster songs she sang off-key while she was cooking.

He shook his head. With everything he'd felt tonight, all the words between them, and all the thoughts and feelings they'd caused him to think and feel, his sotted brain had brought him back to *that*— her pledge to him in the run-down hotel lobby. *My God*, he thought drunkenly. His love for her; what a relentless thing it was. How could he not admire it, the way it just kept coming for him?

He heard again the other thing she'd said. *That she could be a better mother too.* He'd leaned toward her in her ugly, high-backed chair and watched her blush, her face turn a pale rose shade that lingered, as if she felt embarrassed to have said it, embarrassed by her boast.

Her words would return to him, with the remembered charm of her blushing, when they learned late in January that she was pregnant.

1918   *Two Years Later*

CHAPTER TWELVE

October 15, 1918

At the supper table, the four of them lingering over coffee and Emily's chocolate cake, she was telling of entering the grocery that afternoon to let Macauley know she'd arrived with the delivery of their eggs and finding two soldiers talking to him. She described them as both tall and lanky and looking very much alike. She'd heard them say they were stationed at a base in Kansas. Fort Riley, she believed. She hadn't heard them say why they were there, in Hinton, passing through.

"Where was the rest of their outfit?" Rooster asked. "Their convoy, their platoon. Their regiment, whatever."

"I don't know that, Daddy."

Earl shook his head. "Just the two of them, that doesn't make sense."

"Maybe they was deserters," Rooster said.

"Maybe the others," Earl said, "were seeing the sights of Hinton."

"Listen," Emily said. She was impatient to get to what she wished to tell them all. "They were saying the war will be over in a month. The news was spreading like wildfire, they said, and traveling mouth to mouth, nothing official, was the proof it was true."

From his high chair next to Emily, baby Henry smacked the chair's wooden tray with both hands.

"Henry likes the news," Rooster said.

"Henry's a pacifist," Earl said. "We've had long talks about it."

Emily reached over to Henry and pressed her hands to his fat cheeks. His face was smeared with chocolate frosting, a painterly streak across his forehead, and she reached for a napkin. He would be a year old in two weeks. He met life mostly as a variety of games, and now he wiggled in his high chair and ducked his head, feinting skillfully to avoid the napkin.

Emily paused and looked at Earl. "I was thinking all the way home. Thinking it again, I think it all the time. How grateful I am you're not in the war. 'Grateful' doesn't begin to say it. I was watching the two of them strutting back and forth with their news, and I thought, this is the way boys act. And they *were* just boys, I know, but I mean *young* boys, when they've got ahold of something that makes them feel superior and they walk around all puffed up."

Henry was wanting more of the napkin game, but his squeal seemed also like a comment.

"You're so right, Henry," Emily said to him, and she held her smile as she looked again at Earl. "When I saw them that way, as boys, I saw Henry, grown up, the spitting image of you, and I thought of him in a uniform too. Both of you." She set the damp cloth on the tray. "The nightmares of a mother of a soldier in a war."

Lottie was seated across from Henry. She said, "When I talk to Ethel now, I can tell she doesn't hear me, barely sees me." She was speaking of her best friend, whose son had been sent somewhere over there and dead within a month.

Earl followed the war in the Sioux City *Journal*. The tone of its headlines as he read them was as if the world was freshly shocked each day to think that men would die if you stood them up in facing ditches, in slop and fetid water, with death-bloated rats and blown-off hands and fingers and cigarette butts and rusted food tins eddying about their ankles, and they shot at each other from distances so close they could see the terror and the madness staring back at them; they could see themselves.

He felt no shame for not being called and not volunteering, and his attitude was helped by knowing other young married fathers who'd also stayed home to farm.

"These are Godforsaken times," Rooster said, "Godforsaken. The war, and on top of it the flu. Which, at least the flu, you don't have to take a boat to France and let some Kaiser bastard shoot you. It comes right to your door, all the way from Spain, real considerate."

Earl heard Rooster's thin static of a voice, etched with fret. He watched Emily finishing with the washcloth and untying Henry's bib, lifting him from the high chair and settling him on her lap. He followed his son's round face, as sober as Emily's as he looked around the table, from Rooster to Lottie, and then, finding him, finding Earl, breaking into a smile, baby-joy, a reflex.

He'd come into the world quickly. Emily's labor had lasted a long morning, with her mother and a neighbor, Mrs. Hilliard, at her side. And from the first, Earl had watched his new son, fascinated. The way he kicked his feet and curled his fingers and squeezed his eyes shut tight like a toad's. He knew they were the first things all babies did with their bodies, but they stirred his pride as if his son had invented them.

But what he'd assumed he would feel instantly—that sweet disturbance in his chest that rose up into his throat and made him stupid with love—it was absent. He felt protective of the baby, but apart from pure emotion.

Troubled by this, his beginnings as a father, he thought of his own. He wasn't fearful for a moment that he'd become anything like him. Earl knew who he was and he knew what he wasn't. But he did fight the thought that there might be something in the Dunham blood, that what he was feeling—or rather what he wasn't—was how that mean old fuck had felt when he, when Earl, was born. That they'd started fatherhood from something like that same place.

Until one morning, five months, six months ago, when Henry was crying in his crib and Emily was elsewhere, and Earl reached in to pick him up and try to calm him. His crying went on, he was squirming and seizing, and then he gradually began to grow quiet, and Earl felt the tiny body relaxing in his arms. It was as if the baby had taken stock of things and decided that resisting was simply too much work, and for what? Earl felt him pressing against his chest, and pressing more, burrowing deep. Relief broke over Earl, and he could feel his body relaxing as well, following his son's cue.

Now he looked around the table, his eyes pausing on each of them: his beautiful wife; his in laws, looking as they sat there like weathered prairie figurines; his nearly year-old son, brilliant from birth in the way he kicked his feet and curled his fingers. And he heard Emily's words from their talk that day, that she was certain they would settle into a sameness she would cherish, a fine day-to-dayness she could only believe he would come to cherish too.

CHAPTER THIRTEEN

October 20, 1918

Earl sat at Emily's bedside, holding her hand. He was covered with corn dust, a golden down, his face and hands and forearms, his shirt and overalls. He'd hurried in from the field with Lottie right beside him and Rooster trailing and shouting to them, "I'll bring the doctor back!"

Lottie had called from the porch, her voice a wild vibrato, then hastened out to them, stepping nimbly over the rough ground of harvested stalks. When she reached the men, she told them that Emily was complaining of what she called a headache, but it was something worse than that, the pain was terrible, and her eyes hurt mortally when she tried to focus on what was right in front of her. Her slight morning fever had risen crazily; when you touched her cheeks and forehead, she felt about to catch on fire. Her cough had become much worse as well, and she'd hardly had the strength to climb into bed. As Lottie spoke, her voice quavered.

Earl couldn't find the sense of it. Emily had been fine not five hours ago, her cough nothing more than *a tickle in my chest*. It was as if a day, two days, a week had somehow gone by, time he couldn't account for. Wouldn't it take days for someone to pass from a tickle in her chest to being as sick as she was now?

He sat, holding her hand, in the crudely needlepointed chair that was much too small for him, his long legs angling awkwardly, as they had as a boy when he sat on the long pine bench in the mines, reaching for pieces of slate and slicing his fingers, and his mother, at night, rubbing them roughly with an unguent of lard and once saying, a tone close to accusation in her voice, that his cuts were like the price you paid in thorn pricks when you reached to smell the rose, and his thinking, at age twelve, *The price you paid for* what? *Life punished you for wanting to smell a rose?*

In the first hours at her bedside, before the blood and before she grew delirious, he was reckless in the way he touched and held her and drew close to her. Again and again, their mouths nearly met, as if he wished to breathe her breaths, to take them into his lungs before they were lost to the heavy bedroom air. (Over the years, Lottie will think that the illness itself was the only thing Emily *didn't* give him in these hours. Everything else, all the rest of her—her strength, her heart, her spirit—she seemed to say to him as the night went on, *Here, I'll have no more need for this. Or this. Or this.*)

At first her eyes flitted constantly about the room, meeting his in passing. She seemed inside herself, seemed to be attending ever more *to* herself, and Earl thought, yes, that's where she should be, that's what she should be doing. But he was certain she knew he was there with her, and he was ashamed to be thinking she'd never looked more beautiful to him, had never drawn him in so intimately. Her skin was as hot as Lottie had described it, and she was moving in her bed in subtle, supple motions, in ways he'd never seen her body behave, as if pain were a clinging garment she was trying to slither out of. Her voice, when she offered it, was a vigorous scratch, and because he knew she wasn't going to die, he allowed himself to see her as set loose and primitive.

At some point he persuaded her to swallow a home remedy of salt and castor oil in water. He pressed cold cloths to her forehead. Lottie came in and out of the room and, with the thought to sweat it out of her, she helped Earl lay still more blankets over her. Another, and another, until they pressed down on her chest like the weight of coffin-covering earth.

Otherwise, Lottie stayed elsewhere in the house with Henry and watched for Rooster to return from the village with the doctor. As she fed Henry in his high chair, she said, "Your mama's caught a cold and doesn't want to give it to you. Your papa's sitting with her. Your granddad had to go into town." She needed to say this to him, baby Henry, knowing full well she was talking to herself, insisting there was purpose and assignment in the world.

Deep into the night, he watched her start to tremble from the chills of her fever. Her hair had come free, sweat was pouring from her, and she looked now as if she'd been baptismally immersed. She suddenly sat up. Her spine was straight. She bent forward and gasped for air and her breath gurgled with blood. She coughed once, and there was a pinkly rabid froth around her mouth. She coughed again, and it came pouring out. Right away, she found a pattern of coughing and blood, coughing and blood, like water from the well as it was being pumped. He called for Lottie to bring more cloths and bowls, but they were helpless to do more than catch as much blood as he could.

She fell back onto her pillows. She lay quietly, and after the violent meter of coughed-up blood, her sudden limpness was the more dramatic thing. Then blood began to flow slowly from her nose, and then more slowly in thin seams from her ears, and then from her eyes, a ghoulish weeping. Tears of blood were running down her cheeks, and they brought to Earl's mind the picture of his father's blood as he'd wanted to see it, and in a moment of madness he'd richly earned, he knew he'd caused this for so fiercely wanting that.

It was then that he sensed her interest and attention turning away, not just from him—that had happened hours before—but from herself. He felt her letting something take her somewhere else, and a bright red jealousy ran through him. He asked himself where she was going and what was taking her there, and even as he asked, he began to know he knew.

She continued to lie still, withdrawn and serene, her coughing now weak, her body not moving with it. He pushed away a thought that made him furious with her for no more than a moment—that she was feeling pleased with herself for all the clever ways she'd found to bleed.

He watched in a trance as she fought for breath, until, as if death were a perverse watercolorist, her face turned in the last hour a frankly lovely wash of blue.

Rooster arrived with Dr. Sampson in the predawn, three hours later. He'd been pacing in the young doctor's office parlor through the night while Sampson was out attending to another influenza patient. He was new to the town and didn't know the way, so Rooster had to wait for him and lead him to the farm. The doctor apologized for getting there too late. He said he didn't think he'd have been able to do much more than help bring fresh cloths and bowls of water to the bedside. (To himself, he thought she must have been, like many he had treated, already past saving before she'd showed any signs, like the soldier who'd appeared on his doorstep a few days before, leaning weakly on his friend and gargling blood and dying in a matter of hours.) Earl thought this spoke to the doctor's skills. *He didn't need to be here to know nothing could be done.* But Rooster and, especially, Lottie heard cowardly excuse in the man's claiming he'd have been powerless.

"We don't know how it spreads," Dr. Sampson said at the door. "Some are saying now maybe houseflies. I tend to discount it. I'd advise burning her clothes and anything she touched routinely."

They did as he advised, turning to the task as soon as he'd left, burning everything, bonnets to stockings, dresses needing mending, heavy woolen things she hadn't worn since winter ended. They worked in silence, without pause. Spoken words had no part in what they'd set for themselves. It was better done right then, while they were insulated in their shock. Imagine their bonfire, their horror, and their trembling, if they'd been aware of what they were doing.

Emily was among the first in Hinton to fall sick. Earl was certain she contracted the illness from the soldier in the grocery, and he was stunned, despising himself to think he hadn't felt terrified the moment he heard the young man had died. It made perfect sense to Earl that his terror would have saved her.

Rooster and Lottie thought it more likely she'd caught it from one of the friends she'd seen the week before she died. She'd been with Maude MacKenzie at their monthly reading circle. She'd visited Sarah Buell, pregnant and due any day, to give her a quilt she'd laboriously sewn for the baby. It was bright with patches of pink and blue and yellow. Maude recovered, and Sarah did not, becoming sick one afternoon and dying at first light in the act of giving birth, as did her baby, a girl her father christened Dawn, for the moment of the day when she had been alive. Dawn Elizabeth. Giving her a middle name emphasized for him that he had had a daughter, that she had lived, if for an instant, and that there'd be a full name to use whenever he recalled her.

Some six hundred people lived in the town of Hinton and on the farms encircling the village, and more than fifty of them died in the fall and winter of 1918. People locked their doors and refused to answer them. In the backyards there were fires beneath big copper vats filled with boiling water to sterilize everything people touched. It looked like a village of witches at their cauldrons. The funeral home ran out of coffins. School was suspended. Shops closed. Public places did as well, among them the three churches.

Lottie and Rooster had been dutiful churchgoers all their lives. As children, they'd stood, small as dolls, sharing a spine-broken hymnal in Sunday school. Even when she was a girl, Lottie's voice was beguiling, a precociously clear and sure soprano. She loved to sing the hymns, and Rooster loved standing next to her listening to her sing them.

As they grew, became adults, husband and wife, their faith remained the faith of those who gave it little thought. But as they came to see it in the wake of Emily's death, when the Lord was needed most, He'd allowed His houses to be shut up tight, as if He'd been afraid the flu would find Him too. Worse, He'd let loose a scourge that mostly ignored the very young and, more baffling still, the old, those who'd have died from a plague that made some kind of normal horrid sense. Instead, it struck young and strong adults like Emily, spreading, as Rooster would think of it, with an Old Testament efficiency, the cunning currents of a Passover.

(When, months from now, the churches reopen, Rooster and Lottie will again attend regularly. Lottie will sing the hymns sourly in the key of grievance, while Rooster spits out the Lord's Prayer and the doxology like a hostile student contemptuously reciting. But he will also find, ironically, that he feels relieved, unburdened, grateful for the hymns and the Scriptures and the sermon, grateful for being able to resent them once a week. He sees this as the way he's found to expend his heart's complaint. And it will occur to him that this was how he'd always assumed a Sunday morning of worship was supposed to leave you feeling. That is, with your mind's muddle lifted, your conflicted heart made sensical. Your mortal confusions briefly clarified. And through all these years of faithful attendance, it had never done any of that for him. But now he feels certain, deeply certain, of God's presence, and he'll chuckle bitterly with the thought that he's become a believer at long last. In idle moments, when he's resting, when he's about to nod off in his parlor chair, he pictures Him as a kind of hot-tempered buccaneer with a booming voice and with thick, ropy veins on the backs of his hands and clean, callused, sandaled feet as big as geese and a blood-meanness in His heart running as deep as Pinky Ingram's. After what He's done—who needed Lucifer?—how could anyone deny that He exists?)

Some weeks after Emily's death, he came back one afternoon from a trip to the village. He was terribly agitated. He saw Lottie in the barnyard and hurried to her to describe what he'd seen. On the front porches of two houses, the Burnetts' and, one block over, the Robinsons', dead cats were hanging from nooses, their bellies' slit, suspended from the ceilings above open front doors. Dripping blood, they looked totemic. They looked like devil worship. He'd been told at the granary that the gutted, bleeding cats were a scheme to draw flu-bearing flies from houses. And Rooster confessed, what bothered him the most was not the madness of what the Burnetts and the Robinsons had done, but that on hearing it explained, the first thing he'd felt was a sharp regret he hadn't thought to do it too.

"I said to myself, why didn't I get the idea to hang a Bernard from *our* porch? I thought, Hell, I'da hanged as many as I could catch. Then I stopped and told myself it would upset Henry something terrible to see such a blessed awful thing."

He looked around and, a sudden bit of panic in his voice, asked Lottie where they were, what had become of Earl and Henry. In his troubled mind, the next horror was all too possible, there was an awful logic to it, but Lottie calmly told him they were both inside the house.

And as she spoke this to Rooster, Earl was waking from a nap, an hour of nightmare in which he'd been falling, falling, forever falling through a featureless sky. Coming downstairs and entering the kitchen, he confronted his son sitting quietly composed and unattended in his high chair. Some seconds passed as Earl stared at Henry. Still partly in his nightmare, unmoored by his sorrow, it made no sense to him that Henry was there, in the kitchen, that he existed in this life Earl had waked to, since the one they both belonged in, with Emily, did not. And as he continued to watch Henry, serenely occupied, Earl began to understand that what he was seeing was the baby's competence—for living, for knowing so much better than he did how to calmly take one breath, then another, then the next.

BOOK TWO

Earl and Henry
Jidge and Lou

1927

—viper of memory,
stab of regret, red light of oblivion.
Hell would be living without them.

—HENRI COLE, "Ginger and Sorrow"

CHAPTER FOURTEEN

//

October 11, 1927   *New York City*

Lou Gehrig walked with his stout, stern mother through the cavernous waiting room of Pennsylvania Station. He was carrying an enormous time-scratched leather portmanteau. It swung easily at his side like a night watchman's lantern. Many other passengers were also heading for their trains, the blink-quick click of heels on the gleaming marble floor, most everybody wearing their traveling best; here and there a creamy color relieved the muted shades. Gehrig's mother, Christina, wore a hideous green-and-red plaid coat. A faded gray wool scarf was tied securely at her throat.

The morning sun shone through the station's grand glass ceiling. The light was soft and beseeching at this hour, and Gehrig complied, looking up into it. A grid of steel, inlaid in the glass, ran overhead for acres and appeared from far below to have the delicacy of a cathedral's filigree. But what Gehrig always saw when he raised his eyes to trace it was a network of great girders and their strict geometry. The sight reassured him. The world was orderly and its ceilings wouldn't fall. He was a young man who needed reassurance wherever he could get it, and he needed it even more than usual this morning. He was glad he was able to hide his anxiousness from his ailing mother.

She'd not felt well for weeks, and he'd worried increasingly about her through the last month of the season, distracted during games and hurrying home afterward. She'd been often short of breath and had difficulty swallowing. It felt to her as if food were stuck in her throat. When she finally saw a doctor, she learned she had a goiter that would need to be removed. Gehrig's first thought had been to cancel his trip, but her doctor said the surgery was common and could wait for his return.

They passed beneath the gigantic Benrus clock, hanging from the ceiling on its thick linked chain like God's own pocket watch dangling down from Heaven. Christina looked up at her son as they continued along. The wire rims of her glasses were perfect silver O's. "Louie," she said, "you will write to me tonight." Her tone was not quite a question and not quite a command. It was as if she were reminding her son how disappointed in himself he would be if he forgot.

Gehrig nodded. "I write to you *every* night when I'm away." They were, as always, speaking German to each other. Gehrig's voice was high-pitched and rapid whatever the language. When he was agitated, it might rise, as it just had, almost an octave. Hearing this confirmed for Christina her son's anxiety, which he hadn't been able to hide from her at all. But she understood his concern. He'd be traveling with Babe Ruth, virtually alone, for three weeks on a train across the country, and she believed the regard her son felt for Ruth was complicated. Indeed, Gehrig's feelings were a contesting mix of envy, bemusement, and awe; primarily awe.

For her part, Christina was very fond of Ruth.

They reached a set of stairs that led to the trains and started down.

On the crowded platform, they moved along at a stately pace. People hurried past them left and right. The air was thick with morning purpose and engine fumes. Steam hissed and made clouds that rose and furled, boarding bells tolled, and there was chatter all around them. No one recognized Gehrig. People didn't picture baseball stars dressed in suits and ties and walking with stout mothers who wore hideous plaid coats.

They continued, silent with their thoughts, toward a Pullman car at the end of the train. In her own way, Christina was worrying about her son's trip as much as he was; the idea that there would be no manager or coaches along to supervise. There would instead be this man named Christy Walsh, who'd organized it all, but she'd only met him briefly, and he didn't seem to her much older than her *lieben*. There would be Walsh, and of course there would be Ruth, the merry barbarian, which, fondness aside, alone gave a mother much to worry about.

As they got closer, Gehrig saw three men waiting at the far end of the Pullman, some twenty yards down the track. He knew the one standing on the top step was Walsh. He could see, even from this distance, his habitual bright green tie. He assumed the other two were reporters Walsh had summoned.

Gehrig and Christina came to a stop. They weren't yet ready for their privacy to end. He drew her close and hugged her. Gehrig's teammates had seen these intimate train station farewells so often they no longer bothered teasing him about them.

From the Pullman's top step, Christy Walsh had spotted them. He looked down at Wilbur Winters, a reporter for the *Telegram*, and Arnold Mercer, one of the paper's photographers. He told them Gehrig was here. They gave back meager nods. They were waiting for the Babe to arrive and claim the very air in some grand, profane, barrel-bellied, burlesque way.

"He's got half an hour," Walsh said, smiling. "It's still last night in his world." He was tall and slender, looking suave as a dance hall crooner in his double-breasted suit and signature green tie. He held his hat in his hands. His thick black hair was brilliantined.

Both Winters and Mercer, in unfortunate contrast, were short and plump and balding young men. Winters's mustache ran above his lip without commitment.

Mercer, the photographer, looked up the platform in Gehrig's direction. "You want to interview him while we wait? I'll take some shots of him and Mama?"

"You ever talk to Gehrig?" Winters asked.

"A few times," Mercer said.

"Maybe you can help me then. In your experience, what's the difference talking to him compared to, say, a tree?"

Mercer thought for a long moment. "Some trees bear fruit?"

Winters smirked. "That's pretty good."

"Boys, be kind," Walsh said.

Up the tracks, Christina asked her son, "You have the sandwiches?"

Gehrig nodded, pointing to the portmanteau.

She patted the wide lapels of his blue worsted suit. The suit was in-expensive—it pained Gehrig to spend money—but even so it flattered him. The full, pleated trousers hid his enormous thighs, the drape of the suit coat his uncommonly big ass. No one benefited more than he from baseball's loose-fitting wool uniforms and the Yankees' slimming pinstripes. In them, as now, he was cinematically handsome. He was twenty-four years old. His brown hair was thick and wavy. When he smiled, his deeply scored dimples gave him a look of impish mirth, though his usual fretfulness was as far from an imp's as a personality could be. His days were driven by an enormous wish to please, his mother most of all, and after her his teammates, and after them the world in general, which, because he was a respectful son, included his feckless father, Heinrich.

"The slaw," Christina said. "You got the coleslaw?"

Gehrig pointed again to the portmanteau.

From the Pullman's steps, Walsh shouted, "Ah-hah! This qualifies as early."

Gehrig caught the sound of Walsh's cry and looked to see him pointing toward a distant cluster starting down the platform. He and Christina turned to watch. They saw people stepping aside to let the group pass. Gehrig spotted Ruth at its head, dressed for winter in October in a camel's hair topcoat and matching driving cap and a flowing paisley scarf. There was no mistaking his dainty, pigeon-toed steps. He was a massive mincing monarch. Two redcaps flanked the group, bearing Ruth's luggage. Men about to board their trains stopped and smiled as they saw who was passing.

Everybody knew who he was. And they knew that the Yankees had just won the World Series, and that during the season Ruth had hit sixty home runs. Sixty! Yes, there'd been a year when he'd hit fifty-nine, but there was something about the round number that made it feel ordained and ultimate.

Many of the boarding passengers called to him. Many turned around and fell in with the growing entourage, thinking, *What the hell, I can catch a later train.* Here was their chance to join a band of acolytes walking with Babe Ruth through Penn Station on an early sunny morning on the eleventh of October.

With Walsh, Wilbur Winters and Arnold Mercer were watching all this, too.

"Three?" Winters said. "Tell me I don't see three."

Two of the women with Ruth wore their hair in stylish bobs. One, on his right arm, was a platinum blonde. One, on his left, was raven-haired. The third, also on Ruth's left—he was a southpaw, after all—her fingers wrapped loosely around his huge upper arm, was a cinnamon redhead. Her hair was an arrangement of coherent curls. All three were dressed in bright harvest colors, yellow and orange and ochre shades.

Mercer said, "I remember once before, him showing up with two."

Christy Walsh said, "Sixty home runs. Three whores for breakfast. Records thought unbreakable continue to fall."

The party marched right past Gehrig and Christina and moments later reached the Pullman's steps. Ruth greeted the reporters as Walsh hopped down to shake his hand. They gave each other big smiles. Ruth's was innocent and larcenous in equal measure. Walsh offered a formal greeting to the prostitutes, and Ruth, pointing at their heads, introduced them as Red, Whitey, and Blackie. If he'd known their names, he'd forgotten them. Ruth, famously, could not remember names. The women rolled their eyes. They were paragons of tolerance. Their cheap perfumes were overwhelming; combined, they made a scent you could peel off the air.

Ruth grinned at Walsh again. "I got no brunette."

Walsh smiled. "Some would call that restraint."

Ruth's laugh, like his voice, was a hoarseness at high volume.

He turned now to the two redcaps and withdrew a thick, money-clipped stack of bills from his topcoat pocket. As if dealing from a deck of cards, he tipped them lavishly.

Standing behind Ruth and the prostitutes, the men who'd come along, thirty, forty finally, began to drift away, tipping their hats, their eyes searching the platform for a final thing in Babe Ruth's universe that might detain them. Leaving, they once again walked unaware past Gehrig as he and Christina approached.

But Ruth had spotted them and now he said, "There's my girl!" He hurried over and bent down and kissed Christina's offered cheek. "How's the mutt?"

"He's fine, Jidge," Christina said. She adored the dog, a yappy Chihuahua, that Ruth had given her last year as thanks for the supper her son had invited him to. She'd prepared several dishes of her leaden German food. Schnitzel and sauerkraut and pickled eel. Four kinds of sausages and loaves of fresh rye bread. A hill of strudel for dessert. Ruth ate helping after helping, shoveling it in at his desperate urchin's pace. Christina watched astonished and delighted as she repeatedly filled his plate. Heinrich smoked his pipe and watched amazed as well. Gehrig smiled, unsurprised. He was glancing back and forth from his mother to the Babe, unable to decide which of them appeared more pleased. At last Ruth finished. His sigh was postcoital.

Once he'd gotten the idea to invite Ruth to supper, it had taken Gehrig weeks to find the courage to do so. At the start of the season, he'd pledged to himself to be more outgoing with his teammates, and Ruth, most of all, was the one he wanted in some way to emulate. He couldn't imagine they would ever be close friends. He couldn't imagine ever wanting them to be. But he hoped that with Ruth, and with people in general, he might come to find something of the ease Ruth felt around every living, breathing, moving thing on God's green earth, an instinctive generosity with his money and his body and his temper and his heart that Gehrig saw as reckless, but finally enviable. He wished for a more modest version of it, and he only needed to look to his mother this morning for proof that he was right to want it. She'd come to see him off, feeling far from her best, bearing her iron love and a dozen bratwurst sandwiches, when Ruth appeared with three hookers on his arm. Their rouge and their lipstick could have lit the dark, but standing next to her, Gehrig was certain he'd heard his mother chuckling. She forgave Ruth everything and offered him her cheek because of the night he'd sat at her table and eaten her food with a ravenous glee.

Ruth turned to Gehrig, smiled and shook his hand. "Morning, kid. You ready to go on this Wild West tour old Walsh has cooked up for us?"

Gehrig smiled and said he was.

Among his money-making ventures, Christy Walsh had been Ruth's business manager for the past few years, and he'd recently become Gehrig's too. He'd put together smaller, regional barnstorming tours for Ruth in the past, but this time they'd be ambitiously tracing the country's glorious latitudes, making twenty-one stops to play exhibition games, Ruth captaining one team, Gehrig the other. There would be some cities. Trenton was the first stop and the largest until Kansas City, then Omaha, Des Moines, Denver, all the way to the West Coast. San Francisco, San Diego, Los Angeles. But most of the towns were fairly small—Lima, Ohio; Sioux City, Iowa; Marysville, California—and a few were smaller than that.

When Walsh had proposed the tour, Ruth's first thought was, Fuck, why couldn't Meusel or Bengough or Dugan come along, one of his teammates who didn't think that thing between your legs was just for watering the shrubs? He liked Gehrig, liked him a lot, how could you not, the kid so shy and wanting to please he'd carry your turds in a towel if you asked him to. And he admired the hell out of him as a hitter. He could *hurt* the goddamn ball. He could shell the fucking pea. But three weeks on a train with him was going to be about as much fun as being stranded in a dinghy in the ocean with the pope.

Christina said, "Jidge. You brought some friends along to say good-bye?"

"Oh, yeah, my cousins," Ruth said, smiling. "They're all three sisters. Came up from Baltimore just to see me off. Ain't that sweet of them?"

"Cousins," Christina said. "And yet no family resemblance." Gehrig gave his mother a quick glance. He'd never heard this perfectly deadpan tone from her.

Ruth didn't try to suppress his happy rasp. "I know. It ain't fair, is it, how I got all the looks in the family."

The pleasure his mother was taking in her teasing made Gehrig feel required, however awkwardly, to join it. "And it's funny, Jidge, their being sisters, how they don't resemble each other either."

Ruth laughed again, a softer wheeze. "Thing is, they all got different mothers. It's a real sad story, kid. I'll tell it to you later if you want, but be ready, like I say, it's real sad."

Smiling, Gehrig picked up his portmanteau and walked with his mother and Ruth the short distance to the steps of the train.

Wilbur Winters, waiting impatiently, said, "Babe, Lou, could we get you two shaking hands?"

Ruth gave Christina another peck on her cheek before she moved away, and Gehrig stepped in and gripped his hand. Arnold Mercer raised his camera. The disc that held its bulb was as big as a hubcap. He told Ruth and Gehrig to smile. Ruth's grin was faintly simian. Gehrig's dimples framed his mouth. The flash went off. Gehrig's smile was the winner. No one could beat Gehrig smiling. The dimples. Then Mercer took another. Then again, with Walsh between them in a three-way, arms-crossed handshake. Winters held his pen and notebook and asked Ruth what Podunk town he was most looking forward to seeing. Ruth smiled and said, hell, all of them, but not as much as they were looking forward to seeing him. Winters asked Gehrig the same question. He nodded toward Ruth. "Like Jidge said, all of them."

Ruth ended the questions by turning to the prostitutes to say goodbye. Gehrig stepped back to Christina and hugged her again and reminded her to take her medicine. "Yes," she said, "and Louie, you be careful now and don't catch a cold." She spoke this loudly in English, her voice publicly maternal. "You know how you always catch a cold this time of year."

Gehrig thought, *I do?*

The redheaded prostitute whispered in Ruth's ear. "Babe, you be careful now and don't catch the clap. You know how you always catch the clap this time of year."

Ruth nodded solemnly. "Thanks for reminding me, kid."

Looking down on this assemblage, what Christy Walsh saw was rich absurdity. Babe Ruth, Lou Gehrig, Gehrig's dour Kraut mama, two cynical reporters, and three handsomely paid if not particularly handsome whores. What a shame they weren't all coming. He was Noah on the deck, his gaze a benediction. He was taken with a kind of brainy buoyancy. When this feeling came to him, he believed his mind was working faster than that of anyone around him, and there were times when it was. He opened his arms and called, "Aboard!"

Ruth and Gehrig and Walsh boarded, and the Pullman steward, whose name was Horace Meadows, stepped forward to welcome them. He was a short, handsome man; bald, broad-chested, mahogany-dark; looking fit and finished in his tailored blue uniform. He said they'd find their luggage in their staterooms, and he pointed the way down a narrow corridor to the observation lounge at the rear of the car.

They'd settled into comfortable, jade-green plush chairs when the train began to move away from the platform. Ruth looked out the window. Gehrig's mother, the reporter, the photographer, they'd gone, but the three prostitutes were waving farcically. Their arms made sweeping, ocean-voyage arcs that lifted them to their tiptoes, and what better evidence, Ruth thought as he watched, of all there was to be grateful for in life than three frisky trollops with a sense of humor.

He sat back again, a man emphatically at ease, relieved to be escaping his life for a while, filled as it was with a wife and a mistress and two young girls, one his natural daughter and one he'd soon be adopting, and two expensive New York apartments and a small farm in Massachusetts, where the hired man, a humorless Swede, kept telegramming with the news that the chickens were dying like they could hardly wait their turn, and the pit bulls had attacked and killed Ruth's favorite cow, a real sweetie that cow, with her big, sad, trusting eyes, who'd never done a thing to those fucking dogs, and Jesus H Christ farming was hard.

They were moving smoothly below ground, a stealthy luxury about it all in the walnut-paneled Pullman with its Oriental carpets and its wall-mounted lights with Tiffany shades.

Gehrig, in his chair across from Ruth and Walsh, was picturing his mother, weary and sad from seeing him off, returning home to a familiar morning. He heard her accusing his father of having beers for breakfast, of his breath smelling like *die brauerei*, and the two of them shouting angrily at each other. To take his mind elsewhere, he worked to think of what lay ahead. Besides being nervous about this time with Ruth, he was concerned that the games themselves would quickly begin to feel dull and dutiful—playing teams of amateurs, and with nothing at stake, less than a week after the high tension of the World Series.

On the other hand, he was being paid five hundred dollars a game, three weeks of work and close to half his salary for the full Yankees' season, and for that, he told himself, he could certainly accept whatever dullness and duty he might feel.

Deep in thought, Gehrig hadn't heard Christy Walsh begin to speak of the Western landscape they'd eventually be passing through. He listened now as Walsh, his voice building, was describing the majestic peaks, the dramatic mountain gorges, the glistening rivers, the astoundingly blue skies. He sounded to Gehrig as if he were rehearsing a presentation of some kind.

"Actually," Gehrig said, "I've never been west of St. Louis."

"Lou!" Walsh said. "No kidding?" He paused to gather his words. "You won't believe what you're seeing. I mean, the bands of color in the canyon walls, they're like . . . they're like rainbows of stone, brought to life by the sun." It was true, Gehrig's sense of Walsh was right, he *was* rehearsing in a fashion, assessing his words as he spoke them. He often did. He felt it gave him great advantage in his work to speak impressively, and hearing what he'd just said, he thought *rainbows of stone brought to life by the sun* wasn't half bad. Late at night, he wrote plays, period melodramas about his favorite subject, the French Revolution. They detailed the gory excesses. Guillotine blades fell. Blood fountained. Robespierre was his man. The plays were dreadful.

Ruth nodded at what Walsh had just said. "We get to the Rockies, it's another fucking planet."

"You put it perfectly, Jidge!" Walsh said. "It *is* extraterrestrial."

"Yeah," Ruth said, "I guess you could say that about it too."

They were all briefly quiet with their thoughts. The train gently swayed; the wheels made their rhythmic clacking.

"Christy? Who are they?" Gehrig asked. He was thinking again of the games they'd be playing.

Walsh frowned.

"How good will they be?" Gehrig asked.

"The teams? The players?" Walsh said. "Oh, you know."

"I don't. Not really."

"Local teams, some semipro. They're pretty good. A few played in the low minors probably."

"They're shitkickers," Ruth said. "The small-towns, anyway. Shitkickers, clodhoppers. They think they're a whole lot better than they are."

Gehrig said he'd decided to imagine the exhibitions as pick-up street games in the neighborhood. Games you played for the pure pleasure of it.

"That's it, kid," Ruth said. "Just have some fun like you did then. Stickball in the street with your little Heinie pals."

Gehrig nodded and didn't say he'd meant the ones he still played when he got home from Yankees games, rounding up some neighborhood boys until it got too dark.

Now the train was gradually climbing, leaving the tunnel and emerging into the sooty morning light. Soon, New Jersey would be sliding past their windows, its flat, weedy wastes and the backs of sagging tenements running grayly unimpeded right up to the tracks. They were heading out into the grand American day.

CHAPTER FIFTEEN

October 11, 1927　　　　　　　　　　　　　　*The farm near Hinton, Iowa*

Henry, very tired, sat slumped on the milking stool, his head resting against the bristly, caramel-colored flank of an obliging cow. In the darkness of the barn, a kerosene lamp on the dirt floor of the stall made a lovely mood of light, palely illuminating much of Henry and enough of the cow.

He'd stayed up late the night before, long after Rooster and Lottie had gone to bed and after Earl had put aside his newspaper, stood, and bid him good night. He'd been studying earlier for an exam in long division. He loved long division, especially loved dividing the larger number into the smaller one. It felt somehow against the rules, or that it should be, but here was their teacher, Mr. Paumgarten, showing them how to do it. Mr. Paumgarten was a chunky young man with chronic halitosis who lived with his widowed mother, and he often grew rhapsodic in the classroom about things like the power of the decimal point in long division. He told his students it was a magical punctuation. A dot, like a period, but instead of marking the end of a statement, it worked the opposite way, allowing you to continue when it looked as if you couldn't. Decimal point, then a zero, and on you went toward the answer, just as in life.

Henry loved it when Mr. Paumgarten made his lessons a fable.

The milking stool was low to the ground, but Henry's legs were short, so he sat comfortably. He was new to the chore, his fingers fumbled with the teats, but he felt a kind of wizardry when he *zinged* a stream of milk into the pail. His temperament, then, was a dreamy and agreeable one, though away from school he was sometimes lonely. But he also felt quite loved, because he *was* quite loved, and he sensed his loneliness from a kind of romantic remove.

When he'd finished studying, Henry stayed at the kitchen table reading Zane Grey's novel, *Riders of the Purple Sage*. It had been Mr. Paumgarten's copy until, one afternoon last week, feeling particularly thankful to Henry for his reading skills in a roomful of dolts, he'd impulsively given him the book at the end of the day as a reward. Mr. Paumgarten had himself gotten swept up in the story, and only later that night, while helping his mother wash the supper dishes, did he worry that Henry, nearly ten, might be too young for it—its frontier violence, its sexual allusions winking out at the world, hidden within all that *yes, ma'am* Western courtliness.

At the table, in the lamplight, Henry had come to a description of a mysterious masked rider who'd been shot and badly wounded. Unmasked, she was revealed to be a beautiful young woman. She was burning up with fever and speaking delirious nonsense. Henry knew immediately that she was going to die because he'd learned this was the fate of beautiful young women who were on fire with a fever and lost in delirium. Many times, when his father and his grandparents thought he was out of earshot, he'd overheard them remembering a moment of his mother's dying. Her shocking fever, her animal groaning, the ingenious ways she'd bled.

His understanding of her had been formed as his young mind began to reason. She'd lived here with them all, and then she'd gotten sick, and frantically as they'd tried, they could not keep her from dying. This was very sad, because she'd loved him so much. It was as if she'd fit a lifetime of love into the year they'd been alive together. And if she were in his life now, he would love her just as much.

He knew she was beautiful because there were framed photographs of her here and there in the house. Formal poses in front of velvet backdrops, with hints of her smile peeking through her serious expression. There was one on the sideboard in the dining room, another on his father's bedside table. He sometimes sneaked into the bedroom to kiss this picture, and when he did, a forbidden thrill ran through him.

But he knew nothing of how his mother had lived, how she'd gone about her days. The life she brought into a room. Her low, pulsing laugh. The few things that annoyed her (the ancient kitchen stove she called treacherous to use; Mildred Olmstead's incessant sewing circle gossip; her father pissing off the end of the porch; not much else).

He didn't know the quick sound of her footfall. He didn't know which parlor chair she favored. He didn't know she hummed and sang to herself as she went about her tasks—hymns and ragtime tunes and, frequently, "They Didn't Believe Me." Neither his father nor his grandparents had thought to offer him such details, and he had no idea what questions he could ask that would have given him a sense of her.

It was her dying that Henry felt he had a claim to. Like a scavenger, he'd kept everything he'd overheard about that day and night, kept it in a special place that wasn't just in his mind and wasn't only in his heart.

And then last night he'd read in Zane Grey's novel, *Hour after hour she babbled and laughed and cried and moaned in delirium.* He'd paused. It was as if his mother and her death had found its way into the story. As if something private had escaped the special place he kept it and was right there on the page for anyone to read.

And then: *The fever broke on the fourth day and left her spent and shrunken, with life only in her eyes.* And then: *She awoke stronger from each short slumber; she ate greedily.* And: *her recovery would be rapid.*

He'd closed the book and pushed it away. Sitting at the table, feeling very confused, he'd become aware of the surrounding country quiet. He normally loved this sound, as—he didn't know—his mother had. But he'd heard it last night as the silence secrets make, secrets the world had been keeping from him, and he'd wondered as he sat there how Zane Grey could think anyone would believe the beautiful young woman hadn't died.

In the barn, he stood and lifted the heavy pail of milk. He was unusually strong for his age and his size, as his grandfather had been for most of his life. He carried the pail to a corner and set it down by the cream separator. As he walked toward the sliding double doors, he heard a *thud!* from outside. The sound surprised him. His father was starting early this morning.

He stepped into the crisp October air. The sky was barely light. He heard the ball hitting the side of the barn again.

As he came around the corner, he saw Earl firing a pitch at the rectangle Emily had hurried to paint—she'd already done the research to learn how wide home plate was—the day Earl had told her he'd be playing and getting semipaid.

Earl repainted it each spring before the season started.

"Morning, Dad," Henry said.

Earl nodded perfunctorily.

The two of them had the same long, fine-boned face. Henry's fat baby cheeks had disappeared as he grew. They had the same brown hair, straight as straw, and the same large ears that lay flat against their heads. Henry's small size to this point in his life was the only feature he'd inherited from his mother.

He watched his father reach into a pail next to him for a ball. Harold, the family's obese beagle, was lying nearby in a shallow trough he'd dug in the earth. He was following Earl's pitches closely, his chin resting on the ground, his eyes moving back and forth like a shrewd old pitching coach gone to fat.

Earl wound up and threw. The sound of the ball as it struck the siding was sharper, less cushioned than inside the barn, more a *crack!* than a *thud!*

Six weeks earlier, the mayor of Sioux City had driven up to Hinton and gotten directions to the farm. Arriving in his new Studebaker sedan, he found Earl walking through the barnyard toward the house. He stepped from the sedan and introduced himself; his name was Leonard Enright. He was a slight, fair-complexioned man with a waxed mustache turned up at the ends to curls as fine as fishhooks. He looked like the tenor in a barbershop quartet. He managed a prosperous Sioux City haberdashery that had been started by his father, and he was dressed in a handsome gray houndstooth vest and matching trousers. He appeared to be uncomfortable standing in a busy barnyard in the early afternoon.

He spoke to Earl in high-pitched gusts. "I just received a telegram from a man in New York City! When I read it, I thought of you immediately. That's the honest truth, I did. You're the first to know. I didn't even stop at home to tell the wife before I headed out to find you!"

Earl shook his head. "The first to know *what*? You didn't tell your wife *what*?"

"Yes," Enright said. "I'm getting ahead of myself." He took a breath and began to explain that Babe Ruth and Lou Gehrig would be arriving in Sioux City on the eighteenth of October to play an exhibition game at Stockyards Park. Yes, he'd said to Earl, "Babe Ruth and Lou Gehrig, you heard me right." The teams would be made up of players from the local league. Sioux City was their stop after Des Moines. "They're crossing the entire blessed country," Enright said. "Just imagine!" He paused, waiting for Earl's reaction, and, getting nothing, he looked around the barnyard. He watched a hen who'd plucked out half its feathers, its ass pecked raw, roaming about like a shunned leper. Enright felt a surge of pity, seeing this man Dunham surrounded as he was—the leprous hen, the mud-caked pigs in their nearby pen, their absent-minded snorts like professorial asides, more chickens clucking drolly as they squatted in the dirt—after what he'd just described of Ruth and Gehrig's tour, starting in New York and all the way to California. There was that romantic notion, the sweep and glamour of that life; and then there was this one, Earl Dunham's.

Earl's mind had already raced past what Enright hadn't said yet. He was filling things in for himself, with memories and sensations that had been stilled, had gone quiet, years ago. He looked at Enright standing there, delicate and dandy, as the mayor was saying that Earl would obviously be pitching for one of the teams, "since you're the best pitcher in the league."

Earl nodded and thanked him. "I don't know if that's saying much."

"Oh, but it certainly *is* saying much! And I know what I'm talking about. I come to the games. I've watched you pitch."

And what Earl heard, and why he'd hesitated, and the blood rush he was feeling, was Saul Weintraub saying he knew talent when he saw it.

Enright talked on, now the bumptious politician, saying what a great day it was going to be for Sioux City. He would declare it a civic holiday, businesses closed, school let out.

He grew quiet, apparently lost in reverie, then said, "I should be going. I need to let some others know." He offered Earl his hand, turned, and started toward his new sedan, speaking over his shoulder. "I'll be talking to you soon, when I learn more."

And again a parallel memory came to Earl—Weintraub fading into the lavender twilight as he'd walked away toward his Model-T.

Leaving the sloping path of rutted driveway, Enright honked the sedan's horn, and as it headed down the road, it disappeared in a cumulus of dust, though the engine could still be heard, and Earl stood listening to the fading sounds.

The wave of adrenaline that chilly April Sunday had seemed to lift him from the bleachers as he felt himself surrendering to hope, to the threat and lilt of it. Watching Saul Weintraub as he'd waddled away into the early evening, Earl had told himself he was not inside a dream. He remembered saying it aloud, *I'm not dreaming*, thinking it a way of making sure he wasn't. Thinking that people in dreams didn't say they weren't dreaming.

But what the fussy little mayor had just described to him seemed too much like a dream not to be one. It felt to Earl that he could say the words again, *I'm not dreaming*, he could hear himself saying them, and he would not believe he wasn't.

Still looking up the road, although the engine's sounds were gone, Earl was feeling the same skirmish of emotions he'd felt that afternoon. The same wild agitation was sounding in his ears. And for a moment the power of these feelings seemed to him, what? somehow disloyal to the years of time and talent that Saul Weintraub had offered him. For here he was, standing in his barnyard, with his heart ricocheting exactly as it had that hour in Riverton, maybe harder, yes, even harder. He'd already decided he would ask for the team that had him facing Ruth. He'd be standing on the mound pitching to Babe Ruth. It didn't matter, not to his ricocheting heart, that it would be a single afternoon of artificial innings, that all the years he hadn't had would be distilled into a day.

In the barnyard, Henry picked up the baseball bat. Tired as he was, it felt heavier than usual as he got into his stance. It was how they'd been starting these very early mornings, a bucket of balls for Henry to hit before he left for school.

"Here you go," Earl said. He tossed the ball casually, and Henry made contact, a slow grounder. They continued, on their way to emptying the bucket, Earl giving him fat pitches, increasing the speed slightly. As his blood got going, he lost his fatigue and, choking up extremely, he began to hit line drives.

Henry's world was the farm and his school, the village of Hinton and the town of Sioux City, a ten-, twelve-mile radius of richly isolated life, and he saw his father as famous everywhere in it. Men stopped him on the street to talk about the games. The Sioux City newspaper printed its accounts. Henry knew that Babe Ruth and Lou Gehrig too were far more famous than that, but he knew this in the way he knew a fact in his history book.

There'd been much talk at school, the other boys' voices catching with excitement when they spoke about the game. Last week on the playground, Roy Wilson, in sixth grade, said to Henry that his father must be scared shitless at the thought of facing Ruth or Gehrig. Henry shook his head and said his father wasn't, that his pitches were so fast no one could even see them, certainly not in time to hit one.

Roy Wilson listened, then made an ugly, buck-toothed face. "Bullshit," he'd said, "your old man's scared shitless."

"Last one," Earl said, reaching into the pail. He pitched, and Henry's line drive sailed past him, the ball hitting the dirt and rolling to the pigpen fence.

They gathered up the balls and dropped them in the pail, and Earl said, "Remember not to lunge. Step into it but stay balanced through the swing."

"Was I lunging?"

"Not every time," Earl said.

Henry started up the driveway toward the house. In his mind he was picturing himself staying balanced through his swing. Nearing the porch, he heard the *crack!* against the barn again, and as he looked back at his father his thoughts moved sideways to another passage from *Riders of the Purple Sage*.

He loved reading of the landscapes Zane Grey described, Utah's cliffs and canyons, its gorges and deserts, a prodigal nature in lavish shades of orange and russet and cinnamon and yellow.

He reached the porch and started up the steps.

But what he *couldn't* imagine in the story were the Mormons. The men were ruthless bullies, threatening women, and stealing cattle in the dead of night. But what had stopped Henry was reading that they could have many wives. He'd tried to picture a farmhouse full of wives, filled to overflowing, and it had occurred to him that if they lived in Utah, his father could be a Mormon and marry several women, and he'd always have insurance in case one died.

The Game

CHAPTER SIXTEEN

October 18, 1927   *The farm and Sioux City, Iowa*

Earl woke before dawn, was quickly alert, and lay listening to the stillness of the world. He was greatly relieved to hear no sounds of rain.
He'd been unable to read the sunset, and Rooster couldn't help, standing on the porch with him, saying he thought he saw some weather
in the sky, but when he looked again he wasn't sure, maybe he did,
maybe he didn't.

"You sound like a politician," Earl had said.

Now he swung his long legs to the floor and sat on the edge of
his bed, the room night-dark. He felt sick to his stomach with nerves
and impatience, and he took this as a good sign; his body had been
preparing, getting ready while he slept, knowing what he needed it to
do today.

Downstairs, he got a fire going in the cookstove while everyone
else, even Lottie, was still asleep. He made coffee and fried three eggs
and some slab bacon and ate slowly, looking out through the three tall
kitchen windows, watching the pinkish dawn taking its sweet time.
Unlike the dawn, his mind was hurrying, thinking about the way he'd
pitch to Ruth, what he'd start him with. No matter what he threw, he
should keep the ball away, give him nothing he could pull.

Next came a sense of Emily, a swoon, an aching filling him. His
usual way was an instant yearning for her, and he couldn't remember
when he'd last felt her so fully. It wasn't merely the wish that she'd be
there to watch him pitch. It was something deeper, a more layered
need: that she was sitting with him now at the table at first light so
he could talk to her about how terrified he was. He imagined leaning

forward and quietly saying this to her, not as an admission, but in a shared, conspiratorial way. That the terror was electric; just what he wanted to feel. And her smiling and saying, *That's good. That's so good. It's what you* should *be feeling.*

He pushed back his chair and stood and carried his dishes to the sink, and minutes later, drinking a second cup of coffee, he rose and left the kitchen and walked out onto the porch and hurried to the outhouse where he threw up violently, tears in his eyes, snot filling his nose.

Afterward, over the next hour, the nature of his terror changed, became an eager dread, which kept him perfectly simple-minded for the rest of the morning, where he wanted to be.

Standing on the mound, three batters into the game, Earl found himself distracted. Stockyards Park was overflowing, a breathy drone coming from everywhere in the stands. They were squatting on the tiers of steps between the rows of wooden bleachers, and they were standing up, leaning back against a railing that ran along the top of the grandstand. They were lining the perimeter of the field as well, making a lively human hem at the outfield walls and behind restraining ropes along both foul lines.

The sun was casting the field in a buttery autumn light.

Earl's shadow hadn't yet extended past the mound toward first base where Gehrig stood, alertly crouched. Earl's stomach had settled and his nerves were calm. The last thing he'd expected to battle was his concentration.

Luckily, the first two batters had been ones he'd faced before, and he remembered they both had trouble with his curve ball. He threw them nothing else and they'd both grounded feebly, one to third, one to second, and Gehrig took the throws and tossed the ball back to Earl, calling, "Atta' way, pitcher. Atta' way to be." Playground lyrics in his nasal New York accent. When Earl had met him on the bench before the game, he was taken by how young, how much an innocent, he seemed, and how he moved carefully, as if his body was still learning how to carry its tremendous strength and power.

Henry and Rooster were sitting in the first base stands. They'd found spots fairly close to the field, but Rooster's back was feeling calcified, and even the short climb had been a steep steps ordeal. They were used to having lots of room around them when they came to watch Earl pitch, but here they were today, crammed in tightly.

"Grandpa, I can't see anything," Henry said.

"I can't neither," Rooster said. He adjusted the prized straw boater, a birthday gift from Lottie, as if angling its brim would give him a better view. "Try and sight between folks."

"Can I stand on the bleachers?"

Rooster shook his head. He feared the boy would lose his balance and he'd be unable to catch him. "It's against the law."

"Really?"

He motioned with his arm, indicating those sitting around them. "Somebody'd turn me in. I'd get arrested."

Earl took a long breath as Ruth stopped just outside the batter's box and looked to the stands. He held his cap high above his head and in every section of the ballpark men stood and took off their hats and waved them back.

Earl had watched him before the game, mixing with the players in his dugout, and even from that distance, with the breadth of the infield between them, he felt the pull of his personality.

Waiting for him to step in, Earl turned his back to the plate and scanned the field, taking stock of his teammates. They were, as Christy Walsh had said, men with decent skills, some better than that, a few much better, and Earl had no doubt the best of them was Lester Semple, the center fielder for a team just over the border in Sioux Falls, South Dakota. He was a compact, muscled man who had, even so, a smooth, unfurling swing and played the outfield like music, and now Earl looked out to where he stood, monumentally still, his hands on his hips. Earl had pitched against him often, and Semple often hit him well. The first time he'd faced him, he'd been warned the man could hit, and Semple went two for four, a single in the first and a double in the sixth, both of them line shots. Later that night, it came to Earl, and to Emily too, that he was Lester Someone, the player the old men in Macauley's had been describing the day she heard them speaking of a league she must tell Earl about.

Finally, Ruth stepped into the batter's box, one foot, then the other, a fussy exactness to the way he placed them close together. He flexed his knees. He took quick, revving practice swings.

Earl peered in for the sign from the catcher, his teammate, Bill Brown, a squat-bodied young man, ideally built for the position he played. Brown called for a fastball, low and away. Earl wound, rocking, the chorus-line leg kick, and Ruth tracked the pitch as it was coming with a close but somehow leisurely attention until it hopped at the last instant into Bill Brown's mitt.

Ruth looked out at Earl and nodded what appeared to be approval.

"Let's go, Babe," Mayor Enright whispered to himself. He sat just behind Ruth's team's dugout with his wife, Louise, a handsome woman, tall and thin, with narrow blue eyes, and her younger sister, Carol Jean, who was shorter, rounder, and even more attractive. He knew he should be cheering for the pitcher, for Dunham. He'd thought often of the day he'd stood in that frightful barnyard with the beanstalk farmer in his faded overalls and mud-strafed galoshes and loose threads dangling from his frayed shirt sleeves, and Enright had wanted to pull out his father's tailors' scissors he always carried and snip them off. And then, when he'd told him who was coming to town, he'd sensed a wave of emotion in the man's response—excitement, disbelief, something altogether phosphorescent—that Enright could only wonder at.

Even so, he wanted to see the Babe hit a homer. Surely everyone here did. Surely that's why they had come.

Now Earl threw a curve, again starting it wide, and again Ruth seemed to watch it coming while considering at great, contemplative length whether or not to swing before deciding, no, he guessed he wouldn't, and it caught the outside corner.

"'S go, Babe!"

"Hit one, Babe!"

Two men were standing beyond first base among the hundreds behind the rope that ran from the dugout to the right-field wall. They'd started their day at a backyard still, and now, as they stood watching, they both pulled rhythmically on flasks. They looked alike in a generic sort of way, apparitional and inbred in their undernourished frames.

"He's scared of you, Babe!"

"Fillin' up his diaper!"

Earl couldn't hear them at all. They were one thin voice lost in the crowd's humming, and he was now in a shell of concentration. He nodded to the sign, another fastball, this one high and tight.

In the stands Rooster offered his hand to Henry. "Here. Be careful stepping up."

Henry had persisted, could he stand on the bleachers, until Rooster turned to the man behind them. "Would you mind? Say 'yes' if you do and for sure we'll understand." The man was large; he sat tall and bulbous, looming cordially on his bleachers seat. It was clear that he could still see everything if Henry were standing in front of him. But the thing to notice was his head. It was cubically shaped to a cartoonish extreme, a Sunday funny pages head.

"The boy wants to see his dad," Rooster had explained, pointing down to the field.

"Your dad's playing?" the cube-headed man asked.

Henry nodded vigorously. "He's the pitcher. Earl Dunham."

"Earl the pitcher," the man had said. "Earl the pitcher." He'd sounded taken with the phrase, as if he were pleased to be learning of some historical figure. Ivan the Terrible. Pliny the Elder.

Standing now, holding onto Rooster's shoulder, Henry could see the field spread out below and his father on the mound in the center of it all. And it *was* a thing to behold, tended like a garden for this special day, the sweeping delta of the infield, the narrow trace of groomed dirt from home plate to the mound, the outfield meadow of infinite green.

Two pitches in, and Earl knew he'd glimpsed Ruth's greatness—his casual focus on the pitch as it was coming that made the ball larger and slowed it down. Earl's blood was rushing, an unsettled strength was filling him, causing him to lose his balance slightly in his windup, and here was the pitch, misdirected, heading for the Babe's midsection, the fabled girth. But Ruth swung in midstride as if to swat the ball away and it came screaming back, Earl ducking, eyes closed, throwing up his hand in front of his face, and it found his glove—old, limp leather, small as a claw—*smack!*

"Whoah!" This from the cube-headed man behind Henry.

"What happened?" Rooster asked.

"Babe tattooed it!"

"Dad caught it!" Henry said.

Ruth stood in the batter's box; he'd had no time to move.

Earl was bent over with his hands on his knees, the ball still in his glove.

Now Ruth gave him a quick salute and started for his dugout. Earl couldn't read the gesture, but as he left the mound, he pointed at Ruth, his hand a friendly pistol, and dipped its barrel, his index finger, in reply, telling himself his glove hand wasn't broken and it would stop stinging and he wasn't dead and Ruth was out.

High in the left-field stands, Audrey Waterston cheered.

She was a pretty young woman, short and buxom with smooth Mediterranean-swarthy skin, who worked as a teller at the First State Bank of Hinton. Earl had slipped a note to her one day as she sat on her stool in her teller's cage, saying, "This is a hold-up. Either give me all your money or a weekend afternoon."

Since Emily died, Earl had seen a few women, three or four over the years, and he'd not been able with any of them to move much past the awkward, bumpkin courtesies. The closest he'd come to relaxing into himself were the several months he'd spent seeing Audrey. Until one spring Sunday, sitting at her kitchen table, with the late daylight in its amber hour and growing intimate if you wished to feel its effect in that way. But Earl didn't, he fought this feeling, telling Audrey he thought it best if they could just be friends.

"Best for who?" Audrey asked. Her voice was chipper, but sincere. It was the voice she used with customers. There was a bounce in it, a rendered shape.

Earl said that as stupid as it sounded, he couldn't shake the feeling that the town was watching them, that when they were together, he couldn't feel they were alone. And Audrey said, no, it wasn't stupid, just sad, very sad for both of them, and it was clear to her whose eyes he sensed were watching them.

Earl was wild in the second inning, walking two and then giving up a double, a low liner over first that kicked up the chalk and cleared the bases. But after that he settled down, getting fairly easily through the bottom of the lineup, the last out a called strike on the inside corner that had the hitter buckling.

He'd thrown a screwball, Mathewson's fade-away, the first one today, and as he headed for the dugout, his step became that glide, that flowing stride, a surety about the space he was taking up in the world. He hadn't moved in this way on a field, in a game, in years.

Ruth's team's pitcher was a jug-eared boy, built wide, solid as an oak credenza. His breaking pitches barely moved, but he threw very hard, he threw BBs, he threw darts, and he kept Earl's team hitless until, with two outs in the second, he walked a batter and Lester Semple shot a liner to the left and Gehrig, whimsically batting eighth, hit a fastball on a 2–1 count, his bat moving viciously along a level plane, his body striding forward and his back knee nearly touching the ground, looking like someone being knighted.

From the dugout, Earl saw the ball off the bat, starting low and rising on a line, soaring toward right center and clearing the fence with a fine economy, as if it wished, like the man who'd hit it, to leave the park in a hurry before anyone could make a fuss.

Earl watched Gehrig circling the bases. He was moving more freely as he ran, hardly gamboling, but not the plodding, dray horse gait Earl had seen earlier, and he wondered at the rush that must lift a man when he'd hit one even *close* to that hard. It could be an exhibition, it could be the World Series, it could be neighbors in a pasture with grain sacks for bases, it would feel just as good. He'd never seen a baseball hit so hard.

His eyes followed Gehrig rounding third, and they watched his dust-covered cleats, wide boats, touch the plate. He had the lead.

On the bench in the dugout, he found himself speaking to Emily, saying, *This is what I meant.* He felt doubly surprised—that he'd thought these words, and that he'd thought them here, thought them now. He'd long counted on the game as a diversion; he'd learned to prize its hours as sanctuarial, grateful that nothing else visited him while he played.

He thought, My *life could have made* you *happy.*

The top of the third, two outs, and Ruth again stepped daintily into the box, got into his stance, and flexed his knees to set his balance. He was all serious preparation this time, no wave to the crowd, no crude jokiness from the corner of his mouth that got Bill Brown, crouched behind him, and the squatting umpire chuckling.

He'd gone two games without hitting a home run, none in Omaha two days before, none yesterday in Des Moines, and this pissed him royally, which he'd never admit. These games, these pitchers, it should be like taking batting practice. And that included Earl, whose fast ball Ruth thought average and whose curve ball impressed him—its sharp dive, falling off the table, hell to hit if you didn't know it was coming. But Ruth did know, because he could glimpse Earl's grip as he released the ball, and Ruth could read it like a headline.

"Let's go, Babe," Mayor Enright whispered again.

His wife's even prettier sister called the same thing loudly. She was wearing a stylish beaded knit cloche hat, and she'd bought smart brown suede pumps with diamanté buckles to wear today. She loved the game of baseball, and she especially loved Babe Ruth. She had his Purity Ice Cream Company baseball card pinned to the wall above her writing desk, and as she'd watched him today her imagination had been wending its way through fantasies of the two of them in the moonlight on the dewy outfield grass.

On the mound, Earl nodded to Bill Brown's calling for a curve, inside. He liked the idea that he might catch Ruth guessing if he came in tight on him again.

Earl wound and snapped off the curve, but the pitch was catching too much of the plate and Ruth stepped into it, released his uppercut swing, and hit a high, arcing fly headed for deep right center.

The drunks behind the rope, one shouting "Whooo!" the other one pointing at the ball as it rose, his finger drawing sloppily on the air.

They'd been nipping continuously, their faces flushed and with that heavy-lidded look of sleepy evil in them.

"Yes!" Enright letting his excitement escape, and his sister-in-law calling, "Yes!" as she watched, the heels of her brown suede pumps making rat-a-tat flamenco stomps.

Lester Semple was running, his legs growing longer with each elastic stride. He'd instantly wheeled, and he was running with his head down, no attention on the sky.

Earl's eyes were turned to right center, to the wall and the sweep of blue above it, the thin clouds cirrusing.

It wasn't how hard Ruth had hit the ball, but how high it was climbing and how long it was taking at the top of the sky. Indifferent to gravity, it could do what it wanted, and what else would a baseball want to do, one Babe Ruth had hit, but be stupendously gone and remembered forever?

Earl watched it carrying, carrying, felt the sickness in his stomach, and he thought Lester Semple looked lunatic racing hell-bent for the ball when everyone could see it was going out. Was he playing it for laughs, which fit with nothing Earl imagined him to be, but the harder he ran, he seemed more and more to be making a show of how far Ruth had hit it.

Henry, looking heavenward, nearly lost his balance, and Rooster, looking up too, tightly gripped his arm. Everyone was looking up. Everyone was open-mouthed and voiceless, looking up. And Henry's eyes were doing more than that; they were fastened on the ball as if he were tracking it for Semple. They were willing it to halt its flight, to back up in the sky, so it could fall on a plumb line into Lester Semple's glove.

Semple closing fast, thirty feet from the men at the base of the fence, no restraining rope out here, and they were shifting and jostling, doing nervous side-step shuffles as they braced for impact, bodies planting themselves and bodies leaning in, and a man being shoved, or maybe just tripping over someone's foot, but two-stepping backward, honky-tonk stomps, four, five, half a dozen before regaining his balance, and at the last instant Semple lifted his eyes, found the ball, and leapt as the crowd of men, enough of them, jumped back to make a narrow lane, and Semple in full flight looked the ball into his glove, then hit the ground and disappeared, the huddle briefly closing as men reached down to help him up.

Seconds of silence. Five, ten, time enough for a nervous excitement to begin.

Ruth had stopped at second base. He'd lost his cap making the turn at first, and he visored his hand to his forehead as he looked out to center field.

And here was Semple reappearing, stepping free and raising his arm to show the ball in his glove, holding it high above his head. His wool cap sat askew, its bill pointing to one o'clock. The front of his uniform was smeared with grass stains.

"He caught it!" Henry shouted, and his imagination took him. He'd kept the ball in the park, he'd called it back as it was leaving.

"Damn," whispered the mayor's wife's even prettier sister, seeing the ball in Semple's glove and his arm raised high, a pose like Madam Liberty's.

The cheering for the catch was a spotty clapping, slapping sounds coming from here and there, not the whole crowd roar you would expect. But people were weighing with their applause what they'd seen and how they felt about it. The man had made as great a catch as you'd ever hope to see, the way he'd left his feet, and what do you call that when you just float in the air like he did? *Lub*ricated, yes, that was the word, he'd lubricated for a second out there in center field. But the way he'd lifted his glove so everyone could see he'd caught it. Who'd he think he was, showing Babe Ruth up like that? It amounted to pig rudeness in the presence of greatness. And then, too, the disappointment that Ruth hadn't hit a homer, as if the catch had robbed him of one, though it would have only been a double if the ball had fallen, maybe a triple if the Babe had hustled, which he hadn't.

Jesus, Earl thought, watching Semple as he straightened his cap and brushed futilely at the grass stains, then started in, the third out gotten, his stride little more than a mosey as he tossed the ball to the second base man, who'd drifted out to shallow right.

Earl thought, *Jesus*. And everything included in that—gratitude, relief, and the feeling that he was himself in someone else's body, or he was someone else in his, either way he was inside an elation, and his wish to stay there seemed a need, something swaggering, rambunctious, and with a gaiety about it.

Ruth was standing with both feet on the second base bag, making a low pedestal of it. Now he threw up his hands, and you could see his wide grin from the stands as he trotted off to retrieve his cap.

"Hey!" and "What the fuck?!" from the drunks behind the foul-line rope. They stared at one another, flap-mouthed, demanding that things be explained, the son of a bitch leaping, disappearing from their view, before he reemerged and struck his statue pose.

They'd gotten louder as the game went on, people moving steadily away from them, from their idiot insults and their rotgut breath, squeezing in elsewhere as best they could, or giving up and heading into the stands to perch on the steps.

Earl made no move to leave the mound. He wanted to be the last one off, and he watched Semple as he reached the infield, the lackadaisy of his stride, hopping over the second base bag, a double-Dutch skip-step that charmed Earl, how easily Semple had found the child in himself, in his heavily muscled body, had found it now. Earl called, "Great catch," and raised his cap, and Semple, looking straight ahead as he passed, said, "Piss-poor pitch." His face was blank as a legume, and it wasn't until he reached the dugout steps that he turned around and offered Earl a smile, a coy curl, conspiracy in it.

Henry stood on the bleachers, resting his hand on Rooster's shoulder. He could see the field, and he didn't mind standing. He liked it, in fact. But he'd been thinking he wanted to get closer, and after watching the man's diving catch, he wanted even more to be standing with the people gathered behind the foul line. Looking down, he noticed a tiny oval-shaped patch of green close to the front, at the rope.

"Grandpa," he said, tugging on Rooster's sleeve.

Top of the sixth, the score still three to two. The game had moved along with a martial crispness, batters up and batters down, quickly put away. Earl throwing all his pitches, the jug-eared boy throwing heat.

Ruth was walking to the plate. His black bat, forty-two ounces. Resting on his shoulder like some Klondike implement.

Henry stood at the front of the crowd behind the ropes in the spot, the little oval-shaped patch he'd noticed from the stands. He was peering out from beneath the brim of his grandfather's dress straw boater with its wide red band. It sat impossibly low on his head. The cube-headed man from the bleachers was standing next to him. The two drunks were just behind them, weaving slightly now and then like saplings in a wind.

"Pitcher's 'fraid of you, Babe!"

"Hit it *out* this time!"

In the bleachers, before he'd got here, Henry had asked Rooster to come down and stand with him.

Rooster shook his head. "If right now I was to say to my body, 'stand up,' what it would say back to me is 'no.'"

Then the large, cube-headed man had leaned forward. "What if I go down with him?"

Rooster shook his head again. "More than kind of you. We already bothered you enough for one day."

The man had flapped his meaty hand, *pshaw*, and introduced himself, Sylvester Loomis, call him Sy, call him anything but late for dinner. "Truth be told, this is me being selfish. I've got two small ones myself, two twins, Morris and Norris, just turned nine, and I'm being honest when I say they're barely civilized. We don't take them any place where there's a crowd. If they were here, Lord only knows; they'd likely find a way to set a fire. But we love 'em to death, and I've been sitting here thinking how I'm missing out on a once in a lifetime father-and-his-sons experience, Ruth and Gehrig *right, down, there*. So let me take *Henry* down there like he wants."

Rooster had looked at Henry and up at Loomis and back at Henry. Then he'd taken off his boater and said, "Wear this so I can spot you."

Henry made a face, sour and quizzical. "Mr. Loomis will be with me."

"Your granddad's right," Loomis said. "I'd want the same if it was me up here and Morris and Norris down there." He cocked his head in thought. "Or maybe not."

Henry had looked down, scanning the crowd behind the ropes. The patch of green was magically still there, even slightly larger. "*Every*body's wearing a hat. You couldn't spot me."

"They ain't wearing this one," Rooster said, and he'd placed it on Henry's head and tapped its crown. "Very handsome."

"Swah-vay," said Sy Loomis.

The breeze in Stockyards Park nearly always blew straight in. But now it suddenly shifted, blowing across the field from right to left, and the flag in center field began to flutter with the change in its direction.

"He's shared skitless, Babe!"

"You said 'shared skitless,' you dumb ass."

"Yeah! You dumb ass!"

"Not the *pitcher's* a dumb ass, dumb ass. *You.*"

Henry was a little bit afraid and working hard to ignore the drunks, telling himself not to turn around, to keep his eyes on the field and the play. He could look slightly to his left and let his gaze travel toward the infield to see Gehrig from behind, the humpbacked crouch of his fielding stance. And looking on past Gehrig to Earl on the mound, his posture loose and lean and belonging, his right foot raking a spot beside the rubber, a coltish digging at the ground, and Henry's eyes continuing still, across the third-base line and into the dugout where Ruth's team sat as the Babe made his way to the plate.

"Hit one it takes his head off!"

"You did last time but you din't!"

Their voices mean and hooting, and Henry couldn't imagine why they were cheering against his father. They'd never even met him. He reached up and gripped the restraining rope, and Rooster's hat slid down over his ears and covered his eyes for about the sixth time since he'd been wearing it. He wanted badly to take it off, but then he'd have to hold it, and he could feel his grandfather's eyes watching from the stands.

"He's shaking his shoes, Babe!"

"His pants're pissing!"

Sy Loomis had been trying to ignore them too, but he was worried for Henry, the ragged heckling falling on his young ears, and felt the moment coming when he'd have to turn around and say something.

He glanced down at Henry. From above, the flat crown of the boater was a straw platter. He imagined Morris and Norris standing there instead, his sweet savages, taking them by the shoulders and aiming them at the drunks and setting them loose. *Go!*

"Smoke one, Babe!"

"Right between the dumb shit's eyes!"

And Loomis thought, *Okay.*

He turned around and nodded at them. Together they gave off a phantasmal aura. They were there, in their bodies, but also they were not. Mostly, they looked just so happy to be drunk. He was struck by their resemblance—gaunt and gleeful, their nitwit, bad-teeth grins.

Loomis said, "Fellas? How about we all just watch the game."

They stared at Loomis, and one of them, the slightly larger of the two, said, "Your *head*, man." He sounded awestruck.

Loomis's eyebrows flared. "What about it?"

"Iss a *box.*"

Earl waited once more for Ruth to set himself. He saw the bodily logic of it now, the upward flow of getting ready—the careful placement of the feet, the flexing of the knees, the quick practice swings that primed and cocked his body. He'd been smiling the first time up, sober-pussed the second, and now his face was expressionless.

Again, Bill Brown suggested starting Ruth with a fastball, high and tight. Earl rocked and kicked and threw it to the spot, and Ruth didn't offer, lifting his arms to let it pass beneath them.

The drunk looked at Sy Loomis sorrowfully. "When you was *born.*"

"Yes, I was!" Loomis said. Keeping a hail-fellow note in his voice.

"Your mama pushing you out, that *head.*"

"Poor mama."

"Not the place or time for insults is it fellows!" Loomis said. His smile continuing, shining it on one and then the other, and they both looked away as if it hurt their eyes. "Just asking you to hold it down." Loomis nodded at Henry, still turned determinedly with his back to them. "We got a boy here he'd like to watch the game."

"Whosayin' he can't?"

Bill Brown called for a curve and Earl nodded, but in his gut he was reluctant. He'd start it wide and hope it caught the corner. He didn't want to go two and O on Ruth. He threw the pitch where he wanted to and Ruth connected, somehow managing to pull it, the ball flying into the right-field sky and sailing barely foul, landing in the street thirty yards beyond the fence and bouncing and rolling over dirt and cobblestones and trolley tracks and trash and litter shifting and lifting on the strong cross-breeze, and the ball rolling on and on toward the stockyards down the block.

The drunk was pointing at Henry. "*His* head a box?" And Loomis understood the fool thought Henry was his son.

"Box-head Boy! Box-head Boy!" This from the other one, again joining in the fun.

"Thass why he's the hat? Hide his head?"

"You should too, big straw hat."

"Wait. No, you need a picnic basket."

Earl got a new ball and held it with both hands, turning it and studying the stitches and telling it that a foul with home-run distance was, the saying went, just a long strike. He was feeling no sort of terror now, nothing that froze him, and not the one he'd welcomed on waking as something he could use. He was breathing evenly, attending only to his need to get strike two.

Picnic basket!! The drunks were laughing, their bodies bending and twisting, small convulsions, propping each other up. They'd cleared more space around them, more people leaving, a little moat of grass surrounding them now. Loomis turned his back to them and put his arm on Henry's shoulder. The thing to do was move away, but subtly, and they likely wouldn't even notice.

Earl looked in for the sign. He shook off a curve. He shook off a fastball. He shook off a spitter.

Ruth called time and stepped out, giving Earl an oversized shrug, a stagey bit of business—*What seems to be the problem?*   that drew laughter from the crowd.

In the stands Rooster was keeping one eye on the game and the other on Henry and the hat, and he was suffering through a feeling like melancholy, but more barbed, more alive in current time. Sy Loomis had said he missed his sons being here to watch, and hearing him say that, the thought went through Rooster that the man didn't know the half of it.

He'd grown to like sitting with Emily watching Earl pitch. He'd tried at first to keep this a secret from himself as he came to understand his pleasure was selfish, seeing he'd been right to want the future he'd wanted for them all. And right to say to Earl it's the one he should want too, for he'd found a way, Earl had, the perfect way to have the game in his life without its *being* his life.

Earl was going to throw a screw ball. The one to end the top of the second had had a biting life, and the hitter's legs had wobbled and he'd leaned on his bat to keep from lurching forward.

The drunks were laughing with a new energy, or the same energy with new sounds, babyish and gurgling, and it made Henry even angrier, made him feel more afraid, and at last he spun around. He looked up at them from beneath the boater's brim.

Earl threw a thigh-high screwball that broke classically away, and Ruth swung weakly, his bat feeling the air for where the pitch might be.

The crowd's great surprise at swing-and-miss-strike-two on Babe Ruth, and a noise, a choral *Hmmm!* ran through it.

Mayor Enright in his seat could feel his rooting interest shifting. The count was one and two, and his new thought was a headline. LOCAL PITCHER STRIKES OUT BABE RUTH! What publicity for Sioux City! He felt a magnanimity, and he was proud of himself for feeling it. Let the farmer have his moment in the sun. Ruth had had a million of them, and he'd have a million more.

Henry was glaring up at the drunks with everything he had, but it didn't feel to him like nearly enough. He imagined yelling at them, "Shut up!" You could see his lower eyeballs beneath the straw brim.

He looked demented and gargoylish.

The slightly larger drunk peered down at Henry. "Who we got down here?"

Sy Loomis took a step and stood in front of Henry. "We'll move over there and leave you to your fun." Loomis nodded to the open space of grass.

Babe Ruth looking foolish with a bat. For everyone watching, it had the force of revelation. It would be one thing for him to take a vicious cut and get nothing but air. A swing like that, its brutal grace, happened often, and it stopped a pitcher's heart. But the flailing wave just now had pulled him off balance, nearly causing him to stumble.

The first bright beat of what could happen. Earl felt it, felt a fine heat building.

He signaled for Bill Brown.

The drunk was trying to reach around Loomis and snatch the boater from Henry's head. He hooked his index finger, beckoning *C'mere*.

On the mound, Bill Brown spoke through the grill of his catcher's mask. "Throw it again."

Earl said, "He's maybe looking for it now," and Bill Brown said, no, he sensed Ruth was looking for the curve, he wanted the curve, so Earl should throw the screwball, which broke the other way.

The drunk reaching around Loomis and feeling blindly, his fingers wiggling. Stealing the hat was the funniest fucking thing he could possibly imagine, the kind of stunt you woke up from tomorrow, half blind with a hangover, and there was somebody's straw hat with a wide red band lying on the floor beside your bed and you thought, *How the fuck?* But that was tomorrow. Right now the mission was getting the hat, who cared about the shape of the little goober's head? It could be square, it could be round, it could be as flat as planet Earth. Just grab the hat. He tried to reach around Loomis again, and Loomis took a slide-step, still shielding Henry, and the drunk moved with him and said, "Wanna dance?" and this was the most hilarious thing so far.

Ruth set in his stance.

Earl leaned in for the sign. Bill Brown went through the sequence, hoping he could get Ruth trying to guess what was coming. He

signaled it last, four fingers wiggling, like the drunk's as he was grop-
ing for the hat.

A feeling rising in Earl's chest, the sweet astonishment of strike
three. He remembered the rush he'd felt was Gehrig's when he'd
homered in the third, and he knew his was going to be the same. No,
greater.

The mayor's wife's even prettier sister, nervously patting her thighs
as she watched.

The drunks, giggling idiots, took Sy Loomis by the shoulders and
pushed him aside. He stumbled and fell backward and found himself
sitting on the grass watching the larger one pluck the hat from Henry's
head and with a backhand whipping motion send it high into the air.

"Whoo!" and "Whee-yah!"

Henry heard their shouts making ugly fun of everything, of his father most of all, and he didn't turn to watch Rooster's boater floating
toward the infield, going and going, impressively going on the breeze
blowing strongly right to left. He kicked the drunk in the shin as hard
as he could, and it took the pain a moment before the cry, "Shit!"
and the drunk dropping to his knees. Henry pivoted and ran, and the
drunk looked at Loomis still sitting on the ground. Their eyes met,
a man on his ass and a man on his knees, and Loomis smiled and
nodded. He was so proud of Henry. The twins could not have done
it better.

Earl was in his windup, his left leg starting its high kick, when the
umpire came out of his crouch and raised his arms and shouted,
"Time!" Earl stopped his motion, his leg came down. The umpire was
pointing out past Gehrig at first base, out to the crowd behind the
foul-line rope in right field, and Earl turned to see a boy, some little
brat running onto the field.

"Goddamn it." He felt his body going in opposite directions, his
coiled strength retreating, diminishing, and the rest of him—his
brain, his blood, his breaths—racing on to Ruth's swinging and missing again.

He stood, looking out to right, the scene becoming circus-worthy,
the boy running toward the infield, with others just behind him

now, dozens more running and the number growing. They'd broken through the rope, the boy weirdly out in front, their leader, and more were hurrying down from the bleachers.

Earl watched. He was inside the finished instant he'd been about to pitch to, looking out from the perfect center of it and feeling it so powerfully because it hadn't happened. "God*damn* it!"

Rooster had seen his hat go flying, the red band come loose, a flapping ribbon in the sky, and he thought, *What the hell, that can't be good.*

Gehrig had turned to watch them coming. There were shouts and screams and laughter, all the attitudes of laughter, and he saw a little kid leading, his short legs churning. Gehrig wasn't surprised. There'd been versions of this scene in every game, young boys mostly, rushing onto the field to get to him and Ruth and jumping up to try to steal the caps right off their heads. In Des Moines, a boy had run to him and wrapped his arms around one of his enormous thighs, and Gehrig had had to give the kid a ride to second base, peg-legging it the whole way, before he'd let go.

Henry was running for his life and to retrieve his grandfather's hat. He didn't turn around; he could hear the pounding feet, he could hear the shouting, the cattle-drive falsetto *hee-haws!* He knew the drunks were at the front and gaining on him. He could hear their goony cackles. The shape they were in, they couldn't catch a turtle, but he didn't know that. He didn't know the one he'd kicked had fallen and the other one, bending down to help him up, had fallen too, and there they were at the bottom of their long, dumb day, sitting on the grass like debauched picnickers, puzzled by the tumult all around them. A hat sailing through the air and a boy loose on the field—the permission people needed to break through the rope and run.

And Sy Loomis pleasurably trailing, a bounce of satisfaction in his boulevardier step.

On the mound, Earl felt his anger taking him as he watched the kid in full, chopping stride, leading the stampede. He panned the scene left to right, and he spotted a straw hat lying where the grass met the infield looking like a stage-set prop that didn't belong. And he could never say which he recognized first—Henry's way of running, his short legs pumping, or Rooster's boater, the birthday gift from Lottie, which she thought made him look like Calvin Coolidge, who was a very handsome man in Lottie's opinion. Or maybe the two reached Earl together to make it clear it was his *son* running madly, away from something and toward Rooster's hat, reaching down to pick it up as he ran, and stumbling, falling, landing face-first in the dirt. A splat, a toddler's sprawl, and the crowd, people caught in the current of their momentum, but goofily, the lawless joy of it, and Earl was sprinting to Henry, knowing in his gut it had taken him too long to see what he was seeing. He'd been elsewhere with his anger as he watched, and he knew he was too late.

Henry lay on his stomach and, looking up at Earl, too frightened to move, his eyes were huge with knowing it too.

And there was Gehrig racing in from somewhere out of the frame and kneeling as he ran, a dip, a curtsy in full stride, and scooping up the boy with ease and hurrying him off the field and on, into the dugout, as the rowdy wave started past.

He sat Henry down as if he were a piece of his mother's Old World family china, and they looked out like spectators taking in some odd, impromptu rally.

At home plate, heading for his dugout before he got mobbed, Ruth said to Bill Brown and the umpire, "That little fucker was just about his mama's memory." He was suddenly bone weary of this dog and pony show, the tour and these numbskull rubes running onto the field every fucking game. The thought flashed of the easy money he could be making in a vaudeville act, three times what he was getting for this, like the one Walsh had put together for him last year, when all he'd had to do was burst through a tissue-papered hoop and toot duck-call sounds on a saxophone and toss a baseball in the air and tell jokes about preachers' daughters and pretty maids just off the farm, and it didn't matter if he forgot the punch lines. The audiences laughed their asses off because he was the Babe.

The crowd had slowed to a trot, those at the rear forced to run in place, as it reached the quickly filling infield with nowhere farther to go. People stopped and began to mill about, and Earl pushed and squeezed, his body his wildly working heart, trying to get through them to Henry. There'd been a strange, unnameable sense to it all, larksome and anarchic, but now the air of a reunion was taking hold, as if this thing, still happening, was already the anniversary of it. Men spotted acquaintances and shook hands, strangers introduced themselves, and Earl was struggling to get through them. He couldn't see Gehrig patting Henry on the back. He couldn't see Henry's effort at a smile, the one he was no good at—it was tremulous and thin—when he was very upset and trying not to show it.

Rooster was making his way down to the field, taking each step at an angle, one at a time, left foot first. He could see that things had quieted, the infield packed with people, but he couldn't spot Henry or Earl, or for that matter his straw boater. He was upset and he hurt and, made more upset by how much he hurt, he thought, as he hadn't for a very long time, what an asinine game baseball was.

Earl reached the dugout, down the steps, and squatted in front of Henry. He was speechless, out of breath, as he reached up and cradled his son's sweaty face in his hands.

"I tripped," Henry said.

"I know," Earl said. "I saw."

The mayor had left his seat, telling his wife and her sister to stay put. He couldn't judge the crowd, couldn't read its disposition, and he wouldn't think of putting the women at risk. He was headed for the dugout where the boy sat with Gehrig. The little bastard, whatever had possessed him, appeared to be fine, tragedy avoided, and what a thrilling rescue with Gehrig hurrying in like that! And a small part of Enright felt sorry for poor Dunham, the game ending as it had. Such a hapless soul, it seemed somehow fitting, *so close and yet . . .* And anyway, Ruth no doubt would have focused with two strikes on him and hit the next pitch to Omaha.

Still in a crouch, his eyes holding Henry's, Earl shifted them to look up at Gehrig. "Thank you." He had to clear his throat. "*We* thank you." His words were still trembling a bit from his adrenaline.

Gehrig smiled, the dazzling dimples. "Time I got there, he was ready to pop up on his own." He looked at Henry. "*Weren't* you." He squeezed Henry's shoulder and gave his hair a Roosterish mussing.

Earl said softly, "I saw what I saw. I'm more than grateful."

Henry looked at his father then. "Where were *you*?" His nerves still jangling, he said this sharply, a stern disciplinarian.

"I was coming," Earl said, "I was on my way to you," and hearing himself, he felt the child to Henry's parent.

"I was *scared*," Henry said.

Earl nodded. "Of course you were." He cleared his throat again. "But what were you thinking, running onto the field?"

Henry breathed deeply. He considered for a moment how he might try to explain it all, at least begin to. But he realized he had no wish to make the effort, and besides, he shouldn't have to. All he'd wanted was to get closer so he could see better. He'd done nothing wrong. In fact, he'd done the opposite, yes. He'd been defending his father, trying to rescue him from the things the stupid men were saying. To stand up for him, same thing. He felt suddenly greatly put upon. He wished Mr. Loomis were here. He'd be able to explain it.

Audrey Waterston had hurried down the grandstand steps, squeezing past people, asking brusquely, rudely, to be pardoned. She'd watched from high in the stands, Henry falling, Gehrig arriving, Earl some steps away, all of it unfolding, timing and sequence, like an act they'd rehearsed. She'd reached the bottom step and leaned against the railing, and she could see across the field into the dugout where Earl was squatting in front of Henry, and she thought she saw him cradling Henry's face in his hands. She couldn't tell for sure, but it looked from where she stood as if Henry was unharmed, and she could only think how frightened he had been. He'd been so open to the world, so sweetly undefended, when he was seven, when she'd known him, and surely he still was. She was thinking of the day he'd come with Earl to the bank, and seeing her behind the bars of her teller's cage, he'd asked her if she was in jail because she'd robbed a bank, and then he'd cracked up at this really great joke, which he'd made up with his father on their trip into town.

In the dugout, Henry looked out at the people on the field lazily milling, supremely satisfied with themselves, but not knowing what to do with it now, and he saw Rooster nearing the first base bag, holding his straw boater to his chest. From what Henry could tell from his distance, it had been flattened, the red silk band dangling from it like a tail. And he knew that wasn't his fault either, it was his grandfather's, for making him wear it. He'd only been trying to rescue *it* too.

Lester Semple had started in from center field, the other two out-fielders had left a while ago, and as he reached the infield and per-formed his little jump-rope hop over the second base bag, he was thinking, as he had been, standing alone in the shadow of the outfield wall, that the whole crazy thing he'd just watched, with the boy and Gehrig, and the crowd running, jostling and dazed, then massing stu-pidly, that if none of it had happened, the thing people would remem-ber about this game was his catch. He'd felt a bite of bitterness when this thought had come to him, what the kid had done to rob him of his day.

Nearing the dugout, he was remembering, hearing once more the crowd's reluctant cheering as he'd lifted his arm to show the ball in his glove. It had pained him, angered him, *What the hell?* when he'd heard it, such miserly approval, so much less than he'd deserved.

But hurrying down the dugout steps toward the rat-infested tun-nel leading to the clubhouse, he was thinking, even so, the catch had simply been too good. Maybe not yet, it might take time for people to sort it all out, but that's what would stay, that's what they'd remem-ber. As he ducked into the tunnel, he glanced at Henry, surrounded, wondering why the pitcher especially was paying the little shit such close attention.

Sitting next to Gehrig, with Earl still on the step in front of him, Henry felt both men's caring company, and he felt, compatibly, his fear. It was as if the four of them—he and his fear and his father and Mr. Gehrig—were all bound by the experience they'd just had. The *reasons* he'd been so frightened—the awful men, his falling down and thinking he was going to be trampled—they were done. And what they'd left for him was the pure feeling of it all. Which was still fear, but starting now to feel an ally; again, a companion, and like some-thing he had won.

He saw himself lying on his stomach and he saw his father's ex-pression, the panic in it, and now it seemed—a clearer image forming

—that his father had been wrong to feel the terror Henry had seen so clearly in his eyes. He'd been wrong, and Mr. Gehrig, what *he'd* said, had been right. Henry was picturing it, remembering it, his senses shaping it. It was like something he'd lived and at the same time he was reading, like a grand climactic moment in a serial he was listening to on the Atwater Kent in the farmhouse parlor. He saw himself gathering his body as Mr. Gehrig had described, set to jump to his feet, the effortless spring, the lifting grace of a Bernard, and hurrying away on his own from the danger, just in time.

CHAPTER SEVENTEEN

Sioux City, later that day

Ruth's hotel suite was two high-ceilinged rooms, this parlor where he and Gehrig were sitting in leather chairs patinaed with age to a soft, dark luster and a bedroom beyond. The walls were papered in a Roman pillars pattern, and the woodwork was painted a handsome pearl gray. Ruth was getting paid $30,000 for this tour, and his contract specified the largest stateroom on the Pullman and the luxury suite at every hotel, though the idea of luxury in a couple of them had been an extra spittoon.

Gehrig smoked a cigarette, Ruth a large Cuban cigar. They exhaled together and their smoke curled and merged, Ruth's predominant. Gehrig watched it, then looked past Ruth to the suite's tall windows. Through them the sunset was sending a clean and clarifying light. The mullioned panes were luminous with it. Ruth was wearing his tailored, paisley-patterned silk dressing gown with black velvet lapels and matching belt. He was wearing his English handmade elkhide slippers.

They'd been talking a short while. Ruth had asked him in the taxi as they rode back from the park to come up to his room and fill him in. He'd watched it all, of course—the kid running, if you could even call it "running." He'd never seen anybody work so hard to run so slow and the herd of yahoos whooping it up behind him and Gehrig's rescue like your basic winged hero out of some bullshit myth-type tale by a famous cornholed Greek. But everything had been decided and agreed to by the time he'd left his dugout and made his way to theirs. He'd crossed the infield through a few dozen fans still wandering around, signed some autographs, shaken some hands, chatted with a dame, a classy looker with shiny buckles on her shoes who'd smiled and quoted him his batting average for the season. "Everybody knows the sixty homers, but how many know you hit .356?"

So when he made it to their dugout at last, that's when he learned that the boy and his father, who, it turned out, was the *pitcher*, for Christ's sake, they were coming along on the tour, riding with them in the Pullman for a while, and Ruth didn't know why the news of this had left him feeling vaguely pissed off. Maybe just because he hadn't been consulted. Maybe it was as simple as that. Or maybe he didn't like the idea of the sad sack kid and his father getting in the way, whatever might pop up that they'd be getting in the way of. Although now that he was thinking, the kid reminded him some of little Ray Kelly, his good luck mascot in the Yankees' dugout. He was older than little Ray, but his spastic fall had looked like a toddler learning to walk.

"How long they coming for?" Ruth asked.

Gehrig leaned forward and stubbed out his cigarette. His chair's leather cushions made a mewling squeak with his shifting weight. "Walsh said to the father, the pitcher, his name's Earl, Walsh said to him, 'Stay on all the way if you want.' He said to me after they left, it could be great publicity, them traveling with us."

"How so?" Ruth asked.

Gehrig shrugged. "I guess he thinks he can make it into something."

Ruth drew deeply on his cigar, lifting his chin at an effete, patrician angle. "Why'd you ask them? You and Walsh?"

"It was me, really. Walsh said 'Sure,' but it was me. You wish I hadn't?"

Ruth shrugged. "I ain't sure what I wish."

"I'm sorry, Jidge, if—"

"Yeah, I know."

Gehrig hadn't dreamed that Ruth would mind. "I guess I wanted to take his mind off it. He was trying to act brave, but he was *really* scared. He'd calmed down a little by the time you got there." He shrugged. "It seemed, I don't know, like he deserved something."

"A kick in the butt, for all the shit he caused."

"Jidge, really, it never—"

"I know it didn't."

Gehrig reached for his pack of cigarettes lying on the low coffee table between them. He lit one and took a drag. "His birthday's coming up."

"The kid's?"

"I was saying to them, why didn't they come, and the pitcher, Earl, the fa—"

"Earl the pitcher. I got he's the father."

"He was saying, no, they couldn't. Thanks, but no. Then the grandfather stepped in and said it'd be a hell of a birthday present for Henry." Gehrig said, a musing tone now, "Maybe that's some of why I invited him."

"Because it's his birthday?"

"Because his name's Henry."

"So?"

"*My* name's Henry."

"Since when?"

"Henry Louis," Gehrig said.

Ruth raised his thick eyebrows. Nearly touching, they formed a bushy chevron. "Did I know that, kid? I probably did." He leaned back into the cushions of his chair again. They made that same mewling squeak. He crossed his legs, an ankle on a thigh, and his dressing gown fell open for a moment. Gehrig was relieved to see that he was wearing underwear, which you could never just assume. Navy blue silk boxers, as it happened.

"His mother died," Gehrig said. "The Spanish flu."

"Jesus," Ruth said, "you got the whole sad story."

Gehrig nodded. "Walsh was wondering where she was, if she was at the game, and Henry said she died and Earl said how she did." He paused and smoked. "Pretty matter of fact. Both of them."

"Well, the kid, he probably don't even remember her."

Gehrig looked down at the carpet. It was a pattern of green octagons framing fat cabbage roses. Still feeling slightly chastened, he said, "They seem like nice folks."

Ruth nodded. "They'll stay on what, a day or two?"

"Tops, I suspect," Gehrig said.

"Then home to pick the corn with little Gramps." Now the late-day sunlight through the windows was finding every surface, and Ruth, as Gehrig saw him, was sharply outlined by it. He drew on his cigar and, scooting forward in his chair, chose a flirtatious wink from his store of them. "Okay, kid. I got some place I need to be."

In his room two hours later, Gehrig wrote, *Dearest Mama, My team won today. It was low scoring for a change, although I did manage to hit a home run. And like all the games so far, this one ended early when some in the crowd ran onto the field and stopped the play.*

He paused then, thinking through what to say about the mayhem and Henry and about his own part in it.

But what happened today was unusual, to say the least.

Or:

Today, I met the young son of the pitcher for our team, but to say I "met" him hardly describes it.

Or:

Everything today was going along as usual until the sixth, I think it was, when I heard a lot of shouting behind me.

He decided he'd say nothing about it, at least not tonight. He opened the desk drawer for another sheet of the hotel stationery and wrote to her just briefly, continuing to hope she wasn't in a great deal of pain and reminding her to keep in mind that she was blessed with a strong as iron constitution.

Ruth sat by the mullioned windows in his silk dressing gown drinking whiskey. Carol Jean, the mayor's wife's even prettier sister, had gathered up her things and slipped her slender feet into her smart suede pumps, which she'd worn while they fucked, an inspired touch in Ruth's opinion, her legs pointing to the ceiling and the diamanté buckles catching glints of the light from the chandelier.

She'd paused at the door, arranging her beaded cloche hat, fitting it smartly, and said she hoped he'd hit another homer the next place he played.

He frowned. "I didn't hit one here."

"Sure you did," she said, and gave the doorframe a tap, a vaudeville rim shot as she left.

But now, looking down at the small-city quiet, the empty streets, he was feeling gloomy again, sunk in self-pity, which he hated to give in to, except sometimes when he was as drunk as he was now and invited it in.

To his annoyance, his blurred mind was moving around in the world of Earl the pitcher and the kid and the late Mrs. Earl. A dismal and depressing subject times two. A man had lost his wife and a boy had lost his mother. But he was nothing if not a fierce competitor, and he was thinking, in his own case, it was his mother, plus his old man, plus his brothers and sisters, six of them altogether, some he'd known and some he hadn't, but they all counted whether he had or not, so the total of dead Ruths in the ground came to eight.

No contest.

He poured more whiskey and looked away from where he sat to the huge hotel bed, where he pictured Carol Jean lying naked, her furry twat like an accessory to match her fancy shoes. He drained his glass and labored to stand and made his way to the bed.

He collapsed heavily, loosening the velvet belt of his dressing gown, looking up in the dark at the chandelier, its crystals like sculpted icicles ornately not melting. The booze was making it move, swaying and spinning, or it was staying still and *he* was moving as he lay drunkenly beneath it. He shifted on the bed and put one foot on the floor to stop whichever one of them was spinning. He wiggled his pedicured toes but couldn't feel the rug.

So which start in life was worse? Your mother dead before you knew her? That, or living your first seventeen years knowing your old lady was alive but too loony, too gone in mind and body to come and see you even once, forget taking care of you from the get go? Forget, *You hungry, baby George? Here's my tit.* Forget getting any of that. He couldn't say for sure who won that one, which one was tougher—probably his. In any case, he wouldn't have minded taking a crack at the one he hadn't gotten.

What the fuck, he'd have the kid sit next to him on the bench and be in charge of his tobacco pouch, like little Ray was in the dugout at the stadium. Getting ready to bat, he'd pat the kid's head for good luck like he patted little Ray's, not to mention the way Carol Jean had patted the top of his when she got out of bed to get dressed. Well, no, maybe not; maybe not quite like that.

CHAPTER EIGHTEEN

The farm, much later the same night and very early the next morning

Earl sat at the kitchen table with a mug of coffee from the pot he'd just made, thinking as he drank that he was bookending the clamorous day. It seemed another life—his having sat in this chair with his coffee at first light, imagining telling Emily he was terrified in just the way he hoped he'd be. It seemed he'd lived a lifetime between that ignorant hour and now. He'd spent much of the evening, he and Lottie, trying to settle Henry down and help him pack, knowing it was a waste of breath to order him to bed. He couldn't think when he'd seen his son so energized, and why wouldn't he be? But it had nowhere to go, his energy, not until the morning, and as he careened through the rooms, in and out of the house, Henry kept asking Earl questions about their trip. How long they'd be gone, what they'd be doing minute by minute, if they'd have beds on the train, if they'd be sitting in the dugouts or watching from the—it had to be the dugouts, didn't it? Could he make sure it was?

Questions too about Gehrig. Did Earl know if he was married and, if so, was he a father, and didn't Earl think he was just as good a player as Babe Ruth, maybe better, since he's the one who'd hit a home run today, so why wasn't his picture in the newspaper as much?

"Henry, my heavens!" Lottie said at one point. "You're a headless hen tonight." She had a way, which could confuse those who didn't know her well, of voicing her rare disapproval with a genuine warmth, and earlier tonight, speaking this to Henry, her irritation was real while sounding also entertained.

It was past 10:30, nearly eleven, when Henry, propped up in bed, read for Earl what he'd written to Mr. Paumgarten, explaining his absence from school. In a postscript he promised not to "lay down anywhere or lie something on a table" while he was gone. Mr. Paumgarten was as passionate about grammar as about decimal points in long division, and recently, to dramatize proper usage, he'd stepped around from behind his desk and dropped to the floor as if shot and asked the surprised classroom, all the students, all the grades, if he was lying down or laying, "And if you say 'laying' you're lying," and two others besides Henry got Mr. Paumgarten's joke.

When Earl turned to packing for himself, he couldn't remember where he'd stored his battered suitcase. He hadn't used it since the day he traveled to Sioux City to marry Emily, and she'd chauffeured him to the farm in the Model-T. It was surely in the attic, but he couldn't find it there, and finally Lottie had spotted it in a dark corner where the slanted ceiling met the wall. Cobwebs had made a lace that draped and hid it.

At the table, he drank coffee. He often did at night; caffeine didn't keep him awake, and anyway he'd surrendered all hope that he could get some sleep. As he'd lain in bed, his body was alive in the same way as Henry's—edgy, anxious, the titillation of not knowing.

When Gehrig, then Walsh, had invited them, Earl met Henry's eyes and held them, looking to see how alertly he was listening. Sitting on the dugout steps, with Henry next to Gehrig, Earl had sensed the look on his son's face was made of many feelings—beguiled, expectant, thrilled to be confused, wide-open to the mystery of what he'd just been offered.

Earl had said to Walsh, "We thank you kindly. Don't we Henry." He'd heard himself say this, *Thank you kindly*, and wondered why in God's name he was talking like a character in one of Henry's dime Westerns.

In his first grief-hectic months, Earl had moved through days and lain through sleepless nights that reduced him to a boy. He'd felt a child's powerlessness, a child's ignorance, a child's panicked abandonment, and it had led him to see that life made your choices for you. He'd tried to have it the other way—him doing the choosing—and his mistake had been forgetting that you were always looking in on it, your life. Reaching vainly out to touch it. Living at the mercy of it.

But just then, in the dugout, with Walsh and Gehrig assuming how he'd answer, it seemed to Earl that life was daring him, ceding him a turn, and he'd felt lost in hesitation, lost and somehow threatened.

"But," he'd said to their invitation, "we'll have to say no."

"No?" They'd said it together and with the same lift of surprise.

"What reason could there possibly be?" Walsh asked.

"Missing school?" Gehrig asked.

"If it's missing school," Walsh said, "surely a few days away won't cost Henry anything." He'd turned to look at Henry as he said this and given him a smarmy smile. "We're just meeting, Henry and I, but it's clear to me he's a boy who can make two and two add up to six."

Earl looked again at Henry and saw that his expression was now simple, imploring him to change his mind.

Earl said, "Plus the farm. I couldn't—"

"Sure you could." Rooster, listening impatiently, had stepped on his cue. He'd said to Earl, "We're done in the fields, which you already know. There's only the chores." He'd nodded sharply toward Henry and added, "It'd be a hell of a birthday present." He'd waited for Earl to agree right away, and when he still hadn't, Rooster said more quietly, as if he thought Henry, sitting right there, somehow wouldn't hear him, "You can't disappoint the boy."

Earl had seen in Rooster's face that he was pleased to have put it this way, making the adventure entirely for Henry's sake. And that's when he understood he'd felt the instinct to refuse because he'd just finished playing these carnival innings with the game's great stars, and it had brought him far too close to what he'd once been sure he'd find his way to. But they were being invited now, he and Henry, just to ride along, so he'd be kept at its edge, merely its guest, and that would be the worst place of all to spend time in, even if it were for just a few days.

He'd felt all this in his gut when Walsh said, *Come along.*

"No, you're right," Earl had said to Rooster. He looked at his son and, as Rooster had, spoke of him as if he weren't there. "I couldn't disappoint Henry."

He heard the sound of slippers on the parlor's wood floors, Lottie's quick, light steps, and he looked up from his coffee to see her in the doorway. She was wearing her faded, rose-colored flannel robe over her nightgown. Her hair was down, fell loose and careless past her shoulders, which made her look like a very kind witch, not the least inclined to cackle.

Earl said, "My noise woke you? I'm sorry."

Lottie shook her head, "I was awake," as she walked to the stove and reached for a mug on the shelf.

She settled into her chair at the end of the table. She blew on her coffee to cool it and asked, "How are you?"

"He's fine," Earl said. "Calmed down finally."

"*You*," Lottie said. "How are *you*?"

Earl closed his eyes and smiled. *Ahh, right.* He said, "I'm fine too."

By chance they raised their cups together; it seemed the motion of a toast, and he touched his to hers.

He said to Lottie, "He wouldn't tell me why he ran out on the field."

Lottie frowned. "To get Frank's hat, I thought."

Earl tilted his head left and right. "And maybe that's all it was."

"It was foolish, Frank was, letting him go down there."

"I get why he did."

"So do I," Lottie said. "That doesn't mean it wasn't foolish."

Their eyes met, and he looked at her unhurriedly, the way it seemed to him she always looked at people—her plain gaze with the wish to learn things in it. "Can I tell you something?" Earl asked.

Lottie said, "You know you can."

"A confession?"

She smiled. "We all have things to confess."

Earl made his eyes huge, pretending to be shocked. "*You*, Lottie?"

He waited through a moment they were both enjoying, then said, "I was angry."

"What are we talking about?"

"When I saw him running on the field. And that crowd. I was furious."

Lottie set her mug down and made a gesture with her hand that said, *Say more*.

He imagined telling her that the count was one and two, that he had Babe Ruth set up, and as he'd gone into his wind-up, he was already picturing Ruth once more swinging through the pitch, the one he didn't get to throw. But that would all be lost on Lottie, who knew next to nothing about the game, not enough to think of its cadences, its splendid narratives unfolding.

He took a breath and exhaled loudly. "The way he . . . he and that crowd stopped the game right when they did."

Lottie said, "Well, I can see how 'furious' might be a little strong. But then again I wasn't there."

"It took me a few seconds, too long, to see it was him."

"It's about the last place you'd expect to see him—leading a riot."

Earl leaned forward, his elbows on the table. He drank the last from his cup and again looked closely at her, his exhausted eyes all fondness. Her hair was white. Her face and neck were busily lined, like the fine crosshatching of a silverpoint print. She was fifty-four years old, and more than once he'd had the thought that it was as if she—her body, her face, and her skin—were in a hurry to be old. A foolish notion, he knew, and one she contradicted every hour of every day as she moved nimbly about the house, from room to room, up and down the stairs, and all around the acreage and the barnyard, a woman with many things to do and doing them briskly, youthfully. The day he'd hurried beside her from the field to the house where Emily lay with her headache getting worse and her mild fever rising, she'd scampered light as a sprite over rough, uneven ground, and he'd barely been able to keep up with her.

He said, "This trip, their tour. I didn't want to go."

He assumed she'd look surprised, but she didn't, not especially. "Frank said you took your time." She said, "You had to think it through."

Earl shook his head. That wasn't it. "I was looking for excuses, and they kept saying it was only a few days."

"Well, they're right about that, obviously," Lottie said. "So why do you think?"

He lifted the empty mug and absently sifted the dregs. If he tried patiently to explain it, to say the words aloud, it would give them too much life. He said instead, "Then Rooster chimed in and said we had to go, for Henry's sake."

Lottie merely nodded, noting that he hadn't answered what she'd asked him.

She and Rooster had talked earlier in bed. He'd said he knew his telling Earl they had to go only meant they'd be taking a ride on a fancy train with these famous fellows. That urging Earl to say yes wouldn't make up for that hard, mean thing he'd done, as she had put it at the time, all those years ago, which, in case she was wondering, he'd never forgot and never would, of that she could be sure. But at least Earl could enjoy a few big-time baseball days some way or other, just how he didn't know. And Henry would be thrilled and pampered and get to live the high life.

So he'd wondered to Lottie why Earl had hesitated even a moment.

Earl picked up his empty mug and nodded at Lottie's.

"No more for me," she said.

He felt suddenly overwhelmed with fatigue, a physical weakening. Nearly a whole day had passed; it was close to the hour he'd risen to start this one. He gave over to a disorderly buzzing in his thoughts; it would soon be yesterday, and somehow, because of that, he felt the past and the moment and the future pulling at him, all of them at once and each one wanting to claim him for itself.

He shook his head to try to clear it of this nonsense.

Seeing him, Lottie said, "Go on up and get some sleep. An hour anyway."

He said after a moment, "*Here's* a thing. In the game." Exhausted as he was, really *because* he was, his mind was running on untethered, and he felt a need to offer up more parts of the day. "Gehrig hit the home run, so we were ahead, and I realized I'd started talking to Emily, sitting on the bench and telling her all about it. Telling her to look around, take it all in." He gave a snort of a laugh. "What do you make of *that*?"

Lottie asked, "It surprised you? That you were thinking about her?"

Earl looked into his empty cup again. "It's been the one place I could count on. Where I didn't."

"The 'place'?"

"A game. When I'm pitching."

Her shrug was the same as a sympathetic smile. She said, "'What I make of that' is pretty simple. You were wishing she was there." She crossed her legs beneath her faded, rose-colored robe. She gathered its collar at her throat. She felt no chill, the gesture was a habit. She ran her free hand lightly through her long loose hair, and watching her, Earl thought she looked very beautiful. He'd never thought of her as that, or of having been when she was young. He'd seen her face as open, alert with intelligence in the way it responded to what she sensed, to the sounds of life, to the things people said, and what they felt but didn't say. But right then her beauty was quietly ascendant, her gestures so feminine and free that they took his breath.

Now she rose slowly from her chair. "At least lie down for a bit, even if you don't sleep."

He said he would, on the couch in the parlor.

He watched her leaving, her tiny rose-robed body, her long white hair.

It sounded to her that he'd wished Emily was there. The words were Lottie-pared, precise as a prophet's, and he was especially grateful for them. It was as though she'd sensed that at this complicated hour he needed their simplicity, that they were all his mind could hold.

In bed, next to Rooster, whose sleep was quiet tonight, Lottie listened for Earl moving around below. Noise passed easily through the floors and walls of the old house, but she heard nothing. She knew she wasn't going back to sleep; she'd get up shortly to cook breakfast and see them off.

Earl. His games had been, among many things, a refuge, the one place where he could escape her. That's how Lottie had heard it, though he hadn't said that word.

He hadn't said, either, the other thing she was sure had been alive in his thoughts, or as a presence, like a pulse. Counting from this early morning hour, the date she'd died, it was tomorrow.

Now she was thinking of the day he and Emily had met to talk at the hotel. Emily had described some of it after she'd returned from seeing him. Her voice had sounded, not fluttery with excitement, as Lottie thought it might have, but anchored instead with the weight of her relief, and her thoughts of the two of them and their life here already with a momentum.

She'd told her mother how he'd risen from his chair and asked her to dance to the Victrola recording. How he'd confessed he'd thought about her, pictured her going about her day, and she'd sensed he hadn't for some reason meant to tell her that, so she'd held herself from saying anything in reply. And how he'd made the hour light-hearted as their afternoon ended. It was the mood he'd wished to give her for her drive back to the farm.

Lottie lay there with the very song they'd danced to sounding in her head, and she saw Earl that day, standing and opening his arms and freeing his need to love her daughter from everything he'd used—his thoughts, his heart—to try to keep from feeling it.

And that was how he'd decided. He'd opened his arms and set his senses free, let them have him, and they'd chosen what they felt he couldn't bear to lose. But the life he'd let go of and the life that had let go of him in the time the bleeding took, Lottie had long understood that in the sequence of his grief they had fused, become for Earl the same life and the same loss. She knew, she remembered all too well, that for a long while he'd seen it, he had lived it, just that darkly.

She moved her head slightly, back and forth on her straw-stuffed pillow, feeling in her chest how much she'd come to love him as if he were her own. And what did that even mean? With all the life they'd lived in common, of course he *had* become her own, hers and Frank's. She held this feeling tightly, crossed her arms and pressed it to her breast.

A confession. He'd said at the table that he had a confession, and now she was remembering another one, on a winter Sunday afternoon a year or more ago, the two of them drinking coffee after dinner in the parlor. She'd made a fire, a neat bouquet of flames as always. Outside the sky was a blanketing gray, snow falling lightly through it. Rooster napped upstairs, Henry read in his room.

Over time, she and Earl had come to think and talk freely in one another's company, so that a subject could be raised without any need to explain what had prompted it. Often nothing had, nothing traceable at least. And that day, drinking coffee and watching the snow, Earl had suddenly said, "I have a confession." She'd turned her eyes from the window and the snow to look at him. He said, "I had this awful thought, when it happened, that I couldn't get rid of."

She'd known right away what he was referring to.

"I kept thinking," Earl continued, and she remembered now the nervousness that had come into his voice. How it had made him sound and seem so young. He said, "I kept thinking right after—I'm ashamed to say this, but I did—the way I saw it, the two of you were old, and I couldn't stop thinking, 'Why wasn't it one of them?'" He shook his head. "I forget that I thought that, but then it comes back. It was there this morning, really strong when I woke up, maybe it was part of whatever I'd been dreaming. And I thought, okay. Today."

She remembered pausing to be sure he was finished, and then she said, "You've been thinking all this time we *didn't*?"

Earl had frowned. "Didn't what?"

"Didn't wish for that very thing."

Lying in bed, with no sounds from below, her eyes were closing, and she was seeing Earl's face going blank with his surprise as he'd leaned toward her in her chair and reached to take her hand. *No*, he'd said, *he hadn't thought that's what they'd wished.* He'd sounded chastised, and he'd felt relieved to be. *He hadn't for a moment.* And hearing this, she'd had the thought that *that* was his confession: not to have known it's what they were fiercely feeling.

CHAPTER NINETEEN

October 19, 1927

They boarded very early. The morning sky was starting, the chilly air still mostly night. The steward, Horace Meadows, stood in the open door of the Pullman to welcome them. He introduced himself and said, "Let me have your bags, and I'll show you to your rooms."

As they climbed the Pullman's steps Earl and Henry saw their breath, and they saw Horace Meadows's breath too, which Henry watched escape and thinly vapor, and he thought it looked somehow much more interesting than theirs, as if Horace Meadows were performing a bit of prestidigitation.

"Mr. Ruth and Mr. Gehrig and Mr. Walsh have not arrived from the hotel." Meadows's voice was harmoniously layered.

They followed him with their bags along a narrow corridor.

"Your rooms are cozy," Meadows said, as he led them back. "But they're beautifully appointed. The way they're arranged, there's the first room, then the one behind it, then the one behind that, and so on, five in all. I like to say, I like to tell people it's laid out like the shotgun house I grew up in, in New Orleans. Just a whole lot fancier."

Henry studied Horace Meadows's broad back in his handsome Pullman jacket, thinking what a thrilling life of danger he must have lived as a boy, to have a house with a shotgun in every room.

They reached the two smallest state rooms, and Meadows opened the first door. Earl saw that he'd told the truth, the space was outhouse tight, but what an extraordinary outhouse, paneled in rich walnut and trimmed in brass polished to a low luster. There were two wall lamps with cut glass shades. There was a narrow bed, a chair, a washstand

and a toilet. No, not an outhouse. It was like a playhouse mansion. A rich boys' clubhouse.

"We're snug as bugs," Horace Meadows said. "In my experience down through the years, folks like to stretch out just a bit in the observation lounge. Mr. Ruth, Mr. Gehrig, Mr. Walsh, that's often where you'll find them."

Meadows said that once they'd settled, Earl and Henry should come to the dining room at the front of the car, where he would cook them breakfast.

Earl declined. He wanted to lie down for a few minutes.

Meadows nodded, then turned to Henry. "Young sir?"

From his chair at the table in the small dining room, Henry watched Meadows moving back and forth from the kitchen and pantry to the tiny stove. He was sitting on two red velvet pillows to be higher at the table.

Meadows's way of walking was smoothly deliberate, looking consciously balanced, as if he were still and always carrying suitcases in both hands. Henry had seen Negroes, though he'd never spoken to one until now. There were Negroes in Sioux City. There was a Negro janitor in the town's railroad museum, the first one he'd seen, on a country-school trip in first grade, when they'd entered single file through the heavy double doors, and he'd stopped in his tracks to watch the man move past pushing trash barrels loaded on a wooden cart, his long, wide-brush broom rising from one of the barrels like something heraldic.

Nawlins.

Henry had heard Meadows say he came from some place called Nawlins, and he imagined an entire town floating on the air because that's how the word had sounded to him, as if it were floating, as it came from Horace Meadows's mouth.

Meadows placed a plate of scrambled eggs and bacon and toast in front of him, and as he thanked him, Henry glanced at Meadows's large wide hands. Their palms' pinkness looked to him like brand new skin, a newborn's skin, and very tender.

Now the dining room door opened, and Gehrig appeared.

"Morning," he said, sitting down next to Henry. He was wearing a light brown sweater and brown tweed slacks. He shook Henry's hand, and his grip felt like a huge rough glove.

Meadows went into the kitchen to get the coffee pot.

"You're all settled in?" Gehrig asked Henry. "Your rooms are all right?"

"They're cozy," Henry said. "But they're beautifully appointed."

Gehrig laughed. "And so they are—*both* those things." He looked at Henry. "Well, I'm glad you made it," he said, and placed his hand on Henry's head. Henry braced to have his hair mussed; that's what adults did to it, and Gehrig had yesterday in the dugout afterward. But he just rested his hand briefly, as if he didn't know quite what to do with it, the gesture oddly baptismal.

Henry ate Meadows's eggs and bacon and spread strawberry preserves on his generously buttered toast, and Gehrig drank coffee. It was a fine domestic moment all around, as if this were the way every morning started for Lou Gehrig from Yorkville and Horace Meadows from New Orleans and Henry Dunham from Hinton, gathered at the breakfast table before their days began.

In his room, Earl couldn't sleep. He'd raised the window for fresh air before he lay down, and from his bed he heard the voices of boarding passengers on the platform. Their talk was bright and buzzing. They sounded like a city of pleased bees.

He got up and looked out, and he saw Ruth making his way to the Pullman, moving past passengers who, as always, stopped before they boarded when they caught sight of him, and others who'd come to the station just to catch a glimpse. Earl was watching Ruth be his public self supremely, the Babe among his people, greeting everyone as he moved toward the door with the raffish case of a bayou politician. Many were wearing their Sioux City best. There were flustered hellos. There was fawning and glad-handing. There were bold backslaps and dumbstruck smiles.

And Ruth's voice, a bardic croak, sounding through it all.

CHAPTER TWENTY

October 19 and 20, 1927   *Across Nebraska*

They left Sioux City, heading south, and spent a day of farcical delay in Council Bluffs. A connection, a ghost train apparently, that never arrived from Kansas City. An engineer who spent the afternoon getting drunk on bootleg bourbon before he was taken away by two station agents. The several hours until his replacement got there—a handsome young man, blond and improbably tanned, radiating a great outdoors kind of health, looking like an Alpine mountain guide.

It was nearly midnight when they crossed the Missouri and began the journey west. In the Pullman, the clatter of its wheels and the rhythm of its rocking made a regular tempo, presumed as a pulse, as they passed through scattered settlements, Valley and Fremont and Schuyler and Columbus, past section-gang bunkhouses every six or seven miles, hour after hour, and the flat and empty landscape a kind of achievement, a thing of barren grandeur becoming visible in dawn light.

Henry woke confused, not knowing where he was, then felt disappointed that he'd been asleep at all. He reminded himself that they'd all been sleeping, but surely *something* interesting had happened while he slept.

He would hope to make up for what he'd missed by lingering at breakfast to ask Horace Meadows about growing up with shotguns in Nawlins.

Through Central City, Grand Island, Gibbon, and Kearney.

Earl came awake as they arrived in North Platte, the train slowing to a stop, its great weight groaning, its sighs of steam. He rose from his bed and looked out to the empty depot platform in the muted light of morning.

Before he'd gone to bed, he'd sat with Henry in his room. They'd begun to review their very odd day, its comical events, and after just a few minutes, Henry fell into a heavy-breathing sleep. Earl had watched him as he slept, his stubby fingers twitching, making clumsy little spasms, as if he were laboring in his dream to sew, to knit the very air.

Earl was sympathetic; he was weighed down with the same exhaustion that had taken Henry quickly, and yet he'd felt a sadness, sharply edged, one he knew was ridiculous—the sense that his son, gone so suddenly to sleep, had turned away from him. For he'd been feeling as they'd talked absurdly grateful for Henry's company, sensing how far outside of their life they already were in the first strange hours of this one. And he'd admonished himself, pledging that he must let Henry have these days, have them wholly, live them to their full delight.

He'd remembered then the afternoon, days after Emily died, when he'd waked from a nightmare and come downstairs and been so startled to find Henry in the kitchen sitting in his high chair, calmly occupied, taken up by something blessedly ordinary that Earl couldn't hope to imagine, and how he'd envied that evidence of his son's much greater wisdom.

His room was closest to the lounge, and when he stepped out into the narrow corridor, there sat Ruth in a plush chair by a window, plunking the strings of a ukulele, making tinny whines of sound. To this point, they'd spoken only quickly—*So you made it. Yes, we did.*—and now Ruth looked up and waved him to a chair.

"I need some coffee," Earl said, pointing toward the dining room.

"There's a pot here," Ruth said. It sat on a cart in the middle of the lounge. "He brings it out first thing."

Earl poured coffee for himself and sat down opposite Ruth.

"He's all recovered from his stumble?" Ruth asked about Henry.

"He seems to be," Earl said.

"He have any idea how close he came?"

"He hasn't said much," Earl said.

Ruth was wearing his tailored dressing gown and his handmade elkhide slippers. Earl didn't know that one of Ruth's tabloid nicknames was the Sultan of Swat, but you didn't *need* to know that to think he looked as he sat there like something of the sort: a sultan; a swami in swaddling silk and velvet.

Ruth chuckled, a fissured, graveled sound. He said, "His little ass was pounded flat if it wasn't for young Lou," and Earl felt quickly defensive on Henry's behalf.

The ukulele looked tiny as a toy in Ruth's lap. He strummed it, sounding a chord more or less, then set it carefully on the floor.

They sat in silence, looking past one another, and Ruth reached for a cigar in the dressing gown's breast pocket. Earl watched him light it, heard his puckering mouth making soft popping sounds as he drew smoke in to get it going.

"So you been a farmer with your old man all your life?"

It took Earl a moment to understand. "Old-man-in-*law*," he said.

"The runty fella with the stomped-to-shit boater."

Earl nodded, then said, "No, not all my life."

"He seemed real torn-up about that boater," Ruth said.

"His wife gave it to him," Earl said. "She thought he looked handsome in it."

"I hate 'em. Boaters. They make my ugly mug look fat."

Earl tried to picture it. Ruth with a big straw pan on his head was the image he got.

"My ugly mug *is* fat, so what do I need with a boater that makes it look fatter?" Ruth smiled, and holding his cigar, he inspected its length. "I shoulda' known he wasn't your old man." He raised and lowered his flattened palms, a set of scales, its trays extremely imbalanced, showing the difference in Earl and Rooster's sizes. He said, "I just never understood little guys." He looked away, pained annoyance on his broad and rubbery face. He sounded genuinely puzzled to Earl, as if he thought small men *chose* to stop growing for some unearthly reason. Again Earl felt defensive, a pugnacity, this time for Rooster's sake, and he was ready to describe their neighbors' recalling Rooster; what they'd watched him lift and pull and carry in his prime.

"So how long you been pitching in your league back there?"

"Ah," Earl said, calculating. "Ten, twelve years?"

"Long time," Ruth said.

Earl nodded but said nothing. He looked out the window at the way the Great Plains did a bright and cloudless morning. All it had to work with was the sky, and the sky was all it needed, the same as Iowa. In his mind he saw Ruth swinging feebly through the pitch, looking like a blind man feeling the air with his cane, *strike two*. In his mind he heard Ruth saying to him now, *That screwball fucking fooled me.*

He said, looking back at Ruth, "Before that, I played—I pitched—in the Three-I League."

"No shit."

"No shit," Earl said. *Come on*, he thought. *Let's hear it. Say it.*

"Who—"

"The Cubs," Earl said. "A scout for the Cubs was the scout, he signed me. Saul Weintraub."

Ruth shook his head as if he'd been asked whether he knew Saul Weintraub, and Earl felt pressed to sound persuasive. Why, he asked himself, irritated, did he sense any need to do this?

He could tell of the little fat man arriving, grieving his Aunt Bessie, and of his spirits being lifted as he watched Earl's pitches leaving his hand and spinning and dancing on that perfect afternoon.

Ruth asked, "How long'd you play?"

Earl's mouth tightened, his lower lip extending. "A year."

"Huh. Just a year." Ruth smoked and wiped the corners of his mouth with the tips of his thumb and index finger. "So what happened? You get hurt?"

He could tell of Saul Weintraub christening him Mr. Cocksure and of his going to the library the next Sunday to look up the meaning of the word and, when he found it, thinking, *Oh, okay. If you say so.*

He could tell of sitting with Donnie the night before he left and hearing the shrewd coyote offer up its trembling howls.

"Life," Earl said. "My life happened."

In the dining room, Henry was listening to Horace Meadows say the best thing about New Orleans was its several kinds of people with their several different hues. Meadows spoke of those he called Creole, a word Henry hadn't heard, people he hadn't known about. They were, Horace Meadows said, handsome men and beautiful women with cream-in-the-coffee-colored skin, whose blood came partly from France and partly from Spain and partly from some islands close by to New Orleans.

"It's the Lord's best recipe, Creole blood." Meadows smiled at Henry, enthroned on his red velvet pillows. His eyes were fixed on a prominent vein that ran jaggedly along Meadows's left temple, a raised line that looked like an adornment, like a script written in cursive on his skin. Meadows's smile appeared to animate it.

Listening, Henry saw princely Creoles promenading.

Life. The man's life had happened to him. Ruth nodded, tapping his cigar into the pedestal ashtray standing next to his chair. He hoped he wasn't referring to how Mrs. Earl got the flu, but he probably was.

This new silence lasted only a few seconds, long enough for a mood, a stubbornness, to take hold.

Ruth looked at Earl and said, "I ain't surprised."

"At what?"

"You playing some minor league ball."

Well, all right, Earl thought, setting down his cup. He could either hear that as a compliment, as getting close to admitting how badly the screwball had fooled him. Or he could hear it as Ruth saying he'd faced him three times yesterday, three times short one pitch, and he'd seen enough to know that the most Earl could have been was a minor league pitcher. He felt what he'd been feeling these past two days arrive once more; it was a great frustration, that was as close as he could come to giving it a name. He felt it in his chest, and as he waited for

Ruth to ask him more, he was working not to let it go deeper, let it spread into his heart.

"Let me ask you," Ruth said.

"About me playing?"

"About you playing?" Ruth said, confused. "Oh, right." He shifted in his chair. "No, here's the thing. I got a farm in the country—Jesus, 'in the country,' where the fuck *else* would it be?—outside Boston. It ain't as big as yours with your father-in-law there, I'm sure, but, so here's the question for you: Goats."

"Goats?"

"I been thinking about getting goats. You think goats're a good idea?"

Earl turned his head to look out the window, then back at Ruth. "'A good idea.' I suppose, if you're a goat."

Ruth's lips were holding the cigar, so he could only hiss his laughter. He crossed his legs. An ankle rested on a thigh. His calves were white and thin as an invalid's. Earl watched a beautiful elkhide slipper moving crazily on his twitching foot. Ruth said, "So how I hear that, you vote no," as he demurely rearranged the silk dressing gown over his thighs.

The Western foothills at bright midmorning, autumnally blond and patterned with pinion and bristlecone pine, with snowberry bushes and clusters of fringed sage, their silver leaves glinting metallically, making sprays of tiny blades.

Henry sat by himself in the observation lounge as they crossed into Colorado, the landscape rising and the air thinning with the train's subtle ascent, which made him yawn to ease the pressure on his eardrums, his mouth going wide as a grouper's.

Looking out the window, he was imagining a huge cattle drive sending up great clouds of dust, cowboys circling the herd and waving their big hats in the air. They were Zane Grey cattle, handsome, tetchy creatures, alert for Mormons who might come and steal them in the night. They were nothing like the boring Guernseys Henry milked. No one in his right mind would be tempted to steal one of *them*.

The cowboys were shouting their yips and yelps, like the sounds he'd heard coming from behind him as he was running.

CHAPTER TWENTY-ONE

October 20, 1927   *Denver, Colorado*

The stadium in Denver was a small, tidy structure, roofed against the mountain sun, with advertisements covering the outfield walls for candies and lumberyards and athletic goods and mortuaries. Beyond were the gray-blue foothills, the tiered veranda to the mountains.

Ruth asked Henry to sit next to him during the game, watching his tobacco pouch and also his black bat, making sure the barrel end didn't touch the ground. *Lousy luck, really lousy, if it touches the ground.* And Henry was glad to go along. He'd hoped to sit next to Gehrig in the other dugout, but he was starting to like Ruth too, feeling when he was around him as if he were in the company of an enormous, playful boy, and in the bottom of the third he watched Ruth hit a ball that climbed and climbed and reached the ceiling of the sky and appeared to stay right there, moving horizontally against it as it was leaving. Wild cheers went up, they made the little park reverberate, a coliseum for some moments.

Henry watched Ruth rounding the bases, tootling along, the mincing trot, his belly leading, and back in the dugout he plopped down beside him. Ruth let out a satisfied sigh and sat back and extended his legs, his feet resting on the dugout step in front of him. He said to Henry, "I owe you that one, kiddo."

Henry's look showed him he didn't understand.

He gave Henry an *it's obvious* shrug. "You musta' kept the barrel off the ground." He began to move his propped-up feet in tandem, his big black baseball cleats back and forth, left and right as he casually inspected them like a little girl admiring her new-for-Easter Mary Janes.

Earl was sitting next to Gehrig in the other dugout, and he'd been moved to laughter watching the ball Ruth hit as it moved across the sky.

Hearing him, Gehrig said, yeah, Ruth's home runs, he never got used to them, the time they liked to take, and then he answered in the fourth with one of his own. It hurried out true to form, on a line in an instant, and rounding first, watching it disappear, he felt something like light-hearted, as close to light-hearted as—Gehrig being Gehrig—he was able to feel. Yes, these games were exhibitions and the pitching fair at best, but as he'd pledged to himself the morning they departed Penn Station, he'd found that he was playing them for the pure pleasure of it, *like stickball in the street with his little Heinie pals*, even the last game, with the scare the boy had given them, but which had seemed in a way—his fall and the raucous, celebrating crowd, and everything that followed—like some real-life interruption of stickball in the streets.

The game became a show of rocketing line drives—off the walls on the fly, banging detonations; rattling around in the corners where the fences met the stands; singles and doubles, crazy-bounce triples.

Tied at eight through five.

Ten to nine, Ruth's team, after six.

And what most held Henry's attention sitting next to Ruth was the way he spit tobacco juice into a large tin cup.

As he spat, he gave the cup a little dip and lift, like a sommelier rounding off a pour, at the same time keeping his eye on the game and talking to Henry, telling him he was one lucky little nubster, his first train ride and it's a fancy Pullman, where *his* first time, very different, he was nineteen and it wasn't no damn Pullman he took to spring training. And him being such a hick, green as peas, he'd never for instance been in an elevator, didn't know such things existed, and he rode the one in the hotel where they stayed, up and down and up and down for hours, thrilled to his gizzard at the wonders of the world.

Saying, as he looked out to the field, the crazy storm of hits, that the first thing he bought, the first time he got paid, was a bicycle, a red Columbia, he could still picture it, the most beautiful damn thing he'd ever seen to that point in his life and ranking third or fourth even now compared to other beautiful things he'd seen since. And then a wink, like punctuation.

Saying, an inning later, a teasing in his hoarseness, he was wondering who'd taught Henry how to run so slow, he'd never seen anyone that good at running slow, it was a talent, really, and then giving Henry's shoulder a soft cuff. And all the while, Henry watching Ruth not miss the slightly moving cup, wanting him to and not wanting him to and impressed to distraction that he never did, the dip and lift with his eyes partly elsewhere.

Ruth hit his second home run in the eighth, not quite as high or as far, not taking quite as long to disappear.

Gehrig hit *his* second in the bottom of the inning, and it seemed to Earl as if the two of them were having a private dialogue, the elder speaking first and the younger one answering, in a language Earl knew but realized now he'd never actually heard spoken. He sensed its protocol, its graces, its sacramental codes, and his envy was a flavor.

They played nine innings, a rare event, and it ended twelve to ten, Ruth's team winning.

They took taxis to Union Station for the short trip to Cheyenne, where they'd have to wait three hours for the connection that would carry them across Wyoming into Utah.

As they all boarded the Pullman, Gehrig, still close to light of heart, said to Ruth, "I was thinking, Jidge. If only we played every game in this air, maybe we'd both hit a *hundred* homers."

"If only," Ruth said, walking just ahead of him. "But what is it they say? If only my aunt had a dick, she'd be my uncle?"

Earl and Henry were behind them, the last to board, and Earl chuckled to himself while glancing down to see what his son might have heard. But Henry's expression, a little goofy and distracted, was the one he showed when he was somewhere in a daydream.

As the train moved swiftly north, Henry peered out his window into the western distance. He'd been missing his grandparents, and it made him sad to think they didn't know how the world looked, what it became, if you followed it far enough—tilted, tipping, angled, and soaring according to no pattern, its amazing disobedience, nothing like the way Rooster and Lottie assumed the land everywhere behaved.

Looking out, he saw the clouds, plump rose-colored bands, running through the sky like raised embroidery. The mountains were casting deep, late-day purple shadows on themselves, the snow on the peaks a white past pure, and its patterns made Henry think of a burning candle's dripping wax. Which made no sense—frozen snow like melting wax—but he was far from a life where he wanted things to make sense.

CHAPTER TWENTY-TWO

October 20, 1927, 6:30 p.m.   *Cheyenne, Wyoming*

"It's huge," Henry said, standing next to Gehrig beneath an over-arching wooden sign—Frontier Amusement Park in bright red block letters, framed by cartoon cowboys riding bucking broncos.

"It is, isn't it," Gehrig said. "Huge. I'm impressed." He looked down and smiled at Henry. "Shall we? What do you say?"

Henry nodded, and they started toward the roller coaster along a gravel path, one of several that were filled with parents and their children, strolling sweethearts, teenaged louts darting in and out amongst the clusters of people. When Gehrig had noticed a poster for the park in the Cheyenne station, his thought was that they had three hours before their train started west.

He loved roller coasters. He'd gone often as a boy to Coney Island with his father, and even now, even sometimes after Yankees games, he took the train to Rye Beach to ride the giant coaster there—to reward himself if he'd played well and they'd won; to try to forget it if he hadn't and they'd lost.

Back in the Pullman, he was heading for the door at the rear of the car, and there were Henry and Earl in the observation lounge and Henry asked where he was going.

To Gehrig's clumsy invitation, Earl had looked into his son's face for what seemed a long time before he smiled and said, "You two go ahead," and it made Gehrig think of the moment in the dugout in Sioux City when Earl had surprised them all by saying nothing, then saying no, saying thank you kindly, but we'll have to say no, until the grandfather stepped forward and said what a fine birthday present for the boy it would be. As then, this pause wasn't really very long, but that there was any pause at all made it feel so.

"Just the two of us then," Gehrig said in the lounge, looking down at Henry. "It'll be a birthday present," and Henry had said okay, and thanks, though his birthday wasn't for a couple of weeks. Gehrig had assumed it was closer, and in a surge of his shyness he felt relieved the father wasn't coming. There'd be no awkwardness deciding who rode which rides with Henry or if they both should, or if the boy should choose or maybe go by himself.

On the gravel path to the coaster, they passed people eating frankfurters, people holding bags of popcorn. People licking ice cream cones, people eating candied apples. Children with boxes of Cracker Jacks and opening packages of Chuckles and Peanut Chews.

"How about something to eat?" Gehrig asked, and Henry smiled. *Life!* It just got better and better. Peanut Chews were his favorite.

At the roller coaster, Gehrig bought their tickets, and they headed for the last car while other riders were climbing into theirs. He always tried for the last one at Rye Beach, too. He felt self-conscious—a grown man alone—when there were passengers behind him.

Now he turned to Henry. "Ready?"

Henry nodded and said he was. Sitting next to Gehrig, he felt exquisitely afraid. There'd been nothing like this in his life, no moment when he'd been so high in the air as he was about to be. The closest he'd come was a ride called The Mountain—a quick descent, a few modest bumps, down an easy slope in what looked like a toy sleigh—at the tawdry little carnival that came to Hinton for a week every summer and left a vaguely fungal rankness in the air when it left town.

The coaster started forward with a jolt and ran the length of the platform, then began its climb. As he rose, Henry heard the squeals, the happy screams from other rides below, becoming ever fainter.

They were nearing the peak where the breeze was strong and chilly, the night sky washed of clouds. Gehrig loved the feeling that was moving in him now as the car got close to the top. Loved it even more than the lifts and plunges, the rushing vertigo, of the ride itself. Early in the season, a game in May against the White Sox at Comiskey, he'd stood in the on-deck circle taking loose practice swings and watching Ruth at the plate, and it came to him that his impatience to hit was this roller-coaster eagerness, his blood pumping, the way as things gained speed, they magically slowed down as if the moment didn't want to let go of itself, and he'd smiled to realize it—the great game offering him the pleasure of a midway ride.

At the top there was a pause, then the coaster rushed ahead, and Henry felt the surge as he watched the first car, then the second, then the third, then the fourth, disappearing, out of sight, off the ledge, over the falls. He closed his eyes, squeezed them tight, he heard Gehrig shout, "Hold on!" and his mouth was opened wide to let his happy screams escape.

"Feeling better?" Gehrig asked.

Henry was bent over, his hands on his thighs. He nodded and whispered weakly that he was. They were standing in the dark in high weeds behind a large canvas tent, maybe twenty yards beyond the coaster's platform where riders got on and off.

He was still dizzy, his eyes watery from vomiting, his stomach just beginning to quiet. To Gehrig's question, what he mostly felt was thankful he'd survived the longest minutes of his life to date, his face turning instantly white and his stomach roiling and panic rushing to his brain, praying he could keep from throwing up until the cars returned to the platform and eased to a stop, and the attendant seeming to take an hour, his filthy hands fumbling to unlock the restraining rod and lift it free of its groove, before he could bolt from his seat and race to this spot behind the tent.

By the time Gehrig reached him, his stomach was empty and his retching was dry.

He straightened up, a little woozy, and Gehrig steered him by the shoulders away from the foul spot. They stood in the dark. The weeds were damp with night dew and their pants' legs were wet below the knees.

"I'm sorry," Henry said. It was clear to him how badly he'd let Gehrig down. He felt a shame that had him fighting tears.

"No," Gehrig said. "We should have waited till afterward to get you the candy."

Henry sighed. "Peanut Chews were my favorite." He spoke the past tense sadly. His voice was tinged with loss, and hearing it, Gehrig couldn't keep from smiling.

"Let's find a place where you can get a drink of something. Wash that taste out of your mouth."

Henry nodded. "Maybe some water."

The coaster was again flying along the tracks. In the darkness, in the weeds, Henry raised his eyes to watch it screaming past. The riders' shouts and screeches were like ululations, and they sounded to Henry as if they were mocking him.

"How does it taste?" Gehrig asked.

"Delicious," Henry said, and he meant it. The Coca-Cola he was drinking in meticulous sips was the best bottle of pop he'd drunk in his life. He hadn't realized how thirsty he was, and how much he'd been craving sweet flavors. He finished each sip with a punctuating "Ah!" There was color in his face again.

Gehrig held a mug of coffee. They were sitting in a booth in the park's café near the entrance gates. The room was paneled in knotty pine, every last inch of it. There were rows of booths with bright red plastic cushions and there were pinewood tables with checkered tablecloths filling the middle of the room.

Except for the two of them and the waitress at the cash register, the room was empty.

Gehrig drank his coffee and cleared his throat. "I haven't told you yet, Henry. I was very sorry to hear about your mother."

Henry heard this for a moment as though his mother were still living. *You were sorry to hear about her doing what?* He'd forgotten he and his father had told Mr. Walsh about her dying, and the feeling came to him again that his private way of knowing her, what he'd heard and imagined, had escaped once more into the world.

He said, "I don't remember very much about it." He surprised himself in saying this. As if, being a year old when she died, there were things about it he *did* remember.

Gehrig said, "Still. Even so." He lit a cigarette.

The next seconds were alive with silence, and Henry was sure they should be talking and that Gehrig should be the one doing it. He'd brought the subject up and he was an adult, a famous one besides, which meant he knew things, heard things, understood things others didn't, and some of the job of being famous was to pass these things along. But his hesitation now, it seemed a pause that anyone, an ordinary person, might have made, nothing someone famous would do. He leaned forward, his elbows on the table resting near his ears, and asked, "Did *you* know anybody who got it?"

Gehrig took a drag on his cigarette and slowly exhaled. He said, "The influenza?" He thought, then shook his head. "Nobody I knew well. The Tannenbaums, just below us, their son, Robert, I remember."

Influenza. Henry couldn't remember ever hearing the whole word. He said it to himself. He liked the way it sounded, its syllables cresting and falling, the buzzing *z*, and he thought it was probably wrong of him to feel friendly toward it, admiring of it as a word.

He nodded. "My mom tried as hard as she could not to die. My dad kept wiping her face with cold cloths. Grandma did too. And they put more blankets on her when she started shivering. And then some more to make her sweat." He looked away from Gehrig, as if to assess for himself how he was doing before continuing. "That's all they could do. It wasn't like she'd been shot and badly wounded and could have probably recovered in three or four days after it looked like she was going to die. It wasn't like that. Or like my dad was a doctor who got there just in time."

Despite the crazy-quilt illogic of what Henry had just said, Gehrig heard a knowingness in it, the boy's conviction of its worth, as if what he'd offered were sagely drawn from moments of lived life. And Gehrig saw then why he'd invited Henry to come with them on the tour. Not to calm him, not to take his mind off what had happened, certainly not because they shared a name. Nothing he'd offered Ruth in his effort to explain it. No. It was what had come alive in him when he learned the boy had lost his mother, and he'd felt for a moment his own future grief, his grief to come; he'd felt it powerfully.

He said, "I'll bet she felt safe and protected. When they put those cold cloths and blankets on her."

"Mmm," Henry said, wondering for the first time whether or not she had. There was silence again, now one he felt in charge of, until he said, "I got into bed with her, too."

"*Really.*"

Henry said, "She asked my dad to put me next to her," and the picture in Gehrig's mind was as if a posed Nativity.

He drew on his cigarette and tilted his head back to direct the smoke away from Henry. "And you were such a little fellow."

Henry frowned. He didn't understand the point Gehrig was making. He glanced around the empty room, toward the waitress at the cash register. She was a pretty teenager who looked like Clara Bow. She sat on a stool in her candy-cane striped uniform studying her reflection in the window next to her.

Henry said, "She sounded like a cow having a calf."

"What?"

"My mom. That's how she sounded when she was dying. Like a cow having a calf."

It was several summers ago when he'd passed beneath an open parlor window and overheard Lottie remembering this to Rooster. But such a startling description; it had gone deep and it had stayed.

"And you remember hearing that."

Henry paused. Should he say he did? He shook his head. "My dad told me later. When I was older. Three, I think. Or maybe four."

"Ah." Gehrig took time putting his cigarette out. "Well, that was taking quite a risk, wasn't it. Him setting you down right next to her."

"I guess he thought it was worth it."

"I guess he did."

"He must've seen how much she wanted me there."

"He must have," Gehrig said. "But—"

"There was an article about it in the newspaper."

"An article?"

"He read it to me once I got old enough. It said how we stayed with her and we didn't even care if we got sick too." His lies were coming too quickly now for Henry to think them through, to listen for the risk that he'd be caught in one. It was his mouth, it was his voice, but it felt as though someone else was whispering these things in his ear for him to say. "It was a really long article," he added. Thoughts of the roller coaster came to him, the helplessness he'd felt, of having simply to hold on.

"I can see how it would need to be," Gehrig said. "Long."

Henry nodded eagerly. "And there was a picture of my dad holding me. Grandma didn't want to be in the picture. But they kept the article anyway."

More than half the people in Iowa had died from the flu. This great exaggeration lived in the distance of what Henry believed he knew about that time. But he also knew, from no distance at all, that his father had sat with her for hours and he hadn't died.

So death had wanted her alone. This was clearly the only thing to think, and of course he didn't know it's what Earl felt when he'd sensed her leaving and imagined death her lover come to take her.

Gehrig reached across to shake Henry's hand. "You're a brave boy," he said, and it seemed to him that it *was* a kind of bravery, for the boy to take his mother's death where he wanted it to go, to make it the story he needed it to be.

"How come?"

"Sitting with your mother like you did? You don't think that was brave?"

"Well . . ."—and now Henry felt a quick, hard guilt—"it was my *dad's* idea."

"I understand."

"It wasn't like *I* decided. I mean maybe I did, too, but I couldn't even talk yet."

"Still, you must've showed him somehow you wanted to be right next to her."

Henry nodded, saying nothing, and wondered how he might have done that. How his face might have looked. What noises, close to words, he might have made. He wanted to ask Gehrig how *he* pictured it.

He said, simply, "Thanks." He felt the powerful temptation to embellish things a little more. Like Gehrig, he was curious to hear what he'd think of next. But he'd just received this very high praise, and that was more than reason enough to keep things where they were.

They slid out of the booth and started back to the Pullman.

The air had turned crisp with High Plains autumn. The starry night sky was a fabric, a salt-and-pepper tweed. They walked along in a contented silence until they neared the sprawling depot, and then Gehrig said to Henry that since he felt fine now, there seemed no need, none that he could see, to mention his getting sick to his father. So in the end, the visit to Frontier Park had been a great success. Henry had taken the story back from the world, even if he'd had to think new things up to do it. And Lou Gehrig didn't blame him, didn't see him as pathetic for puking up his Peanut Chews. Instead, he'd told him he was very brave, and to Henry these words had the grace of a beatitude.

CHAPTER TWENTY-THREE

October 20, 1927, 10:20 p.m.   *Cheyenne, Wyoming*

Earl stood outside on the Pullman platform. The depth of darkness at this hour made the silence nearly tangible. The temperature had dropped, but he was wearing the cardigan Emily had badly knitted for him and he didn't notice. He turned and sat, perched on the railing, looking back through the window in the door into the car.

Earlier, he'd been sitting alone in the lounge, Walsh in his room, Ruth off somewhere, when Henry and Gehrig returned from Frontier Park. He'd been thinking still about the game in Denver and his watching Ruth and Gehrig trading turns with such an easy majesty, while the ordinary play went on far below them. He'd been asking himself why he hadn't felt that same sense of separation in Sioux City through the innings he pitched. Of course, he'd seen that the two of them hit supremely, just as he'd expected, but even so, he'd felt he and they were playing the same game. But he'd been inside it with them then.

Thanks for Henry's early birthday present. That's what Earl had said, repeating Gehrig, when the two of them got back.

Gehrig said, smiling down at Henry, "I'm a kid too when I get to ride the rides."

Still, Earl had wanted Gehrig to hear his thanks and hear it also referring to what he'd thanked him for half a dozen times or more, and always Gehrig waving the words away.

He'd put Henry to bed, asking him how the night had gone, about the rides he'd ridden, and when Henry said, "Great, it was all really great," and after a pause, "and we talked a lot too." It was clear how much he meant this, and that he was thinking something he wanted to keep adultly private, as if he and Gehrig equally had made the night a success.

"What did you talk about?"

"Just things," Henry had said.

It was almost 10:30. They'd be departing Cheyenne—he couldn't remember the time exactly, but very soon. Earl stood up, the railing made his butt sore, and looking out he saw the tracks' busy stitches, their looping, overlapping weaves, and the several lighted platforms. There were maybe half a dozen other trains. Earl thought of them as asleep, the trains themselves.

The sound of an automobile broke the quiet, its engine clacking like a thrasher. He saw its front lamps coming out of the darkness, and a few moments later a new Model-A pulled up next to the depot, some thirty yards away. A rear door opened, and Ruth's raspy laugh escaped.

Earl watched him slowly emerge as the other rear door opened and a woman stepped out. She wore a long cloth coat that made her shape a mystery, but Earl could see that she was almost as tall as Ruth. They were too far away for him to tell anything more about how she looked.

Ruth gave the hood quick bongo slaps and waved through the windshield to bid the driver good night. The Model-A maneuvered in reverse to turn around, then headed off. Ruth and the woman stood looking into the night in the Model-A's direction, Ruth's arm around her shoulders. Finally, they turned, and Earl watched them stepping over a series of tracks, quick geisha steps, as they headed to the Pullman.

He moved quickly back into the darkness of the car and through it to his room. He waited, his door kept open just a crack, for them to enter and tiptoe down the corridor, giggling and whispering. In his room, in the dark, he felt he was playing a kind of practical joke on Ruth, and then that he was somehow the object of one. He felt a fool, then fiendishly clever, the way a child does, then a fool again.

He waited, waited, hearing nothing. It became clear they'd gone elsewhere, maybe to her train, one of those that Earl had imagined was asleep, and his instinct was parental, a scolding of Ruth. They were about to leave and he was risking being left behind. He quietly laughed, to think he was playing such a role, as he opened his door and walked back into the lounge, heading outside again to see if he could spot them. Chairs and tables were shapes he passed in the darkness, and as he reached the door to the platform he saw, through its window, Ruth and the woman out there fucking.

Ruth was sitting on the railing just where Earl had sat, while the woman straddled him, her coatless back to Earl. She was surely cold, but also surely she was not, her skirt rucked up at her waist, her long, stockinged legs dangling, swinging slightly, playful in their freedom as she rode Ruth. His trousers and underwear and gartered stockings, all lay gathered at his ankles in a puddle of fabric, the woman's coat lying carelessly beside it, and Earl saw his long, white calves. It was the only flesh there was to see, and he thought how strange this world was, strange beyond strange, that his mind instantly identified them, said, yes, those were Babe Ruth's skinny calves all right. He'd know them anywhere.

Earl could see Ruth's face above the woman's shoulder. The night had turned so dark, no moon now, the sky no longer a fabric of stars, no way to see what his eyes were showing. But Earl didn't need to see them to know they were twinkling with a lively misdemeanor.

He watched the woman's buttocks barely lift and fall, her shoulder blades flexing and relaxing beneath her silk blouse. No sounds reached Earl. He didn't hear her ragged breathing keeping time, didn't hear Ruth's voice whispering obscenely, and the silence Earl was hearing made their bodies' movements fluent.

Earl had fantasized holding Emily naked in his arms on the dance floor in soft lamplight. He'd thrilled at seeing her naked by the light of the moon. Their wanting each other had been solemn, ceremonial, their pleasure something they gave and got intensely even so. It was what they'd found at the beginning and never let go of and hadn't wanted to. But here were Ruth and the woman with no need for nakedness; their coupling was functional, primitive, a pragmatic lust. It was a way he and Emily hadn't known, and Earl felt he was watching a recklessness he had no gift for. For several moments, as he watched, he felt instructed—or accused—or that he was being teased by Ruth and the woman, and his mind, as if to come to his defense, remembered the day in the hotel lobby when he'd pictured taking Emily right there in the ugly high-backed chair.

Earl saw the woman leaning back, placing her hands on Ruth's thighs, her arms supporting her, presenting her silk-bloused breasts as Emily had offered him hers. From the first, the night beneath the dance hall porch, Earl had imagined the gesture as that, an offering. He still did, that's how he held it, knowing so well as he watched now, feeling like the voyeur he'd been then, that it was nine years to the night when he'd watched her die.

From where he stood, inside in the darkness, he saw Ruth smiling a smile he hadn't seen before, a beggar's joy in it, then saying something to the woman as he lowered his head to her breasts. And as Earl watched, he heard Ruth's smile asking him what *he* would say to her if she were straddling *him*?

CHAPTER TWENTY-FOUR

///

October 20 and 21, 1927   *Across Wyoming*

Away from Cheyenne on the Gold Coast Limited toward Laramie, where they'd arrive just after midnight and the terrain would start to climb!

Henry lay awake, thinking of all he'd said to Gehrig in the café and wondering why he had, waiting for the guilt to descend, because it hadn't.

He'd been holding competing narratives in his head, and he still was. In the first, he and Earl would stay on the train another day or two until the time for their return. They would say their good-byes and speak their thanks and pledge their memories, and they'd board another train, traveling back across the country.

But he was also traveling across a fabulous expanse, with no sense of a calendar or of days and hours, of anything that measured time and distance as they were passing. So there were moments when he imagined all this just continuing, and since that's what would be happening, why couldn't Mr. Walsh order up a second Pullman for his grandparents?

He saw Rooster arriving in a new straw boater, identical down to the red silk band. He pictured Lottie helping Horace Meadows in the tiny kitchen. As for himself, he'd be moving back and forth between this new life and his old one, living with his father, Ruth and Gehrig, Walsh and Horace Meadows, in this car and his grandparents in the second. He imagined feeling, along with everything that was new, their familiar, secure and all-embracing love.

Thunder faintly sounding in the deep night, in the foothills, and Earl lay awake, fixed on what he'd seen. And feeling still that as much as he'd been watching them, he'd been watching himself, and watching him and Emily in contrast. All of that shown to him, performed for him, as he'd watched.

He'd heard Ruth come into the Pullman, finished with his night, and the moment he'd entered, the train came to life, easing away from the depot platform. The idea that the world could be forever at your service, could *work* for you like that. The woman and the brand-new Model-A, and wherever they went and whoever drove them there and back. It seemed he'd already known who everyone, where everything, was. Everything. Those graceful geisha steps as he and the woman crossed the depot's weave of tracks; they'd hopped over them without having to look down.

The train cleaved the night, the thunder still faint but continuous now, and the world so dark mile after mile that it gave back nothing of the gradually rising landscape, until just up ahead a depot's ghostly light got Earl up and to his window. The train slowed approaching Laramie, where they'd wait briefly, and when it came to its stop, he watched an old man among the departing passengers, shuffling along the platform. He was wearing bib overalls and a tweed suit jacket and his long beard was shaped like a funnel. Now another geezer appeared in a black rain slicker, looking frail and fugitive and skittish as a fawn. The two stood side by side, seeming twinned by their confusion, maybe brothers, maybe strangers, no way to tell. And then the bearded one reached for the other's hand, a shy, Samaritan gesture, and they headed off together, moving like bent dowagers, and Henry, watching from his window too, was thinking there were times when his grandfather moved like that, and if only life were long division, he could place a decimal point at the end of right this second, dividing the larger life he'd found into the smaller one he'd known. And on the world would go, as Mr. Paumgarten said, a perfect problem because it was never finished.

If only.

2:30 a.m., through Elk Mountain and Arlington, with louder thunder and hectic lightning starting and the thunder waking Gehrig, but not Ruth, deep in dream. His legs tucked fetally. His head resting on his folded hands. His pose angelic. The man was a jokester even in sleep.

In his dream, he was sitting at a banquet table with many men he didn't know, all dressed as he was, in tuxedos. He saw nearly empty platters arrayed in front of him, scraps of beef and ham and roast chicken. He couldn't remember that he'd eaten anything, but as he reached for the fancy scraps, a door opened at one end of the room, and a beautiful woman entered. And after her another, and after her several more, all of them walking toward the table and waving the way new babies wave, making curling fingers that barely opened and closed. They wore identical short dresses of a transparent mesh adorned with the fewest possible beads, clusters placed strategically, there, and there, but—oh, how fucking grand—not there, and Ruth heard a sound from the men, a kind of lowing, the hum of connoisseurship in it.

Ruth's eyes followed a very tall brunette he felt sure he'd seen before as she moved along behind the men, leaning down to whisper in their ears, until at last she reached him and sat lightly on his lap.

Louder thunder finally woke him, rumbles of it like a narrative. He lay listening for a moment and thought, *God bowling*, that corny fucking thing one of the Xaverian brothers was guaranteed to say when thunder rolled across the sky like that above St. Mary's School for Boys, where he arrived when he was seven.

Earl, awake, was thinking, *Goats? Jesus.*

The rain beginning and immediately cascading as they passed through tiny Rawlins just after three o'clock, and Gehrig decided to get up and write tomorrow's letter to Christina. His first thought was to describe Henry spinning out his lies in his touching, cockeyed way. But of course he wouldn't dream of writing what he'd been more deeply feeling—that the boy had given him something valuable tonight, a preview of how it might well happen, your mother dying, and all you could offer were your presence at her bedside and ice-cold cloths and warming blankets and the maddening frustration that what she was needing was whatever you weren't offering her right then.

Dearest Mama.

He wrote to her instead about the game in Denver and how far a baseball carried in the thin mountain air, and arriving in Cheyenne, inviting Henry to come with him, and he ended with the thought that *to my surprise the time with the boy has got me thinking of my sisters, I mean the idea of them, of Anna and Sophie, and also of my brother. It feels strange sometimes to remember I had siblings, or would have them if they'd lived, and that I never knew them.*

I guess I'm saying that when I look at Henry I imagine that brother I didn't have the chance to know. But he's the ten-year-old brother, not the grown man he would be now.

Or maybe what I see is myself growing up (his name is Henry after all) an only child, but with the great difference that he remembers no loving mother.

I'll close for tonight with that grateful thought from,

Your loving son, Lou

In the next to last baseball game Gehrig plays, twelve years from now, he will lunge to catch an easy, soft line drive, and, his feet badly tangled, he'll fall forward, landing heavily on his stomach, his limbs splayed like a starfish. And afterward, driving home to New Rochelle, he'll have no thoughts of the game, thinking only of the fall and his embarrassment, and his fear for what it means as further evidence.

He and Eleanor, his wife, will have been aware for several months of his stumbling and tripping on steps, feeling unsteady when he rises from a chair, and trying, as a test, to balance on one foot and feeling instantly a vertigo as the floor begins to tilt.

He'll recently have asked her if she doesn't think they should stop visiting the rink at the Playland Ice Casino in Rye, where he's begun to fall so often that other skaters, sneaking glimpses of his spills, have had a good laugh on themselves for thinking—when they saw him arrive and lace up his skates—*Hey, isn't that Lou Gehrig?*

As he continues his drive home, a memory will descend, whole and unbidden, recalling the day in Sioux City and the boy who fell, whose first name he'll remember being his own, though he won't be able to summon his last name or his father's at all.

As he drives, getting close to his house a few leafy, neat-lawned blocks away, his thoughts will stay fixed on that moment in the game today, and he'll imagine himself becoming two, and one of his selves swooping in to rescue the one who's fallen, picking him up, and whisking him away.

Two hours to Rock Springs, and jagged lines of lightning moving down the sky and flat smacks of rain against the windows, but Ruth was once again asleep, returned to his dream. Which was not how dreams behaved, not like radio serials, not in episodes, but it's how Ruth's was proceeding, with the very tall brunette on his lap, right where she'd been when thunder woke him. And now he traced his fingers along her thigh and asked her how she'd got her legs to grow so long, and she said she'd practiced every night for an hour after supper. He said they were divine, those long legs of hers, just divine, and he asked her where they ended, and she said they ended at her ankles, and he said, no, he meant the other direction, and she said they ended there in Paradise, where all divine things end.

He said he knew they'd met, where was it? and she tilted her head slightly and said she'd give him a hint, then started to recite the nursery rhyme. There once was a woman who lived in a shoe, and she had so many children she didn't know what to do. He raised his hand to stop her—he knew how it went and where was the hint?—but she simply started again, the woman, the shoe, not knowing what to do, then looked at him and said, *But six of them died, then she did too,* and, hearing this, his head snapped back. She stood and leaned forward to whisper into his ear, her voice a mongrel growl, not unlike his, as she said, *I'm your mother, George.*

He woke in wild confusion and looked around his room, and after a moment, asking what the world was coming to when the woman of your dreams turns out to be your mother?

The thunder booming, but Earl was managing to sleep, and he was dreaming too, dreaming he was a miner in a room of coal. He heard its water as a trickle. He heard the hectic skirl of rats. The walls of coal were made of paper money, bales of bills, and each time he swung his pick, it sank deep, and hundreds of bills came flying loose with a sound like beating wings, and his thought was to scoop them up and hurry away, the money clutched to his chest, protecting it. He put down his pick and squatted to gather up the treasure, but every handful turned to coal dust, and he shouted so loudly in his sleep that Henry heard it through the wall, interrupting his thought that his grandfather was the only person in the world he could imagine asking what Mr. Ruth had meant when he said, if your aunt had a dick she'd be your uncle.

The rain a frenzy; the lightning too, a brilliant event.

Gehrig's mind was still going. He got up and found his robe and slippers. Opening his door, he heard the sour plinks of ukulele coming from the lounge, so he headed for the dining room at the other end of the car. He switched on a wall lamp with a Tiffany shade and sat down at the table, mindful of Horace Meadows asleep in his closet of a bedroom, and lit a cigarette.

He was thinking how strange, the lessons you've set for yourself and those you receive instead, and from such improbable sources, in this instance a young boy who'd made wise and useful sense of a sorrow that he, that Gehrig, couldn't begin to imagine how to live with when it came. And he was thinking, again, that he'd seen this tour as the chance to learn from Jidge something of the way he made the world *his* world, something of his skills as a creature moving through it. But what he'd hoped for himself was a more modest version of those skills, and if he'd thought about it for even a moment, he'd have seen there was no such thing. The whole of Jidge's existence had to do with how hungry a man could be and all the things he could be hungry for and all of them at once, and Gehrig remembered now a moment when he'd shown him this exactly.

Two years before, the last game of the Series, down by a run and two outs in the ninth, and Jidge on first after a walk, with Meusel batting, while he stood in the on-deck circle waiting to hit and feeling his roller-coaster giddiness. Now, once again, he sees the pitch and Meusel's swing and miss, and there it is, it's always there, what he'd thought he couldn't possibly be seeing when it happened—Jidge running, off for second and the steal, and the catcher's throw that beats him as he slides to the infield side where he lay, arms spread, like a sick seal come ashore.

He'd wanted second base. It was the next thing to consume. And as Gehrig smoked and watched the rain, he asked himself how he could have thought there was a modest version of such an unsatiable hunger as that.

He stubbed out his cigarette, his mind giving to the rain, its hypnotic effect, and thinking now of Robert Tannenbaum's dying of the flu. He hadn't thought of him in years until he'd mentioned him tonight, a round, clumsy boy in baggy knickers, who spent hours in his room drawing maps of invented continents, brilliant in their drafting, with lakes and roads and mountain ranges winding like graceful vertebrae.

And then one day he felt hot and had a headache.

Gehrig stood and stretched, ready to return to his room and try to sleep. He had the thought—a prideful one, but he allowed himself to have it—that in his mother's commanding love there was surely a measure of gratitude. A gratitude *for* him, yes, but also *to* him, the child who'd lived. It had let her be a mother defined by more than what she'd lost.

He started back to his room with the thought he'd often had—that it was an unimaginable grief, parents surviving the death of a child, and his had had to bear it three times in their lives.

He reached his room and saw his letter to his mother lying on his bed. It would surely upset her terribly, to be reminded, when she read it. What had he been thinking? He tore the letter up and threw the scraps into a wastebasket.

"Divine?" Her long legs looked *divine*? Ruth was thinking he'd never said that word in his entire fucking life. He was sitting in the lounge, in robe and slippers, drinking whiskey, the lightning an even wilder rending now.

Walsh appeared and dropped wearily into a chair. His legs in navy silk pajama drawers showed beneath his robe, a lighter, complementary blue. Here they were, Ruth and Walsh in their lounging wear, like mannequin dandies in the fancy men's store window.

"You look like shit, Christy," Ruth said, "Can't sleep?"

"Ah," Walsh said. "I knew there was something I was forgetting to do."

"Here's how I remember," Ruth said. "First, you eat supper. Then you boink the broad. Then sleep's the thing comes after that."

"Thanks, Jidge," Walsh said. "I guess I'll have to do without the boinking for now."

"Yeah." Ruth nodded. "I'm in the same boat of fish." And as for sleep, he added, the *sleeping* part's okay, but look out for the dreams.

Between Rock Springs and Green River at 6:30, and Henry waking to the rain after a dreamless hour at the very bottom of sleep. He got up and opened his door, looked into the lounge, and saw Horace Meadows moving smoothly about, oblivious to the storm, its flashes and percussions, setting out the coffee pot and cups, the cream and sugar. Henry shut the door again before Meadows saw him. He didn't want to visit with him until he was more awake and ready for the day. From the few conversations they'd had, he'd begun to feel a great respect, an awe, for Horace Meadows, not like the affection he felt for Gehrig and the one emerging in another way for Ruth.

He was starting to understand that Ruth and Gehrig too were

important, were heroes, in a way his father wasn't. This was something about the world, its reach, its many layers, which he hadn't known, and he wasn't sure what to call it, what the word was for how others behaved toward the two of them, though he could see it and sense it in the sound of peoples' words and the look on people's faces. But whatever it was called, he had some knowledge of it now, that much of the reason Gehrig and Ruth went about their lives with such confidence was because everyone they met was eager to tell them things and show them things and give them bits of knowledge without their needing to find out anything for themselves.

But what Horace Meadows knew and how he came to know it—words and stories and so many kinds of people and the places they came from that no one had heard of—this was knowing things in ways that Ruth and Gehrig never could because they couldn't be Creoles and they couldn't be Negroes, which is what you had to be to get to live your life in beautiful Pullman cars with no final destinations.

They'd spoken yesterday, the longest talk they'd had, and Horace Meadows explained that, no, he wasn't married, so, no, he was not a father, no, he had no children. He said he guessed, all these years, he just hadn't found the right woman. And after thinking about this, Henry offered that if Horace Meadows became a Mormon, there'd be several to choose from, many women he might like.

Meadows's slow nod in response had lasted seconds; a history of courtliness was in his gesture. "Well, I thank you, Mr. Henry," Horace Meadows said. "I thank you for that tip." He said he'd definitely keep it in mind, and meanwhile the sun would rise tomorrow and shine down on them both and on the baby's bald head and on the old dog's plumbing if he was laying on his back. And unlike what he'd heard Ruth say the day before, Henry felt he got the gist of what this meant. It sounded in a way like the words to a children's song, maybe one of Horace Meadows's favorites when he was a boy. And he'd had no impulse whatsoever to correct Meadows's grammar. *Lying on his back*. It didn't seem important, didn't seem to matter in the least.

Nearing Green River, the rain pounding the windows, and Earl thinking the rain was desperate to get in out of the rain. He could see through it to the early morning sky darkening still more, thickening like a roux.

He made yet another inventory of his room, the polished paneling and the Oriental-patterned carpet, the brass fixtures and the cut-glass lamp shades, and he caught himself thinking once again that if she had left her life for his, *well, look. This is what I imagined. This is what I saw.* Thinking this even as he knew it wasn't true. He hadn't imagined a world, a life so gilded as this car, this train, these days. Who could have?

He heard her saying, "Eureka?" He'd told her one night, early in his courting her, something of his childhood and that his first mine was named Eureka, and she'd said, "Eureka? That's terrible!" such a horrible place and whoever owned it named it *Eureka*? And he'd said, yes, but didn't she see there was also humor in it? The owners' measly version of Hell, and they called it Eureka? And she'd said, no, she hadn't seen it, the humor, but if he could she would too.

He thought, *Eureka*, and remembered, when he was very young, six and seven, even eight years old, still a few years before he started in the mines, that he'd fantasized the life his father descended into every day. He imagined the mine an enchanted place, bustling with the other miners and with magnificent animals that never left the world below. They resembled no creature he knew of, they were as small and sleek as wolves, with vaguely equine faces, four-legged, silver-hooved, though they walked easily on two, and with fur a brilliant white that coal dust didn't soil. He imagined the miners and the animals intermingling, speaking a private language that was music more than speech. He imagined them conversing in their near songs through the day.

He heard her saying "infectious." She wanted her hope for them and for their life to be infectious. It was an Emily word, but surely the irony was too great for her really to have said it.

All these things coming at him in a rush. Maybe it was the rain. His memories like the torrent the train was moving through. Rain, for where it took them, had often been his favorite weather.

Nearly eight a.m., arriving in Green River, and the rain and lightning stopped, the thunder quit, the storm shut down just like that. From the time it left Rock Springs, the Gold Coast Limited had proceeded over nearly flooded tracks, and here the skies above the little town and the iron-gray range that ran behind it, they were all at once preposterously blue.

CHAPTER TWENTY-FIVE

Earl, Ruth, and Christy Walsh sat in The Ship, a dark, low-ceilinged speakeasy on a narrow street, its potholes rain-filled, its ruts long troughs of mud, a few blocks from the depot. The night was early, but the room was packed; some of the customers already leaning slightly where they stood and a few, their eyes were slits, blinking lazily like frogs! Fishnets hung, draped loosely, from the stamped tin ceiling. There were large, white rubber lifesavers on the walls. Even the air was thematic, cigar and cigarette smoke wafting and trailing like fog off the water.

Near the bar, a tall, bald, malnourished-looking man wearing a red bow tie and red suspenders was playing an upright piano; bouncing melodies, strict and happy strides that moved along beneath the noise, seemed to bring an order to it, to give it here and there a beat. The back of his blue shirt showed a huge sweat stain the shape of Florida.

Walsh looked around and laughed. "How can you say life doesn't have a sense of humor? We're stranded by the floods and Jidge leads us to The Ship."

Earl smiled and sipped his second whiskey. Its fire coated his throat as he swallowed. He'd rarely drunk anything but local beer and Rooster's corn liquor since he'd left the mines for Waterloo, but the bartender had warned him customers complained that what passed for beer in The Ship tasted like moose piss, and Earl thought, *how would they know?* as he said, "All right then, a whiskey."

There'd been the astonished whoops and *whoahs!* when the three of them entered, the predictable eruptions when Ruth was recognized. Then shouts like auction bids to buy him a drink, until he raised his hand and everyone got quiet and he said, why didn't he buy the room a round instead, and they all cheered at this even better idea.

Now, at their table near the bar, Ruth had turned in his chair to receive a long line of idolaters, one by one, in patient papal fashion. Earl could hear his voice, a jolly abrasion within the rabble noise, and he thought of last night, when he'd heard his smile instead.

Walsh said to Earl, "I haven't really had a chance to ask how it's going."

Earl nodded. "Henry's having the time of his life. Which is hardly a surprise."

They were talking loudly, deliberately, not quite shouting.

Walsh smiled. "He must think he's dreaming."

Earl shook his head. "Even better. He knows he *isn't.*"

Walsh extended his smile. "That *would* be better, wouldn't it." He brought his glass to his lips. "And what about you?"

"Same as Henry. I know I'm not dreaming." And hearing himself, Earl thought he'd sounded like an ass.

"I assumed as much," Walsh said.

"I'm along for the ride," Earl said. "A very comfortable ride, and I appreciate it." He looked around, telling himself to let the room in, its talk and its laughter, just let it in. He drank his whiskey and felt its fire and managed to keep from coughing. He asked, nodding at Ruth's back, "How'd he know about this place?"

"He *always* knows about a place," Walsh said. "Or he knows somebody who does. Or he wires Freddie, his bookie, and somehow *he* knows about a place, and I don't think Freddie's been out of New York a day in his life."

That morning, with the sun returned, the air washed to its blue brilliance, they'd expected to pause in Green River and be on their way when Horace Meadows, seeking Walsh, had appeared in the lounge with news from the conductor. The rain may have stopped, but it had been unceasing in this corner of Wyoming for three days, into four, and a few miles up the Blacks Fork had overflowed its banks and washed away a span of tracks. Trains were being held here, and a train was backing up, returning from the point where it had discovered the tracks gone, and a train was on its way from Rock Springs, where it would have stayed if word had reached it in time.

"How long will it be?" Walsh had asked Horace Meadows.

"The section gang's just got there," Meadows said. "In my experience down through the years, they work fast or slow depending."

"Depending on what?" Walsh had asked.

"On what they did the night before." Horace Meadows's face was serious when he said this, but Walsh had heard a jaunty pessimism in his voice.

In the Pullman, after breakfast, they'd retreated to their staterooms. They'd traveled all night, mostly without sleep through the tantrum of weather, and with the world turned calm again, they'd been happy to go back to bed.

The day had proceeded on rumors.

The work was nearly finished and they'd be leaving shortly.

Miles of tracks had washed away. Repairs would take a week.

Until late afternoon, with the sunlight fading, word had come from the conductor that they'd be here through the night.

They were nearly to Utah, and Henry, finally looking at a map, had been eager to get there so he could see how the landscape matched Zane Grey's descriptions. But it was also fine with him that they weren't leaving until later. Unconsciously, as the first day on the Pullman became the second, and with the second flowing now toward the third, he'd gotten used to the sensation of momentum, the train's onward velocity become internal and unnoticed, become a kind of heartbeat. But being stopped, stalled in Green River overnight, he'd also welcomed this news as the day's surprise playing out.

From his room, he'd watched passengers from the other held-up trains filling the platform and the station yard. People stood alone, they huddled, they wandered up and down the tracks, conversations starting, breaking up, re-forming, all of them looking as lost and confused as Ellis Island refugees.

As he'd watched, a sense of wise benevolence came over Henry, and he'd seen himself raising his window and calling out his reassurance, telling them all how exciting it was not to know when you'd be leaving, not to worry if they weren't sure where they were going.

For Earl, the news had sounded only like delay.

Through the last hours across Wyoming, feeling more and more alert, he'd stared out his window, and began to picture, behind the rain, behind the night, a mountain range running pocked and splayed and severe in the distance. He'd just assumed it was there, and as the Gold Coast Limited continued through the storm, the line of mountains became in his fancy the very edge of the world, turned up like a crust.

Every train he'd ever taken, he'd felt himself traveling *toward* something. To Chicago in the box car. To the lives in the windows he passed on the El. To Waterloo and the promise waiting for him there. To Emily on the Land O'Corn Limited, with the countryside nagging him every blessed mile. And back to her again to begin their life.

But as he pictured the rim of mountains, it came to him that now, this trip, what he was traveling toward was his *return*, and he'd felt suddenly, enormously relieved, a sense he didn't understand. And then it came to him again even stronger, this feeling of relief, and with it his impatience to be done with these days.

It's how Emily had felt, return as destination, but Earl didn't have the thought: that their feelings were the same.

He'd been sitting in the lounge shortly after supper, Henry in the kitchen watching Horace Meadows make a pie, when Ruth and Walsh came through, heading out. He'd glanced up from the newspaper he wasn't really reading, and Ruth told him where they were going. "How about it? Wanna come?"

At the table in The Ship, Walsh said, "I meant it when I said you and Henry could stay on. The best of the landscape is still ahead. Utah, my God, the buttes, the caverns, the gorges, they're like rainbows of stone brought to life by the sun."

"Thank you," Earl said. "Really. Thank you." He remembered the first night aboard, watching Henry sleep, and his pledge to let him have this time entirely.

Walsh raised his arm and caught the bartender's eye. He drew a circle in the air and pointed to Ruth and Earl and himself.

Earl looked down at his glass, surprised to see that it was empty. He'd drunk two strong bootleg whiskeys quickly, doubles for the price of a shot at the bartender's insistence, and another round was on its way. A sound, a humming, was starting in his head. He recognized it. Drinking with his father, he'd tried to will it and the numbness that came with it, tried to will them to hurry, before his ugly feelings could get started.

Walsh said, "I just wish I could come up with a way to use you two."

"What?" Earl said.

"You and Henry. To help us sell more tickets."

"You've got him," Earl said, pointing at Ruth's back. "And you've got Gehrig."

Walsh nodded. "That is true."

"You don't need to sell any more, do you? Aren't the games sold out?"

"'Don't need to sell any more'?" Walsh smiled. "I'm not familiar with that concept."

A fat drinker at the bar appeared with the whiskeys on a tray. He'd asked to bring them over so he could tell his grandchildren he'd served Babe Ruth, but Ruth, distracted—at talky ease among the florid-faced men in farmers' khakis or cheap wool suits clustered around him—reached for his glass and grasped it without looking, and the fat drinker's shoulders slumped in disappointment as he walked away.

Walsh and Earl sat for a time, saying little, listening to the piano and steadily sipping their drinks. For Earl, the whiskey's heat was becoming easier. At a point he realized his fingers were tapping the table. He watched them lightly drumming, quick-stepping on their own.

The malnourished piano player struck a pounding chord and ran his fingertip up the keyboard, a rippling glissando. It got the room's attention, and he started a new stride while calling out, half singing, half talking, "Now you see 'em, now you don't, and now you do! Winkin' and Blinkin', the Topper Twins are here for you!"

The swinging doors behind the bar parted, and they appeared in floor-length, sequined gowns, making their way slinkily to a tiny stage next to the piano. They blew kisses and waved and called to familiar faces seated close. The piano player kept his tune going through the applause, and Earl laughed at their joke of saying they were twins. One was tall, voluptuous, her body a series of soft parentheses; the other was small, fine-boned, plain as a sparrow.

They wore identical blonde wigs.

Ruth spun around to face Earl and Walsh, his eyebrows chevroning. "Freddie said if we was lucky, they'd be here."

Earl looked at Ruth, into his big, round face, and what he saw was an enormous innocence, the lively eyebrows and the plump lines of his lips, but otherwise an expression of, yes, simpleton wonder. It was perfectly the man in the moon's, Earl thought. And as a moon, it was a waxing gibbous; it was one night shy of full; he needed something, a quid of tobacco in his cheek to make it full, and if she were here she'd argue playfully that it already was.

Onstage, the Twins were smiling and shimmying in their glittering gowns as they began their introductory ditty, complimenting the crowd, singing, "Such a handsome lot!" singing they should all come and get it while it was very hot. They touched the tips of their fingers to their hips and made the *ssss!*-ing sound of steam escaping. Their voices were low; rich, blended altos.

Walsh chuckled. "The Topper Twins. It looks like Freddie was right. Like they're going to be good fun."

Freddie the bookie. Earl said it to himself. He thought it sounded like a stuffed animal of baby Henry's. Teddy the Bear. Freddie the Bookie.

The Twins, their tune, were rhyming "don't get caught" with "secret spot," and Ruth was nodding along and lighting a cigar. When he'd got it going, he leaned across the table to be heard and said to Earl, "Let me ask you something."

"Don't raise goats," Earl said.

Ruth laughed, inhaling smoke by mistake, and he was helpless to a sneezing fit. When he'd recovered, he said, "No, not that."

"What then?" Earl asked.

"You ever think, when you're pitching, how the ball's got a mind of its own?"

"A mind of its own?"

Ruth nodded. "You decide you're gonna throw a pitch, say your curve. You grip it the same every time, right? You wind up just the same, you throw it the same, but it don't always *act* the same. Maybe *most* of the time, yeah, but sometimes it don't. And that's true—ain't it?—even if you're great?" He emptied his glass and with his back to the bar, he held it up, above his head for just a moment, which was all the signal the bartender needed, since he hadn't taken his eyes off their table. And once again Earl saw it: Babe Ruth's presumption, no need to look, that the world stood ready.

Earl looked closely at Ruth again, and he saw that his eyes were filled with what he'd imagined last night, in the dark, through the window—a kind of alternating light of mirth and mischief, but the mischief more aggressive now. He said, "You're saying it's like when you swing at pitches the same way every time, but you don't always hit them?"

The Twins sang their song's final note, and as applause was ending, the piano started the next one while they did a synchronized twirl, sequins twinkling.

Ruth raised his glass to his lips for a last drop. "That ain't the same," he said.

Earl drank too. "Why not? You take the same swing you always do, but sometimes you don't hit it. Seems the same to me."

Ruth drew on his cigar and watched his smoke rise to join the room's. "I'm saying when it's the fucking *ball* deciding, yes or no," and Earl was more certain he'd been right. That Ruth was thinking of the pitch he'd thrown him and the one he'd been about to, that he was saying they were nothing Earl could take the credit for. And what he was feeling didn't lead him to remember the day Saul Weintraub had watched him pitch better than he ever had for no reason Earl could point to, nothing special he had done.

Ruth said, "I used to think about this. I even asked one of the Brothers about it once, and he said it was just how God works, the ball acting on its own, how else could you explain it? I loved this fella, this Brother, he taught me a lot about the game, but when he said that, I thought, it's the way you explain it when you got no fucking clue."

Another drinker from the bar brought the round this time. He put the tray down and placed the doubles on the table with banquet-setting care. He straightened up and stood next to Ruth, grinning immensely and showing no sign of leaving, and Walsh gave him a dollar to go away.

Earl took a smaller sip. The humming in his head was louder and taking up more space.

Walsh was looking back and forth at Earl and Ruth. He thought what Ruth was saying sounded idiotic. And yet, maybe if you tried to hear it generously you could almost think of it as, what? Theoretical? Philosophical? Which was about the last thing he'd ever accuse the big fella' of.

Also, Walsh sensed that he was agitated, close to provoked and looking to be, and he patted Ruth's shoulder. "That's very sage, Jidge. It's the *ball* that decides, yes or no."

"I'm saying sometimes," Ruth said.

"It has the ring of epigram," Walsh said. "Of aphorism."

"Jesus H," Ruth growled. "Speak English, Christy."

The Twins sang their saucy song, the tempo on tiptoes, quick and light.

When I'm cold and lonely, and she won't show me hers, I get all warm and rosy as I think of you and yours.

Earl leaned forward in his chair to speak to Ruth. "We could finish it," he said, as though he were simply stating a fact. His voice was uninflected, slowed by the booze, the vowels leaning on each other.

"Finish what?" Ruth asked.

Earl opened his hands as if to say, *I really need to explain?* "The count was one and two." He turned from Ruth to speak to Walsh. "We could finish it. The count was one and two."

Walsh took a drink and slowly swallowed. "So what are you proposing, Earl? Some kind of . . . reenactment?"

Earl pointed at Walsh, "There you go," then turned back to Ruth and pointed at him too. "A reenactment." He offered Ruth his open palms a second time.

Nights when you're not here, the sweetest hour occurs, I play naughty games with mine and pretend it's you and yours.

Earl watched Ruth take a drink, then return his cigar to the corner of his mouth.

"I gotta say, kid, it's hard to guess your hat size. Usually, I meet somebody, it don't take me a minute to figure him out and forget his name." He smiled, his lips prehensile as he wagged his cigar. "There's really just two kinds. I figured this out a long time ago. There's the ones that want it all and the ones that wish there wasn't so fucking much to want. What I'm hearing, you're talking like you're the first kind, like you're a greedy bastard. Which there's nothing wrong with that, I'm a greedy bastard too. But I don't know, sometimes it seems to me you ain't. You're a funny kind of greedy."

Earl was ready to say, *How so?* but he stopped himself. He didn't feel like listening to any more of Babe Ruth's bullshit. He sensed he'd gotten under his skin, pissed him off, and that's no doubt what he'd wanted to do, though all he felt for sure was drunk—which for once didn't feel at all bad—and a fresh rush of the impatience that had started. *Return as destination.* He emptied his glass and looked around the room. He sensed the air had become even thicker, the drinkers crowding around their table, and he felt it for an instant like the closeness of a mine; the air, the smoke, was the dust he'd breathed when he was twelve. Even so, he could hear the Twins through it all, the randy lift of their song, and he saw that *that's* what he was impatient for; at least tonight, at least right now, that's where he wished to be.

He pushed back his chair and got slowly to his feet. Ruth and Walsh watched, and Walsh pushed his chair back too. He looked up at Earl, "You calling it a night? I'll go with you," and started to stand as Earl headed off into the room.

"It's this way!" Walsh called, pointing toward the door just past the bar.

"Hey, kid!" Ruth said.

They watched him make his way among the tables. He was managing to move smoothly. Even with the humming and the numbness, he'd found that surety, that glide.

"Where's he going?" Walsh said. He sat down and watched Earl disappear into the crowd.

Ruth was watching him too, then began to scan The Ship. He saw a roomful of phantoms in the smoke, and he said, "Every one of these bastards looks exactly alike." He looked at the few women, sitting here and there with men at tables. "The broads, too. The broads look like the bastards and visa versa. Is that what happens, a little piece-a-shit town? Men, broads. They all start to look the same? I mean, I've been in plenty of piece a shit towns, but I never noticed it before."

Walsh heard Ruth sounding amazed at his discovery, maybe slightly panicked. *Well*, he thought, *Earl's drunk, and I am, and it would seem that Jidge is too.*

Earl was heading in the direction of the Twins, stepping loosely, hearing the piano and their low voices and the humming in his head was searching for the song's key.

And there they were, just ahead on the tiny stage. They'd ended their tune, were waiting through the applause, and when they began again their hips were moving only slightly to the piano's calmer chords. The voluptuous Twin said they were going to slow things down, try something new tonight, a ballad, a love song to the room.

"Because we love you all," the petite one said.

Ruth and Walsh could see Earl again, standing very near the stage. Walsh said, "If he gets any closer it'll be the Topper Triplets."

"Maybe they got an extra wig," Ruth said.

They sat, drinking and watching, listening to the piano play a long, slow introduction, until Ruth said, "That 'one and two' bullshit. He oughta pack it in his suitcase and take it home with him and hang it on the wall so he can look at it any time he wants."

Walsh nodded. He was surprised by Ruth's clever metaphors to-night. He'd never, not once, heard him speak figuratively like this, and he was actually impressed. He'd have liked to say so, but he remembered Ruth, irascible, telling him to stick to English. He said, "I know just what you're saying."

The Twins began, and Earl stood listening with some others right up front. He was trying to get what the ballad was saying, but only bits and phrases could reach him through the humming. He caught *come to me each evening*, he heard *dark skies turn to blue*.

When was the last time he'd wanted to dance? He couldn't remember, and his wish to now was surely the whiskey. Had to be the whiskey. He looked first at the voluptuous Twin, then at the petite one. He focused on her as best he could, and her plainness began to find beautiful details. Her brown eyes deepened. Her long, slender nose was elegant, regal. He saw a lurid purple birthmark on her neck. He knew how it would feel to hold her, small and delicate in his arms, her tiny hand, her fine, thin line of backbone.

Ruth said to Walsh, "It's a shitty thing I did."

"What shitty thing was that, Jidge?" Walsh asked sunnily.

"Missing his pitch. I wasn't fucking with him, I missed it. Almost fell on my ass. But that's as much as he was gonna get and, the dumb shit, don't he see he's already got it?"

"Well said." Walsh nodded. "Extremely well said." *Jidge, Jidge*, he thought. The man lived so heedlessly it was easy to forget that with his greatness came his pride. A kind of peasant dignity was the way Walsh always thought of it.

He was also thinking that Earl's idea was fabulous. A reenactment. *What I could do with* that. They could stage it freshly before every game, David and Goliath, the interest building stop to stop, until they got to California and ran out of continent. San Francisco, Marysville,

San Jose, San Diego, Fresno, LA. Every time would be the first time. The count was always one and two. The release was writing itself. At least another thousand tickets every place they played. More. They could stand in the aisles, on the roofs, he could squeeze them in anywhere, it didn't matter.

And no way Jidge would go for it.

The Twins were singing of love and loss, of heartbreak's pain and things that rhyme with it. Earl was watching the voluptuous Twin. She reminded him of someone, but who, and how did he know her, whoever it was? Maybe he didn't. Maybe he'd just seen her somewhere. Seen her once, a few times, several times but never knew her. Or maybe he'd only dreamed her. And then it came to him. Emily's Aunt Patricia. Sad and proud Patricia, living the deeply unhappy surprise that was her life, and getting a measure of satisfaction from *her* voluptuousness, though of course Earl hadn't known any of that. But, really, he had, just watching her, the way she stood and moved, always giving off a sense of the pleasure she was taking in her fabulous abundance.

Walsh, watching from their table, said, "I'll go get him."

"Nah, let him be," Ruth said. "He looks like he's having fun." And Walsh was glad to hear what sounded like his usually generous voice again.

Earl was staring intently at one Twin, then the other. He was hearing their voices sounding muted, diffused, as if they were coming through the lily horn of an old Victrola. He heard, *I believed you when you told me you were true.* Oh, love; such a sweet, sad thing to sing of. *I dream of waking, there to find you, and you haunt the moonlight too.* He watched their hips barely moving, a suggestive languor, moving them more boldly would be to disobey the song, and then, from somewhere, as they were finishing, Ruth and the woman on the Pullman platform, her body whispering sex as the Twins' were now; a ballad sway to the way *she'd* moved as well.

His last whiskey, he'd taken tiny sips, barely more than moistening his lips, thinking how useful it was to know just how drunk you wanted to get and just how much booze it took to get you there, and he was sure he'd found it tonight, a whiskey equipoise. All those nights with his father at the table after supper, he'd never known you could achieve that. And now, shrewdly drunk, he was going to be able to say to them what he couldn't if he were sober—or drunker. That he'd been standing here, listening to them sing, and he couldn't decide which one he'd ask to dance. He couldn't choose, and he didn't want to, because he was such a greedy bastard.

The final note and light applause (the crowd near the stage had thinned out with the ballad), their waves, their kisses thrown, and then, the song finished and the piano quiet, they turned as one to Earl and he saw them smile. They even *smiled* identically, their pursed lips making the same red-ribboned bows; maybe they *were* twins after all.

The step he took toward them now, he meant it to be his request, and he thought the piano player must have understood, seen it as that too, for as Earl opened his arms to both the Twins he heard the ballad begin again.

They stepped down off the stage, and the voluptuous Twin said, "You been watching us real close." Earl heard this as her explaining why they'd turned to him and smiled, and why they were letting him gather them both in a relaxed, dance floor embrace.

The three of them began to move slowly in a circle, as if practicing their steps for the cotillion, the piano player watching over his shoulder and grinning like a fool as he played. Earl's eyes were on the Twins' smiles that were the same, those red-ribboned bows, just the same, and he could feel his own, spread wide and silly on his face.

"I'm Earl," he said, as they all sidestepped clockwise to the ballad. The voluptuous Twin said, "I'm Edith"; the petite one, "I'm Maxine."

The few drinkers near the stage moved out of the way. They were laughing as they watched—quick, approving hiccups of laughter— and a man standing next to the piano said aloud, "I'm in here every goddamn night. I shoulda' thought of that."

Earl was feeling slightly dizzy now, but even so he was managing to move with that lithe and lucid confidence that Emily had once seen as a stranger's. Looking first at Edith, then Maxine, he thought, *one of me and two of them. The count's one and two.* And just then he felt a tap on the shoulder. He flinched, surprised, and turned to see Walsh smiling too. He and the Twins and the piano player and now Walsh smiling; everyone was smiling and Earl thought, *What a happy time I've made!*

"It's almost midnight," Walsh said. "The magic coach is turning back into the pumpkin."

Earl shook his head. He could find his way back on his own. It was only a few blocks, and he was done with Walsh and Ruth for tonight, done with listening to the wish that he and Henry could be used, done with hearing how the ball decided, yes or no. He was just the right amount of drunk, and all you had to do was pick a rut of mud, stay in it like you were following a furrow in a field, and it would lead you back.

He looked again at the Twins and said, as if explaining, "I couldn't decide. Who to choose. I couldn't decide."

"I'm sure we're flattered," Edith said, and she didn't have the slightest wish to ask him what he was talking about. He seemed sweet and harmless, this Earl, a cute drunk, at least he was tonight, with his smile and his big ears she was tempted to reach out and softly squeeze. They'd had some fun, just leave it there.

Maxine was thinking this too, thinking they heard things at least as dumb as what this Earl was saying every night here in The Ship, in Green River, sucking as it did on the hind tit of nowhere, and the steady run of dumb-ass proclamations; over time, they dulled a woman's curiosity, they just goddamn killed it. "Shit," she said to Walsh, "ain't it Cinderella gets the ride?"

And Edith said, "Magic coach, my ass. When's the last time a magic coach come to Green River, Max?"

Earl, listening, was utterly smitten. Slinky sequined gowns and sexy songs with blushing, *Oh my!* lyrics, and when they spoke they sounded like a couple of miners. He said to them, "It's true. There's a magic coach here now."

He looked at Walsh, "See you back there," and past him to their table where several men were once again encircling Ruth, who was peering through them toward the stage as if through a stand of trees.

Now Earl turned back to the Twins, Walsh standing behind him, and said, play and lightness in his voice, "Edith, Maxine, dance me to the door."

At the end of the night, Maxine relaxed in the small frame house with blistered paint siding she shared with her parents. It sat unprotected from the constant winds at the very edge of town, plopped down, she liked to joke, right on the border where civilization ended and the land of the feral pigs began. She was sitting in the room's comfortable, upholstered chair, picking stuffing from a hole in one of the arms, sipping rum and water while her mother massaged her pretty, child-sized feet. It was their nightly ritual; they looked forward to it equally, Maxine feeling her body calming, moving toward sleep, and her mother—with the sparrow-plain looks she'd given her daughter, the long, narrow nose, the quick brown eyes, a bowl cut of graying hair, so that Maxine saw just how she'd look in twenty years—asking her about the night, how it had gone, and asking tonight how the new ballad had been received, the thing she was most interested to know since she had written it for them, as she wrote all their songs.

"The usual," Maxine said. "Farmers and cowboys." She sipped her rum and water. "Except we danced with Prince Charming, me and Edith did. He liked your ballad."

CHAPTER TWENTY-SIX

///

The mound was a hillock of mud, impossible to throw from, so Earl
was standing next to it on the wet infield grass, toeing the splinter of
wood he'd found by the bleachers, happy to pretend it was the pitching rubber. He wiggled his fingers inside the glove he'd borrowed
from the very fat, baby-faced boy squatting in a catcher's crouch and
waiting for him to throw his first pitch. Earlier, he'd handed the glove
to Earl with some ceremony, saying, "I'll warm you up," and adding,
"Name's Buck."

"Well, thanks, Buck."

"The glove," the boy had said. "The *glove*'s name's Buck. My name's
Arthur." Then he'd smiled sheepishly, as if to say, *Yeah, I know, but
that's its name.* He'd been orphaned at eight, his parents lost to the
influenza, and raised by his grandparents. He adored them both, especially the old man, who'd started naming everything as his demen-
tia worsened. He'd named the kitchen table Gerald; he'd named his
pillow Ruby, which was also his wife's name, so that she and the pillow
sometimes exchanged identities; he'd picked up his grandson's baseball glove one day a few weeks ago and handed it to him and said its
name was Buck.

A second boy, Clyde, stood ready to bat. He was tall, slender, and
fair as an albino, which made his facial features appear waiting to be
finished. He'd taken off his sweater and laid it on the grass, not caring
that it got wet, and attempted to fold it in the shape of a home plate.
Two more boys, Ellis and Walker, stood in the outfield. They were

stocky, redheaded brothers a year apart in age, their hair sticking up, disorganized, like something horticultural.

The four were close friends at Green River High School.

Earl hadn't set out to find a baseball field this morning. What he'd needed was to take a long walk in the early morning air. He'd waked with a hangover, which hadn't surprised him, and lain in bed listening for the faint clattering of cups and saucers that meant Horace Meadows was wheeling the coffee cart into the lounge.

When he'd gotten back from The Ship last night, he checked on Henry, found that he was sleeping, then fell into bed himself, and when he woke this morning, daylight just beginning, his head pounding, still dressed from last night, mud drying on his pants' cuffs, wearing his wet wool socks, what he'd thought of was Maxine's birthmark on her neck, how beautiful it looked, like an artful blot of ink, when he'd gotten close to it, their slow carousel, the three of them, along the bar to the door.

He'd drunk his coffee and thanked Horace Meadows. Just the two of them were awake, and he'd asked him to tell Henry he'd be back soon.

"I'll be going for provisions, just a few things," Meadows said. "If he'd like to come along, would that be all right?"

Earl had said of course it would.

"Don't go far," Horace Meadows said, and smiling, "like you could if you wanted to. But in my experience down through the years, I have a feeling we'll be cleared to leave early afternoon."

He'd stepped outside, picked a street, and started walking.

The sky was the sky it had been the day before. It was hard to believe there'd ever been another kind of weather. He paused to lift his face to the sun, its early heat and Meadows's coffee helping quickly. He'd walked aimlessly, turning left, right, block to block. His spirits were bright. He passed The Ship's unmarked door by chance—*Edith! Maxine!*—which made them even brighter. The village was quiet; it would begin to open in an hour or two, and what he heard was the river that gave the town its name. It traced a wide U, the settlement had grown inside it over time, and its waters, normally a lazy trickle, were racing and boiling.

As he walked, he'd kept his eye on the horizon line of mountains. There they were, looking just as he'd pictured them, behind the night, from the train. At other times, in other light, their grayness was severe, and it was easy to think there was no more world beyond them, no world worth seeking, that they were the pitted, crevassed face of the end of things. But the sun this morning was giving them a pearlescence.

He started along a muddy street, and after a block he saw a small, stooped figure moving slowly up ahead. As he got nearer, he could see that the man was elegantly dressed in autumn-colored tweeds. His silver sideburns shone beneath a black velvet derby that fit him like a crown. *Another stranded passenger, and a rich one*, Earl thought, and he was about to call to him when the man turned down an intersecting street and disappeared.

Earl continued on, and after a few blocks he'd seen the baseball field laid out at the town's northern edge, bleachers along each foul line, the fenceless outfield running until it turned to scrub grass. As he approached, he'd seen the boys playing catch behind second base, the field a virtual wetlands glistening in the sun.

He'd stopped to watch, leaning against the bleachers along the first base line. Their form as they threw and caught the ball was engrained, expert, smoothly calisthenic. This was true even for the fat one; in fact, especially for him.

He'd watched them unobserved, with pleasure, grateful to be feeling human again, feeling strong. He sensed that impatience that had started in him, sensed it going deeper, and mattering, an even greater clarity about it.

He'd watched for several minutes until an impulse took him.

They'd seen him from a distance walking toward them, and they thought he was someone from the school sent out to look for truants. When the deluge had ended so abruptly, it felt to everyone in Green

River like a holiday. So the four had decided yesterday they would skip school tomorrow, and here they were, first thing in the morning, with their gloves and four baseballs and Clyde's black bat.

"Shit," said Ellis, one of the redheaded brothers.

"Anybody know him?" Clyde had asked.

"Ignore him," Walker, the other brother, said.

"Great idea," Arthur said. "That way he won't see us." His smile had been a friend's, his voice teasing, not sarcastic.

When Earl reached them, he'd introduced himself, and they had too, wary, monotone grunts with their names somewhere in them. Earl explained he was a passenger, waiting to leave, which gave him at least some credibility in their eyes, for they all four felt the only excuse for being in Green River was if you were waiting to leave.

Earl asked, "You all heard about the washed-out tracks?"

They all said they had, and Earl had smiled at the thought of what they'd say, how they'd react, if they knew Babe Ruth and Lou Gehrig were here. It would be as if he told them God and Jesus were stranded in Green River.

Then he'd asked, how about his joining them. "I'll throw you all some pitches to hit, take your turn."

They'd looked at him suspiciously. He was wearing the old brown cardigan Emily had crudely knitted and his stained gray fedora, and together they made him appear older than he was and frankly like a tramp.

"You ever done it?" Clyde asked.

"Not really," Earl said. He shook his head. "I was watching you all. It looks pretty easy."

They'd exchanged glances, amused at his ignorance, and wordlessly agreed they'd indulge him until his arm got stiff and sore, which would not take long. The day and their freedom made them see themselves as generous, and the sky helped too, the sun sending down its beneficent light.

It was then that Arthur said, "I'll warm you up," nodding toward the bleachers where his catcher's mitt lay while taking off the glove he'd been using and offering it to Earl along with the smile that said, *I know, but that's its name.*

They'd started throwing to each other, Earl and Arthur. The spongy earth behind second base made squishing sounds when they planted their feet on their follow-throughs. The other three were watching, and they'd all been shocked to see that Earl was not what they'd assumed. They'd followed his arm coming through and the ball leaving his hand with a life they couldn't spot the source of. He'd claimed to be a passenger from somewhere going somewhere else, and that at least helped explain it. Because you'd need to be from somewhere to know how to throw a baseball like that.

"Where do you like it?" Earl called to Clyde, and the boy looked vacantly back at him.

"Your pitch," Earl said. "You like it high? Low? Outside? In?"

"Oh, low and outside," Clyde said, and he pointed with the black bat to a spot in the air.

Earl wound and threw and Clyde watched the ball coming at an easy speed just where he'd asked for it, and he sent a line drive to right field, where Walker scooped it up and wiped the ball on the bib of his overalls, then threw it back.

They did it again, and then again, and again. Ten pitches, fifteen, twenty. The swing, the echoing knock of sound, the ball in play, the cadence so simple, each time just the same, and each time new inside the sameness.

Clyde finished, Walker hurried in, and Earl was feeling a warmth that wasn't only the sun's. This was what he'd sensed he needed—this thing unfolding purely through a morning nearing noon—when he'd leaned against the bleachers and watched these enviable lives, poised unknowingly between their boyhoods and the world.

The pitch, the hit, and the ball lifting, the ball skidding through the soggy infield, the ball moving through the air on a low line. They began to cheer for Earl, and when one of them swung and missed, the others chided him for swinging like a girl, like a rusty gate, like Ellis and Walker's mean grandmother brandishing her broom. They'd forgotten that Earl was a passenger from somewhere going some-where else. They'd forgotten that the only reason to be in Green River was to leave it. What mattered was this stranger's being here now to throw his perfect pitches, and it had begun to matter to Earl too, beyond the simple way he'd thought it would. There'd been the lure of his returning growing in his mind, the push when he'd sensed he was traveling toward just that, toward his return, and the pulse of impatience taking hold and getting stronger. But now there was this as well—what was it?—this wish, and not a simple one, to stay right here, inside what he'd found, with nothing come before it and nothing coming after.

Ellis, redheaded Ellis, had been hitting for a while when he stepped away and pointed down to Arthur in his catcher's crouch and said to Earl, "Artie ain't hit yet!"

"Oh," Earl said. "Sure." He'd in a sense forgotten about him, the boy catching him so subtly he'd become invisible—yes, very large, kind Arthur, disappeared into his quiet skills—and too polite to stand up and say it was his time to have a turn.

First, he needed to stretch. He bent to touch his toes, then stood straight and flexed his knees. He took some practice swings, exhaling loudly, air through his nostrils like a horse. As he waited, Earl looked to the bleachers where maybe twenty people were gathered. He'd been aware of their arriving, one and then another, two or three couples, more refugees from the trains no doubt, taking a walk and looking for anything to pass an hour before they left this afternoon, if Horace Meadows's experience down through the years was right.

There'd been a smattering of applause if a pitch was hit hard, but it was dutiful clapping, a kind of patrons' amusement, nothing really heartfelt.

Arthur gave Earl his bashful smile to signal he was ready, and Earl asked his question. Where did he like the ball?

"It don't matter really," Arthur said, but he said it deferentially.

Earl's pitch was down the middle and just above the knees, and Arthur's swing so quick and violent all you saw was its completion, his gaze already lifted to find the ball in the sky, and the black bat in his left hand trailing as casually as a song-and-dance man's cane.

There were sounds from the bleachers, the calls genuine now, real whistles of surprise.

Earl had spun around to watch Walker chasing after it and sending up sprays of water from the soaked grass with each stride. He heard the boy's laughter sounding thrilled as he ran and ran to retrieve it.

Surprised, impressed, Earl looked back at Arthur, who seemed neither. He was taking slow practice swings, his eyes following the bat through a patient sweep, making tiny adjustments like a tinkering machinist.

Earl pitched, and Arthur hit half a dozen balls to left and center field, none as high or as far as the first one, but carrying so much farther than any his friends had managed. Clyde and Walker had backed up twenty yards, and their shouts and laughter each time Arthur hit one said that they, like Ellis behind the soaking home-plate sweater, had been waiting for this. That they'd witnessed their friend's great gift in so many games, and every time their excitement was the first time they'd felt it, for how could you truly remember someone's being that good? No matter how often you'd seen it, it was always a surprise.

Now Arthur swung, and the cheers from the bleachers were involuntary *oooh!*s as the ball rose. Earl lost it against the backdrop of pearl-lacquered mountains, and he could only watch Walker running far into the scrub grass, where it came to rest against a glorious bush with long stiff spears, sprouting up confused like Walker's hair.

Earl gave his next pitches even more—airing out his fastball, his curve dropping twelve to six, just the same drop every time, and *him* deciding, not the ball—and Arthur's strength and his timing and his eye were alive to the challenge of baseballs coming at him with a vicious finesse. A kind of catechism with each pitch and swing, and Earl was feeling it strongly—their deepening duel, they were rivals and allies, their focus more and more intense and taking the two of them to a place where they were by themselves.

Arthur's friends were feeling it too. In the outfield, Clyde and Walker sensed they should run harder, try to catch whatever Arthur hit, while Ellis was ducking every pitch Earl threw. The ball's speed, its baffling movement, there was no way he could catch one, but he hustled after it uncomplaining as it caromed off the wooden backstop. *Thud! Thud!* This was a game the boys had never played, and they weren't sure of the rules. They weren't sure it *was* a game. They weren't sure there *were* rules.

Earl threw a fastball with a late, skipping life, and Arthur swung underneath it, then quickly got ready. A kind of solemn elation was driving him. He watched the balls he hit well, watched them soaring, and this pleased him, of course, a muscle-pleasure running through him and finishing in his chest. But when he swung and missed, it meant there was another thing to learn, and in a real sense this felt even better. All there was he hadn't known, hadn't seen, and Earl giving him the chance by wanting to throw it past him and wanting it to teach him, and Earl starting to know too what this was teaching *him* when he threw just the pitch he wanted, watched it bite and dive exactly, and Arthur hit it to Montana.

It was unfair to his friends, how long he'd been hitting, and Arthur felt guilty for it, but he sensed that if he stopped, if he held up his hands and said he'd had his share of swings and more, he'd be leaving something incomplete, unfinished. When, until not that long ago, his grandfather's mind was sharp, he used to tell him that his good humor was his strength, and his weakness was letting that good humor get in the way of what he needed when he needed it, and he had to learn how not to let that happen. And here, Arthur's instincts told him, was what his grandfather had been talking about.

Earl's first spitter ambled through the air like an ancient, seemed not so much to break as lose its balance on the way, and Arthur, badly fooled, had finished his tremendous swing before the pitch arrived. And only then did Earl see it. Arthur's great size and with it somehow his agility. The ferocious ballet of his uppercut swing. He was Babe Ruth as a boy; right-handed, it was true, but he was Ruth at seventeen at St. Mary's Industrial School for the Orphaned, the Indigent, the Wayward, and the Incorrigible, lost in his love for the game, besotted, and knowing he was blessed to be so skilled at playing it.

Earl shook his head and laughed. A deep, full laugh as at a wonderful joke: It was fifteen years ago, and he was pitching to young Ruth.

He glanced again toward the bleachers. There were more people now, maybe twice as many, and among them there sat Henry, with Horace Meadows, and a burlap bag between them, provisions. For a jarring moment, Earl felt this didn't fit. The stuff of the morning had beckoned him. And he had let it take him, moving further and further into it, and it briefly felt as if Henry were here to interrupt it, or perhaps to watch him leaving, that he'd come to see him off. It could be both, it could be either, and Earl stood still for a moment, waiting for his mind to be his compass, for his thoughts to find their balance. He raised his hand and gave a small wave. Henry returned it, and there was Meadows's sharp salute.

Earl set himself.

He was here in Green River pitching to Arthur, pitching to young Ruth, the three friends gone quiet in their respect for the turn the day had taken.

He was in Sioux City, facing the great man, watching him about to stumble through a hapless swing at the perfect fade-away he was winding up to throw him.

He rocked and wound, and he felt all caution coming free, a permission so clear it was as if he heard its voice. He changed his grip and his arm came through, the screw ball breaking in, under Arthur's hands and on past Ellis. *Thud!*

From the bleachers, Henry heard it as the sound of his father's early morning pitches against the side of their barn, pitches to the rectangle his mother had hurried to paint.

Arthur looked out at Earl. "What was that? What did you just throw me?"

And Earl saw the word printed on the bleached-out page. He said, "A fade-away."

Arthur smiled. "Fade-away? But it breaks *in*."

Earl smiled. *Yeah, I know. But that's its name.* "Not if you hit left-handed," he said.

"Oh, right. Of course," Arthur said.

"I'll throw you another one."

He was in Riverton, and Saul Weintraub just arrived, grateful for the game to distract him from his mourning.

He wound, and he could hear Arthur saying, "Fade-away, fade-away," an infatuated meter as if to help him time the pitch, but he couldn't read its spin or judge its speed or track its movement. He held up his hand and called to Earl. "How do you throw it?"

Earl showed him, the counterclockwise torque, the snap of the wrist.

You hear stories, Weintraub said, but *who knows, all that may be apocryphal.* And the following Sunday Earl had asked the librarian to look *that* up for him as well. *Apocryphal.* He had no idea how to spell it. He'd found *cocksure* on his own.

He threw more screwballs to Arthur, fade-away, fade-away, fade-away, he heard the singsong of the word, whether Arthur's voice or in his own mind, and Arthur started to hit some of them. Swings and misses still, and dribblers on the ground that spun like tops, but crisp liners too, and Ellis and Walker chasing balls down and picking balls out of the air.

He was in Waterloo, standing on the mound and wishing for rain, about to throw a pitch at the batter's ribs, and feeling gut-sick with Emily's words in his head saying she was too afraid.

He was standing on the mound of the weedy infield between the rows of miners' shacks in Evans every Sunday, spring to autumn, nearly dawn to dark.

He felt it all, and all the places. He was everywhere he'd pitched, with no need for where he hadn't, and his fantasy was Henry's—that this simply continue. A pitch and then another to this glad bear of a boy.

Earl glanced once more to the stands, entertained by the idea of Weintraub sitting there in his soiled linen suit, surveying those around him and awarding dictionary names, his lips pursed like a bud about to bloom with something droll. But Earl could not conjure him, and what he saw instead, sitting high up by himself, was the elegant old man in the autumn-colored tweeds, his black derby resting in his lap. In the length of a moment, a deep, slow breath, Earl invented the old man's life, and he'd remember him this way until the day he couldn't. The scout, it's how the finest scouts looked and dressed these days, passing through and stranded in Green River, like all the rest of them, and happening on a game and thanking his lucky stars as he watched this boy—no doubt he'd lose the baby fat, and what he didn't wouldn't matter, that was clear—watched him hit baseballs high into the sky, flying toward the mountains.

Earl threw a fastball, the purest pitch to throw. Not the screwball, the fade-away, not the curve, no arm contorted, no elbow sharply angled. He'd been throwing for more than an hour, almost two, nine innings worth of pitches, and his arm was very tired. So he threw the fastball, trying for more than he had left, for his own sake and for Arthur's and the old scout's in the bleachers, and he heard and felt the pop, the sound and pain together, fire in his elbow and through muscle into bone. He thought he shouted, gave a scream, he wasn't sure, maybe he'd been able to keep it inside him. He bent over, his arm tucked against his body. He held this pose, a courtier's bow, waiting on the pain to lessen so he could stand up straight, but it didn't, so he lowered himself awkwardly and sat down in the wet grass.

He looked past Arthur and Ellis starting cautiously toward him, confused looks on their smooth, young faces, and he saw Henry and Horace Meadows scrambling from their seats. He saw the bleachers behind them slowly emptying as well, the forty, fifty people following after Henry in an orderly fashion. He saw the elegant old man slide-stepping his way to the end of his row.

They all were coming, with Henry out in front, his face blank with alarm, the face he'd shown Earl when he'd fallen. Earl's mind was on the pain, but the quickest thought got through—that if it had been another crowd that day, slow and civilized, decorous like this one, someone would have calmly reached down and helped Henry to his feet, and then the afternoon resuming, people settling in again and waiting as he readied himself to throw Ruth another pitch.

He closed his eyes—he heard the crowd coming, the courteous murmurs of concern, the quick, soft-shuffling steps in the wet grass; he pictured the elegant old man somehow getting to him first—and he opened them again just as Henry reached him.

BOOK THREE

///

Henry

1948

The world your eyes see is the world as it really is,
and you and I are going to live in it forever,
and we will hitchhike to the Painted Hills together,
and hop a freight back home.

—VIJAY SESHADRI, "Your Living Eyes"

CHAPTER TWENTY-SEVEN

Retrospection   *The farm*

My father tore his bicep severely our last morning in Green River, pitching to the boy whose name, I learned, was Arthur. The tendon that attached the muscle to the bone above the crook in his elbow was nearly ripped free; a mere thread of tissue held it. It can happen, he was told by the doctor who saw him there, when a muscle is exhausted and the motion that exhausts it is repeated many times without pausing to rest. He relayed all this to me back in the Pullman, his arm in a sling, and I remember him saying, "Now that would just about describe it, wouldn't it," or something close to that. To my surprise, he sounded more than anything amused, air and lightness in his voice. Sometimes I hear it as self-mocking, as if he'd got just what he deserved for such foolish behavior. Sometimes I hear him poking fun at the doctor for stating the obvious in such detail. No matter which, I see him smiling wearily, feeling real pain I presume, though he assured me he wasn't.

We all crowded into the Pullman lounge to say good-bye, my father and I traveling east, the four of them west on the repaired tracks into Utah, Zane Grey's Utah, and across the Great Salt Lake to the Sierras, then south, virtually the length of California. I felt dizzy, and I was fighting sobs. If I understood that we had to return, my far truer wish refused to see why Christy Walsh couldn't simply hire a doctor to travel with us and tend to my father as we continued west. I'm sure I thought he wanted this as much as I did.

Two moments have stayed with me. I don't recall anything that Ruth or Christy Walsh said as we were leaving, but I remember being tempted to take Gehrig aside and confess I'd told him some things that weren't true. That in her fevered confusion, my mother hadn't asked to have me next to her in bed as she was dying. That there'd been no long article describing the reckless bravery of my father and me as we tried to buoy her spirits and rally her strength. And no newspaper photograph of my father holding me. It wasn't that I wanted to relieve my guilt, one I really hadn't felt, but that, because he'd been so incredibly kind to me, he had *saved* me after all, he had called me brave, I owed him the truth. But I decided to say nothing, telling myself that he'd seemed for some reason to need to believe my wild stories, and so it felt that *not* to tell him I had lied was what I owed him.

Then, as my father and I were stepping out onto the platform at the rear of the Pullman, Horace Meadows bent down to me. He surely saw and sensed my sadness, and he said, "Remember, Mr. Henry, it's not a little Creole boy alive wouldn't wait in line his whole life to have yours for an hour." I heard his words sounding once again as if sung, and I heard them too—with the echo of something unforgettable he'd said to me the night before—as an assurance I would manage the life I had ahead of me just fine, even if I didn't have the Lord's best recipe of blood flowing in my veins.

I remember its being early evening when our eastbound train arrived. We rose from the thickly varnished bench inside the little depot—I'd been fixed on the names, the brainless obscenities, the paired plus-signed initials inside valentine hearts, carved into the wood—and now my feelings were beating inside me like a second, frantic heart. My life was being lifted off the ground and flipped over in an instant, and there was nothing I could do but hold on for all the world. I'd felt this same sensation, of things wholly upended, the morning we'd boarded the Pullman in Sioux City, but with the opposite sense then of a tremulous elation I was trying to contain without really wanting to. I'd felt, as Horace Meadows stepped forward to welcome us, that I was leaving a world I knew completely for one that was filled with everything I didn't. And through the days that followed, I'd felt a blessedness, a kind of christened status. But for all that had been magically conferred, having it end so abruptly reminded me that I was a little boy with no voice whatsoever in the matters of his life.

We were regular passengers returning, no Pullman with all its luxuries, and at first my seat felt hard, punitive, after the deep-cushioned pillows and chairs my pampered little butt had gotten used to. But I soon realized how miserable I would feel in a Pullman with new people, interlopers, squatters, who'd have no idea how poorly they compared to the company I'd known, and I'd have to be polite to them even so.

We traveled, then, back across the country, following the very route that had taken us far away. And it came to matter to me, as I looked out and watched the landscape in reverse, that I make sure our retracing it did not erase it, did not erase those days. That this effort was somehow essential. Actually, this seems too sophisticated a thought for me to have had then, but I'm going to give it to me anyway, a boy turning ten who'd just lived a lyrical adventure of dream and desire across a time outside of time. Which was the phrase I heard my father use in the next few years when someone asked him what that time had been like.

"Oh, well," he'd say, "it was a time *outside* of time," then smile, and often say no more, let it stand as that, seeming very pleased to be offering this enigma.

Rock Springs, Rawlins, Arlington, all the other little towns I hadn't seen traveling west in the darkness and the rain. But when we reached Nebraska, this was countryside like what I'd known, and what I'd watched streaming past in daylight. And now it seemed to me that we were sneaking up on it from behind, on the settlements we passed through, surprising them for arriving at their back doors when they'd been expecting to welcome us at their front. I'd have this sense of misdirection all the way home.

When I picture my father after we were back, I see his movements as watchful, appraising, feline; yes, that's it, moving with the patrolling elegance of a Bernard. As though, if he stayed vigilant, whatever disappointment, whatever might be threatening to go wrong, wouldn't happen. And along with my emotions, I continued to assume he must be feeling just what I was. So I might have watched him pause on the stairs, halt his step, looking around, affably attuned, and presumed I was seeing him mapping in his mind everywhere he'd been and where he was once again and asking himself how it all could make any sort of sense, those days flowing somehow reasonably into these. For I was doing that very thing in *my* mind.

With all I'd experienced, the world of change I felt inside me, it was as if I'd been gone for years from—as Horace Meadows had said of our accommodations—my cozy and, in its way, handsomely appointed life.

I don't recall that my father had surgery, and if he didn't, I don't know how rare that would have been. And I don't remember a cast, only the sling—can that be right?—until, I think, some time that winter, which would have made him virtually useless as a partner in the work of the farm. I'm sure he managed to pull a cow's teat and wring a chicken's neck and toss the slop vegetables at the feet of the hogs, but nothing much more skillful, more dexterous than that.

The day he returned from the doctor with his arm freed, we gathered in the kitchen to celebrate. My grandmother had made a chocolate cake. I'm sure I'm wrong seeing lit candles on it, and I remember my grandparents and me clapping as he slipped his arm out of its shirt sleeve and presented it to us, flexing the muscle jokingly like a boxing movie brute. The arm looked delicate to me, exposed, fresh as something newly born, and I reached to touch the bicep. "Does it hurt when I do that?" I asked him.

He smiled and said it didn't, but that he couldn't believe how much strength it had lost. He said, "And it feels like it's separate from the rest of me. I have to say 'Hey, arm!' and get its attention before I tell it what to do." He laughed then and said, his face lifting as if on some brightly lit past moment, "Maybe I'll *name* it, and it'll come when I call it." I see him; I see his healing arm; I see all of him feeling freed that day.

And I use it, that day, to mark the change in him, from the watchful sentry to a man emanating an ever more accessible ease. That is to say, the person he'd *always* been for me. But even more and beyond that to a new realm of calm, an agile simplicity in his bearing. Of course, this change as I describe it would have occurred not in a day but gradually, and beginning when it was still undetectable.

I ask myself how, at my age, I could have recognized it, even if I had no guess as to the cause. I think I likely saw and heard nothing really tangible, no altered ways or words that could have signaled this change. But when you love someone as I love him, I might, as a child, have simply willed into being what something—call it a primal intuition—told me he deserved; the clarity of a settled heart, which he had more than earned.

Looking back, I believe what had taken hold was his knowing at last that he was done with a dream that had long been done with him. That he'd found a way, his way, to live not in the past but with it. Which may have set him free to miss only my mother and his life with her.

At one point on the train, returning, he began to reminisce. Maybe the aspirin he was taking wasn't helping enough, and he was trying to talk over the pain, to take himself away from it. Maybe there wasn't so much pain after all. But all I heard was his affection for what he was remembering as he described his first times on a train. (And I thought of Ruth's telling me as we sat in the dugout in Denver of *his* first train, and that I'd better believe it was, unlike mine, no damn Pullman.) He remembered riding in an empty boxcar across the Midwest countryside, or at least nearly empty, just him and a family of courteous rats who stayed mostly nested in loose straw in their corner. And then he spoke of riding the glorious elevated trains in Chicago, of passing incredibly close to tenement windows. One, and then the next, lined up as if for the event of his moving slowly past them.

He said he'd never been quite sure just why he'd found this so compelling, beyond what was obvious—the chance to peek in, to spy, for a blink of a moment. But he felt sure it was something about the *news* of other lives he felt the people living in those rooms were showing him.

(Other mysteries, I hear him saying now, other fierce immersions in the blunt work of survival.)

I believe, as I've just said, that our trip, *his* trip, his experience of it, caused him to leave behind any vestige of his life before the one he began here with my mother. That he came to see it as like the lives he'd glimpsed in those rooming-house windows, and still compelling to him because it was no longer his. He could *wonder* about it, the mystery of it.

I listened raptly to him recalling those times, those trains, and I imagined them as like amusement park rides on a magically more ambitious scale than the roller coaster whose giddy challenge I'd failed to meet. "Dad!" I said. "I never knew you did any of that!"

"And now you do," he said. His smile was mischievous.

I didn't consider what this said about him as a vagabond in his young life. In fact, I don't remember what, if anything, I imagined about him, his life as a boy, of being particularly intrigued to learn about his childhood, and I would never know all that much, truth be told. I think that, growing up, I felt him in the present, entirely, and the notion of his life before—beyond, outside his being there in front of me, surrounding me—it didn't really occur. You might think it would be the opposite. That because he defined my life so fully, I'd be keen to know his history. But I suspect there are some children, I know I was one, who aren't all that curious about the pasts of the essential people in their lives, don't really understand the past as a world of its own, filled with fortune and loss, blessings and calamities, with richly inhabited, unfathomable events, since they themselves haven't had one yet.

As for my father's parents, or rather their absence, I suspect I just assumed he'd lost them to the Spanish flu.

But lately, with all that has happened, and with what I *do* know about the hard years of his growing up, from allusions my grandparents have made, which they'd gleaned from those he'd made to them, I can't help but wonder if at some point he went back.

If he ever did, I imagine him making this decision some months after we returned, with both his arm and his past newly freed from what had held them. That he felt, with this freedom, a kind of emotional momentum, the idea that he had the chance, that he could turn now to the other unfinished experience of his life. And so he journeyed back, knowing nothing of what he'd find. I imagine him stopping several times along the way, pulling to the side of the road, becoming highly animated and vocal as he argued with himself that no good could come of it. Arguing that if his father had died, that would only be as he'd thought of him since the day he left. Or, if he were very ill, that would invite the temptation to treat him with a certain deference, that dignity the dying deserve, but not him, not his dying. Arguing that if his meanness had kept him energetically alive, more or less who he had been, why would he wish to revisit that for so much as an hour, unless for the chance to thank him for making it so clear he had to flee?

I know nothing that helps me imagine what he found. But when I think through the likelihood of his traveling home, I can and I do believe that, once he returned, he'd have felt all the more how thankful he was for the ways that Rooster had long been his father.

That first spring back, he told us the doctor felt, and he agreed, that the risk of reinjuring his arm if he pitched was too great. I see the two of us that summer—and for some summers after—very rarely sitting in the stands to watch games. And him watching, when he did, from a quiet remove. And what followed inevitably the next year was his decision that simply too much time had passed. That he couldn't hope to reclaim what he'd had. I hear his voice explaining this calmly, evenly, saying in this manner what only made sense.

We still played catch, and he would pitch to me almost whenever I asked him, and as I grew I came to be able to hit what he threw pretty well, pretty far. The day I'd watched him throwing to Arthur in Green River, going to the edge of all he had and pitching past it, the two of them urging each other to a contesting eloquence, I'm sure I assumed that's what I could look forward to. That there'd be many times as I got older, stronger, when he and I would be lost in our version of that contest.

But those times never came. If I asked him to throw harder, put more on his pitches, he'd say his arm was a little stiff, and anyway what he enjoyed was a casual catch, an easy batting practice. He good-naturedly refused to make it more than that, and eventually I gave up and stopped asking.

For years, after we returned, my grandfather's days started with him helping—the milking, the feeding, joining my father in the fields—and after a few hours, when gripping reins and levers and handles became too hard, retreating to the porch to watch the world aggressively.

I would look for him there when I got home from school. And while we talked and sat in silence and I rolled a supply of cigarettes for him, a task I took to be an artisanal craft, and we looked out past the sloping lawn and the barnyard to the fields, I began to ask him questions about the way the work got done. Why a field lay fallow. Why corn in this one and not soybeans. Why those hogs, rooting unwittingly with all the others, sent off to slaughter. I'd always helped with simple chores without giving them a thought. But my interest began to be lively, as if the farm were a subject in school that had suddenly caught my attention. I don't know entirely where my enthusiasm came from. But with my grandfather less and less able, and my father newly mended (and it was how I thought of him for some time after he'd healed, as *newly mended*), I'm sure I held fast to the romantic notion that I must come to their rescue. For that was the sort of adolescent I became. In any event, I began to immerse myself in my new subject.

A rare very hot early afternoon in spring; I've no idea the year, but at some point after my interest had started. My father was plowing the field closest to the house when he reined the mule and called to me in the yard. I thought this meant he was thirsty, and I hurried to the pump with a bucket and tin cup we kept ready on the porch, then out to the field, stumbling in places over the loosely clodded ground, water sloshing in the bucket.

When I got to him and set the bucket down, he took the cup, then pointed at the mule. "What do you see?"

I looked, confused, where he was pointing. "Just Charlotte," I said, meaning the mule. I felt sure it wasn't the answer he was looking for, but I couldn't imagine what was.

He bent to dip the cup, nodding as he did, and drank, several swallows, his Adam's apple moving, then handed the cup to me. While I drank, he said, "I feel obliged to point out, what a farmer sees when he looks at the world all day is not the vast horizon." He swept the sky with his arm as he said this. "When I met your grandfather, and he was trying to tell me how great farming was, that's all he could talk about. Glorious days under the skies. The vast horizon." He shook his head, "Unh-uh," and his smile was starting as he raised the cup to his lips again. "You're right," and he pointed to Charlotte. "What you see all day is the ass end of a mule."

He started to laugh, and I did too. The phrase by itself was enough to make *me* laugh.

He signaled Charlotte, who started off, and I walked along beside him through the field toward the infinite wonder of my grandfather's horizon. I was chuckling to myself—*the ass end of a mule; the ass end of a mule*—now that he had said it, there *was* nothing else to see.

We continued along inside a smiling silence, the plow turning the earth and drawing a furrow, bright birdsong in the distance. The sun, as I said, was very hot. He was sweating freely, and had been, his denim shirt spotted with wet stains, but my own sweat was just starting, and I was glad for it, for the comradely sense it helped me to feel.

I hear us trading small talk, nothing memorable, and we were nearing the end of the field when he said, "I was thinking this morning, how long it's been since I pretended a mule was anything but a mule."

I looked at him then, confused and deeply curious, waiting to hear more as we got to the field's end rows, but his concentration went to steering Charlotte and the plow as he moved them through a turn around and we started back.

We were walking west now, into the full sun, but it was high and we didn't need to squint in its direction. And then he said, adding, "I mean how long it's been since I pretended I was doing something else."

"What are you saying?" I asked.

"Just that." He said this with a no-big-deal tone in his voice. There was a faraway but highly pleased expression on his face, and that told me he was done, that there was nothing more he wished to say about it.

Over the years, I've heard those words in my mind many times, and wondered what inspired him to share them with me, just then, that day. I've felt that he was asking more of me than I had at that age and with my inexperience, more than I could possibly bring to bear on what he'd said, expecting me to hear it in its context, sense its nuance. And I've never been able to decide if he spoke them with nostalgia or regret or satisfaction. As much as I can hear them in my memory, his tone has some of all those things. And why wouldn't they all be in it? Aren't they the very stuff of our complicated feelings toward so much of our lives when we see them in review?

When I think of the span of his working life, I first see a boy who performed the most brutal of men's work in the mines, and then, once he became a farmer, a man doing a man's. And in between he was a man whose work was a boy's; at its best, it was play that mattered utterly, and he found his way to it again for a morning in Green River.

So the next years passed.

Each fall, with the other boys—some my age, some older, a few even younger, more than a dozen altogether—I left our country school classroom, none of us returning until our families' and our neighbors' harvests were finished. These became my happiest days, days of lessons and learning I'd come to want far more than school's.

Somewhere in these years, our ancient obese beagle died. I found him by the corncrib, lying on his back, the sun shining on his plumbing, as Horace Meadows's refrain had it.

I helped my father more, and once I graduated, our partnership grew, increasingly one of equals, until that's what it became.

My grandfather talked of feeling some days that the land was mocking him for what he couldn't any longer do. And other days, that it was asking for his care as only he could give it. And most days, that it didn't give a good goddamn one way or another.

There were times, most often unusually busy harvests, when we needed—and frequently still need—help beyond our neighbors', and we were lucky to find Thomas Vanderkamp, a Dutch immigrant who somehow ended up in Hinton and who's been happy to work for us, and for several others, according to the needs of a farmer and his season. He's a quiet giant of a man, looking perennially sunburned, and with a magnificent scar that runs diagonally from his forehead, across his nose, to his jaw. None of us has ever felt it was our place to ask him about it if he didn't raise the subject, and in all the years he hasn't, so we haven't. But of course we've all imagined, made up stories, how he got it. Mine has him fighting, bayonet to bayonet, a German in a trench in a raid in the Great War.

On a warm night in July in 1939, I was sitting in the Orpheum Theater in Sioux City. I forget the movie that was showing, forget entirely, for first a newsreel of Lou Gehrig's farewell filled the screen.

It showed a hot, muggy Fourth of July at Yankee Stadium, its three decks, with their scalloped trim, completely filled. I'd read that he'd announced his retirement, his record of consecutive games played coming to an end. But I was stunned at his appearance as he stood shyly near home plate, where a man was arranging a copse of microphones. I'd watched him on the same theater screen just a year before, playing, and really not all that badly, a cowboy in *Rawhide*, looking fit and powerful in his Western outfit. But here I saw a wraith—gaunt, slumped, his pinstriped uniform hanging loosely from his frame, his belt tightly cinched, his pants billowing like pantaloons. He was holding his cap in his hands and wringing it nervously, staring down at the ground as the man spoke into the microphones. He looked like a boy about to get a scolding he knew he deserved, as if his life of strapping strength, his physical brilliance, had all been a whopping fib he'd told the world, and now he'd been caught red-handed.

Many of his retired teammates were there, forming a line of tribute behind him, and I spotted Ruth right away, standing out in a white, double-breasted linen suit.

I watched Gehrig being coaxed to the microphones. He shuffled forward, scratching his head as if he'd just woken up, the aw-shucks ignorance of a Grand Ole Opry hayseed.

The tale of my father and me—the game, my fall and very near miss, our traveling on that fancy train with Lou Gehrig and Babe Ruth—was the best one Hinton had ever had and ever would. There was something in the color and settled legend of it, as if we'd been swept up by famous aliens and as suddenly returned, with my father injured and never pitching again. For the most part, the story had become like an heirloom in the attic that the family no longer needed to get down and pass around, though it was highly pleased just to know it was up there.

But every now and then I was asked about it. To settle an argument: Was it Ruth or Gehrig who'd scooped me up? Or even a request to give a quick but detailed retelling of the day, as someone asks the piano player to play a favorite tune, then hums along and mouths the lyrics. I'd honed the story over time, some details falling away and others, more vivid ones, coming forward, always starting by saying that my grandfather had a hat that made him look like Calvin Coolidge.

But the very sick man I watched on the screen that night was not the one in my story, and I decided that to tell it any longer would be, among other things, a lie. I haven't been asked more than a few times since, but when I have, I've said it happened so long ago and I was just a kid, and I really don't remember much about it. People seem to believe me when they hear this, not that it matters to me if they do.

When I was very young, my mother often spoke to me in my imagination, offering her praise for something completely ordinary I'd done. The panache with which I laced and tied my shoes. My bravery when I tossed a madly pecking hen from her nest so I could get to the eggs she was sitting on. That sort of thing. In my fantasies, she was a kind of spectral admirer, certainly my greatest, commenting on my brilliant successes from where she sat in her prime viewing location, a low mezzanine in the sky.

She returned to me at times once I became my father's real partner in the fields. She complimented me for the way I could read the earth's details. Could see how finely it had broken, note the gradient depth and several blacks of the newly turned soil. Could feel the resistance of a plow blade and know immediately whether it was set too deep or too shallow. I heard her praising me lavishly for all of this.

I still do. It's not so much that I imagine her voice, hear her watchful praise, but at times I sense the harmony of her presence when I'm otherwise alone in a field with the work (which does lead to her speaking her approval now and then, I admit. *That's a pretty field of beans you've planted this year*). As a child, I felt I knew her only as someone dying, an awful intimacy; I had no sense of her alive in her life as, from everything I've gathered, she so richly was. But over time—with what I've understood and intuited about my parents' history—I've come to think of her as someone whose absorbing ambitions were, like mine, local ones. For me, the fascination of a field is the illusion it gives of running to earth's end, until you're reminded that finally it's fenced, and then it gets still more interesting, that paradox you can feel it offering—an endless freedom within the limits of the land. And I think, though I can't know, of my mother as a woman who saw life in somewhat the same way. That what drew her to hers was the chance to find new and deeper pleasures in repeated rewards. Or to realize the pleasures were in great part in their sameness.

The sixth of May 1944, at the day's-end milking, I was working in the stall next to my father, a rough-hewn, loosely boarded wall between us. I heard him moving on his stool, and when I raised my eyes I saw that he was standing; the wall between us came just to his chest. The expression on his face seemed to be in conflict with itself, as if he were trying to explain something complicated to me, but he didn't know quite what that was or what to say about it. "I'm dizzy," he said finally.

I stood and reached across and took him by the shoulders. "You okay?"

"Everything," he said.

"What, Dad? What about everything?"

"Everything . . . moved, too far away."

One of his hands was resting on the Guernsey's flank, and he was holding the full pail of milk in his other.

He said again, "Too far away." His eyes were looking past me in the barn's gloaming light. Then the pail was on the floor, tipped on its side, and we both watched the milk spreading and soaking the straw. We simply stood there watching it, each of us confused for our reasons by what had just happened.

"I'll have to take it out of your wages," I said.

"How'd I do that?" he asked, and, unlike mine, his voice wasn't straining to make a joke of it. He sounded mystified, but also impressed with himself, as if he couldn't believe he'd pulled off such a difficult trick. He began to move his hands, up and down, back and forth, his face curious now, as much that as concerned. He looked like a marionette of himself, as though guiding his hands and arms with strings from above.

He said, "Like the *sling*," and I somehow understood. He meant the way his arm had felt separate from the rest of him when it was first free. He managed a weak, confounded laugh. He raised a hand to his mouth and began to pat it as if to brush away cake crumbs. "Am I smiling?" His speech was beginning to slur.

"Yes, you are," I said. "Of course you are."

"Good."

But I was lying; his expression had become just one thing, he looked purely afraid, and I sensed him going limp. I felt this starting in his shoulders, and I watched it moving, shimmying down the long length of his body, I swear it was visible, his body drastically relaxing, and then he fell.

CHAPTER TWENTY-EIGHT

August 23, 1948   The farm, Sioux City, and the country roads between them

I read that Babe Ruth died in his sleep a week ago. He'd been failing for some while, and all the world could see how thin and frail he was when he was honored a last time in June at Yankee Stadium. I saw it, that frailty, for myself just one week later, when we talked for maybe half an hour, but even so, when I read that he had died, I was startled to think how close to death he was that day. I shouldn't have been. For I felt a kind of shy magnificence coming from him for the time we sat together. I say "shy," and who could imagine choosing that word to describe Babe Ruth. What I mean is that I sensed he was self-conscious about his weakened strength, its quieter reach.

But magnificent too, his willful spirit coming through what I'll call his hesitation, as if he wanted to make it clear he wasn't interested in being dead before he died.

Cancer had eaten deep into his throat, and referring to it, he said, "I got a hole in the back of my mouth. It's as big as a cave. Fucking bats could live in there." He shook his head. "And my teeth hurt all the time." It was the only moment of complaint he voiced to me, and he spoke it with an air of begrudging awe at what your body could think up to do to itself. As if you had to tip your cap to it, the shit it could come up with.

The stroke my father suffered paralyzed his left side and made his face immobile. Over time, he's come to be able to offer us a speech of hard stops and moist elisions. There are helpful patterns in it that act as emphases and give shapes to his words, and when I talk to him I often imagine I'm hearing an untraceably primitive language that is not without its music. But his emotions move unpredictably, from grateful to volatile, from seemingly joyous to nearly opaque, behind the mask of his expressionless face. And it's still sometimes impossible, at least for me, to find a logic to them, to know why he reacts a certain way and not another. One day, the morning sunshine through the tall east-facing kitchen windows delights him; the next, his chair positioned in the same spot, it brings impatience, a sunlit agitation.

We learned that his heart routinely pauses for a quick off-beat, very quick, but that it happens over and over, and each time it does is likely time enough for blood to pool and form a clot and for the clot to fly up to his brain. They think that's what finally happened and, for that matter, could happen again at any time.

The doctor who explained this to us said we might think of my father's pausing heart as like a dancer who loses the band's beat and the rhythm of his steps and stops for an instant until he picks it up again. He seemed pleased with his metaphor, which sounded practiced to me, strained and fatuous. But it infuriated my grandmother, who said later he reminded her of the fool who got to the farm too late to save my mother.

We share his care, but my grandfather stays with him for most of the day, bathes and dresses him, which is an effort on those mornings when his own hands are especially stiff and painful. He makes their breakfast and their lunch; he sits and talks with him. I remember his observing, just after my father came home and our routines began to form, that the duties of the farm were the same, only reassigned. Now I was the farmer, my grandmother did the barnyard chores that didn't take great strength, while he presided, if you could call it that, at the stove and in the house, and I remember hearing this and thinking caustically that he hadn't thought through what my father's reassignment was in this new domestic order. I was being unfair to my grandfather, but the shock was so new, and I was thoughtless in my outrage. All three of us were, in our characteristic ways, taken up in bleak confusions, in dark and stunted disbeliefs.

I remember a sleepless night, early on, when I paused in the doorway before entering the kitchen from the parlor, surprised to see my grandmother sitting at the table in the dark. I'd thought she was upstairs asleep. She didn't see me; she was sitting right there, but far away in her anguish, and as I watched, I heard her quietly say, "Not again." I was sure I understood just what this meant. That this heartbreak couldn't be happening. That it couldn't *have* happened. Not again. Her sheer refusal to accept it. Or maybe she was giving a warning, saying—too late—*Don't you dare.* For it was plain that she was in a conversation, though I couldn't presume to know who—or what— she thought was hearing her. But her faintly whispered bitterness in the dark was a scream.

Later, I would think that because I hadn't known my mother, I hadn't lived the loss of her as my grandparents had. For me, this wasn't *Not again.* Mine was a first and, in that sense, a simpler, cleaner grief, at least as deep, but unlike theirs not doubly textured.

When I'd noticed the newspaper lying on the kitchen table, saying that Babe Ruth was coming to Sioux City, I thought it was a copy, more than twenty years old, from the day of the exhibition game, which my grandmother had saved and now, for some reason, had set out for me to read. But when I picked up the paper, I saw the date was June 18, that the year was this year, and I read that Ruth would be visiting in two days to promote an American Legion junior baseball program. The Ford Motor Company, one of its sponsors, was paying him to travel the country, holding clinics, talking about the program and his fabled baseball life.

After reading the article, I sat back and memories came. I do remember quite a lot, young as I was, and with so much coming at me, impressions colliding, overlapping as I lived them, and not one thing I wasn't avid for. Random moments, sensory flashes, are always there to be retrieved. The rough warmth of Gehrig's huge hand enveloping mine when he shook it. Running to darkness behind a tent where I could be sick before he reached me. Being mesmerized by Ruth's tobacco juice spitting style, the dip and lift of his cup a moving target, as though he were tracing a quick U in the air. The purple shadows on the mountains, that wondrous, gaudy purple, a color I hadn't dreamed nature had the wherewithal to make.

I remember my falling, in the moments I lay sprawled, and the sound of deadly hoofbeats, a herd stampeding. This is how it's stayed fixed in my mind. And along with that, my father's eyes when I met them, his fear a mirror of mine. And then the great dream-shock of being lifted up, held in Gehrig's arms, pressed against his chest, cocooned in his strength.

Two days later, the twentieth, a Sunday, was dry and hot; there was serious summer in it, and as I turned from our rutted path onto the newly graveled road, I rolled down the window. I felt the sun and smelled the loamy air. I heard the crunch of tires on the gravel as if it were the sound of moving time, breaking into its million tiny bits. Leaving the house, I'd told my grandmother I was going for a drive, and I felt as I said it that that's all I had in mind. I take these Sunday morning drives often, all through the year, each season has its pleasures, losing myself in the lift and roll and plane of crisscrossing country roads. I suppose it's what I've found as my hour of Sunday worship. But if I believed what I was telling her that morning, I doubt that she did for a minute. I'd been talking with her about seeing Ruth again.

I was highly curious, which was hardly a surprise, though the *depth* of my interest, my intrigue, was. But what I couldn't settle, really, was what to say to my father. It seemed a betrayal not to take him with me, and it seemed it would be every bit as cruel if I did. It seemed both these things, making their arguments, and I couldn't think it through to any sort of wisdom. His thoughts live far inside him, and his feelings, as I said, are just as hard to predict. Surely, he'd be upset to have Ruth see him so compromised. Frustrated to engage him in such a limited way. Or would it please him to be able to return for an hour to that special province of our past? But was that return remotely possible for him?

The evening before, with my father and grandfather asleep, I'd sat talking with my grandmother, and at some point I said, "I *could* just go and not tell him."

"You could," she said, and her pause was meditative, clearly for my benefit, pretending she felt the issue was elusive. "I suppose you could." And I understood that she was asking me if I honestly thought I could do that without feeling I'd deceived him.

I'd decided not to go.

As I drove, a mix of memories were once again going in my mind. Ruth's voice, its buoyant growl; his many ways of winking; how he filled a room with the big-hearted cunning of his personality; sitting next to him in Denver with my assignment to make sure the barrel end of his bat didn't touch the ground, *lousy luck if you let it touch the ground.*

I came to a crossroads, turned left instead of right for no reason, and I was thinking now of a moment at the end of Gehrig's farewell newsreel, after he'd finished speaking, after he'd said he'd caught a bad break with his health but had an awful lot to live for, after he'd acknowledged the fine-looking specimens of young men, the players, gathered around him. And just then Ruth came up and wrapped him in a clumsy embrace, almost knocking him down with the force of his affection, and whispered something in his ear that made Gehrig laugh, his dimples flashing.

What could you say, what could you whisper into an ear, that would bring such sudden life to such a lifeless face?

And even as I thought this, I knew I wouldn't ask Ruth what he'd said to Gehrig. The notion was absurd—his words as an elixir. It was fairy-tale alchemy. Besides, chances were better than good that he'd have no memory of it. And that's what I was thinking as I turned and headed the short distance to Sioux City. It was apparently what I'd needed: to know the thing I wouldn't ask him.

I'd just assumed he was giving his clinic in Stockyards Park, on the field where they'd played the exhibition game. But I arrived to find it empty, and I drove around, stopping several times to ask people, before I found a boy behind a lunch counter in a drugstore who knew where Ruth was appearing.

It was a high school field, with sets of bleachers behind home plate and along the foul lines. I could see as I was walking toward the infield that the clinic had finished. There were a few boys lingering, three or four of them listening to Ruth being interviewed behind home plate by a reporter with his notebook. Another man stood with them. He looked from a distance to resemble Ruth, his height, his size, his thick pomaded hair. The fluorescence of his bib-wide tie shone from twenty yards away. A paper banner for the American Legion, another for the Ford Motor Company, had been tied to the span of protective wire-mesh fence behind the batter's boxes.

I reached the bleachers and sat down. I was close enough to see Ruth's face and to note how thin he looked in a silk short-sleeved shirt and linen trousers. And this surprised me too—the way he was dressed. Without thinking, I'd pictured him in a baseball uniform. I leaned forward to try to hear what he was saying, but his voice was barely audible and I couldn't catch a word.

When the three of them shook hands, Ruth and the reporter and the man with the fluorescent tie, I stood and began to walk toward him. I wasn't hesitant or nervous, wanting very much to talk to him, however briefly, however much of his voice he had left to give me. I wasn't sure quite why, only that I did. I wasn't sure what I would ask him, only what I wouldn't.

I watched him shield his eyes from the high sun and cock his head as I approached. He looked expectant, ignorant, maybe vaguely annoyed, as if this stranger coming up to him meant there was some last thing on the schedule he'd forgotten.

The man and his tie stepped in front of Ruth to shield him. "And what, on behalf of the Ford Motor Company, can I do for you, young man, on this fine summer day in God's country?" His smile was a salesman's, an implement he kept handy and ready to flash. I could see now that he didn't really resemble Ruth, or maybe a little as he'd looked twenty years ago, when his face was round and his cheeks were fat and cancer hadn't eaten a hole in the back of his mouth big enough for fucking bats to live in.

I tried to look around the salesman to meet Ruth's eye. "Hello, Babe," I said. This sounded strange to my ear. I'd only called him "Mr. Ruth," and no more than a few times at that.

He frowned, but not in a hostile way. He must have assumed now that I was just a wayward fan who'd gotten there too late to hear him reminiscing. I thought I saw him looking for whatever I'd brought with me for him to sign.

"We're all closed up here," the Ford salesman said. "The Babe's had a long morning, he needs to get some rest, and after that we have to be some place." His words were bouncy, like a jingle's.

"Of course," I said. And I surprised myself, feeling something in me that was ready to risk rudeness. "It won't take long."

"*What* won't?" the salesman said. "I'm sure I'm not following. Who are you anyway?"

"I'm Henry Dunham." Again I looked past him so I could say this to Ruth. But it too sounded ridiculous, like an announcement I was making, and I would read in his obituary that he had no memory for names anyway. That he'd found a way around this, calling everyone "doc" or "kid." I hadn't remembered that, if I'd even noticed it at the time.

"Nice to meet 'ya, kid." He held his frown.

I said it was nice to meet him too. "But we've met before. I'd love if we could talk a few minutes."

"Like I was saying," the Ford salesman said. "Maybe Babe can sign an autograph for you, but then you really—"

"Oh, yeah?" Ruth said to me. "Where was it? Where'd we meet?" He laughed weakly, seeming surprisingly entertained, as if this were an exchange he'd had so many times over the years—someone saying they'd met and his asking where—and the predictable repetition as he recited his lines amused him.

"Here," I said. "We met here."

"Here?" Ruth said.

"Here?" the salesman said.

"When you played the exhibition here. I was a kid. It was twenty years—"

"Wait." The reporter had been silent. "Your name's Dunham, you said? Are you *Earl* Dunham's boy?"

I said I was, and the reporter stepped forward and shook my hand. He said his name was Hubert Hodge, but everyone called him Hub.

He said he'd bet my father would remember him. Hub Hodge. He'd stayed quiet, in the background, listening, and I hadn't really taken him in. He was as tall as I, and very thin; he seemed mostly his long neck. He looked remarkably like Ichabod Crane in my illustrated copy of the story.

"So that makes you the kid who took the tumble." I heard an uncertain note in his voice, as if I didn't fit the picture, his idea of that foolish little boy who'd grown up to be the man he was talking to.

I said, "Guilty as charged and clumsy as ever."

His head sat like an arrangement atop his very long neck, and he was shaking it slightly. "*Damn*, he was good."

To this I nodded, and my smile was lighter than his.

Ruth and the Ford salesman were walking away, and I feared they were leaving. But I was relieved to see them heading for the bleachers, and I noticed only then that Ruth was using a baseball bat as a cane, leaning on it, the barrel head pushing into the grass.

Hodge said, "I do other things at the paper now, but I still cover sports when I want. I watched your dad pitch, what? Five, six years? More?" His mouth was now a line of serious smile. "He got hurt if I remember. *Do* I remember? Am I right?"

"Yeah," I said. "He did."

"I forget now. It was something else, right? I mean, it wasn't in a game. He hurt it doing something else."

Such nostalgia coming at me, a veritable ambush of it. "No," I said, "he hurt it pitching."

"Really. You're sure. I mean, you're his son, of course you're sure. So he hurt it pitching. In a game."

"A *great* game," I said. "I never saw him better."

"Huh," Hodge said. "The things you think you know, and then you find out you don't. I wonder why . . . I guess I wasn't there."

"I guess you weren't," I said, "but I was."

"*You* were. Right! Of course!" He nodded past me to where Ruth was sitting with the salesman. "I wasn't there for *that* game either. I was counting the days. Hell, everybody was. The chance to see the two of them? But wouldn't you know, the wife was pregnant with our first, and damned if she didn't go into labor that morning, and we had our sweet baby girl that afternoon. I always think of her as arriving in the bottom of the third, sliding safely, on her back, headfirst, into home." He laughed. "I had the bright idea to name her 'Ruth,' but the wife put her foot down, wouldn't hear of it."

I looked in Ruth's direction, frankly surprised to see him still waiting for me, and thinking he might reasonably lose his patience any moment. "I really should go."

"I was asking him about it just now," Hodge said. "I asked him, what could he remember about the day, and he said, 'To tell you the truth, not a fucking thing.' He said I should stop and think about it, that I had to realize it was eons ago, his memory was a sieve, always had been, and a whole lot of games, not to mention a whole lot of life, which he couldn't remember either, had got lived since then." He made a wet, clicking sound with his twitching cheek. "I get it. He seems pretty weak."

We stood there, he seemed to be finished, then shook hands again, and he asked to be greeted to my father. "So what's he up to these days?"

Impatient as I was, I needed a moment to think through what I didn't want to say, for my father's sake I thought. "Still not pitching," I said.

"Well, tell him Hub Hodge said hello." A look I couldn't read came to his face, but I imagined he was seeing a picture in his mind of my father performing in a game. Then he made a breathy smile of sound, there was lively fondness in it, and he said, "I mean, *Goddamn*."

He hurried off then, and I stood watching him, feeling incredibly grateful for that *Goddamn*. As I said, its awe was alive, *not* a memory, but the thing he was still feeling about a thing still there to feel. But my instinct was to think that though I understood my gratitude, it was out of all proportion, and I wouldn't see until I was driving home that I was wrong to think this.

I walked quickly to the bleachers and sat down next to Ruth. I thanked him for staying and said I'd meant it; I wouldn't keep him long.

He nodded. "Yeah. I got some place I need to be." I thought, his saying this, that he was making fun of the salesman, who stood then and said he'd take a walk around the block, but he'd be back in a few minutes because the Babe was telling it right; there *was* the next place they needed to be.

Sitting beside him, it was very hard at first to see past, see through his sickly pallor, and I kept catching myself speaking too loudly and smiling too broadly as a way of telling him how well I thought he looked. I even said it explicitly, and that's when he looked at me, a frankness in his eyes, and said, "*How* long ago? Tell me again, *what's* the year we met?"

I told him, and he nodded. He said, "The year I hit sixty." And then, "Well if that's when we met, you're really full of shit, telling me you think I look good now."

I started to protest, but he waved it away and laughed a noiseless laugh, and that's when he told me memorably about the hole in the back of his mouth.

The next minutes, fifteen, twenty, a little longer, started with frustration. I felt it strongly as I described the day and he recalled so little of it. But as we continued talking—*Remember? Kind of. Remember? Maybe. Remember? Hell, I don't know, a little*—I heard it more and more, the rhythm of our back and forth, as like a comic sketch. I believe he was hearing something of the same thing, for I sensed him relaxing, settling in, despite the fact that his teeth must have been hurting, since they hurt all the time.

Thinking now, it might be true that in his life, no matter what, he looked for the comedy at the center of it.

No, he said, he *didn't* remember that I fell on my face, the crowd streaming onto the field, didn't remember it in particular, it was all mixed together since something like that happened almost every game on a barnstorming tour, like the time a mob knocked *him* down and *he* would've gotten trampled if he hadn't grabbed the tail of a mounted policeman's horse and got dragged away to safety, so how could I expect him to remember the close call *I* had, since there wasn't even a fucking horse in the story? And as for Gehrig saving me, he never would have thought slow old Lou could get there in time, which made me one lucky little bastard.

He didn't remember my father, or I should say he didn't remember him as Earl the pitcher, though the memory of the two of us, a father and his son riding with them, it *did* come back to him a little now that I mentioned it. That a couple of extras, as he called us, were in the Pullman for a while.

"So why'd that happen, anyway? Why'd you come along?"

I told him I remembered that it was Gehrig's idea really, and he said, well, good for him, that they'd had their differences later on, but he was a sweet man, all things considered. And good for me and my pop, we got our ride, we had some fun, and I was probably thinking all the time, *This is the cat's sweet cream on Sunday.*

He didn't remember my father's getting hurt, though he faintly recollected us, the extras, going home early, before the tour had finished.

He didn't ask me anything about him or why he wasn't with me now, or about me, the only thing he wondered was, "So you skipped the war?" I said I'd been exempted, a farmer growing grain and raising livestock, and he thought about this for a moment before nodding his head. "Makes sense, I guess," he said. "Everybody had to eat."

I didn't ask him if he had any recollection of what he'd whispered in Gehrig's ear that day, though I confess that in the moment, I was suddenly, foolishly tempted to.

And then he said, "Hey!" abruptly, as if he felt it in his body, the jarring impact of a memory suddenly arriving, a strong memory of the rain, the night of lightning and crazed rain, and of our being held in Green River.

"We was stuck there, what, a *week*, right? Christ. The place was a swamp." Then, "But you know what I'm remembering, *here's* a memory for you"—his voice more energetic now, as if he'd surprised himself, retrieving something from the past—"we found this joint one night, had a piano and a couple of really foxy broads, singers with big blonde wigs and fucking poured into their dresses, and how I remember it I was sitting there thinking, where'd *this* place come from, everybody having a good time, laughing their asses off at the naughty songs, and the booze as good as Canada, as close to the real thing as it gets? How'd it end up *here*?"

He laughed, and I could see he wanted to stay there in his mind, just where he was, taking it all in from his table, listening to the singers and looking around the room, hearing the happy noise. He was far from where I'd hoped he'd be, from what he might remember, though even then I still wasn't certain what I wanted. I knew I had no right and certainly no chance to change anything, since that's where our talking had taken him. But now that a fine, full memory had appeared, I hoped it would yield another and another, and lead him to where we, my father and I, were waiting for it.

"So there you go," he said. "I got you one." He sounded pleased with himself and with his gift to me.

"A memory of the trip." I nodded. "Yes, you did."

He looked at me. He must have heard my disappointment. "Oh, right," he said. "You two ain't in it. Sorry."

But he offered nothing more, and we got quiet then. And in our silence I heard myself asking about Gehrig. But not about that. Just the plainest questions. He'd said they had their differences, and I wondered, then, whether they'd spent any time together in the years before he died. And if so, how he'd seemed—his stamina, his spirits. Once more, I pictured Gehrig in the newsreel, standing slumped and unsteady, looking as if he knew the loudest cheers he'd ever heard were those he was hearing right then, as if it were he and his illness, the two of them together, their ghastly teamwork, that people were applauding. And it felt to me that if I spoke of him now, I'd be asking all that Ruth was working so hard to refuse, asking it to come and sit right there between us.

And then we saw the Ford salesman heading up the sidewalk. He veered onto the field, ambling awkwardly toward us, and I had the thought again that he did resemble Ruth.

"I'll say this for that tie," Ruth said about the salesman's as he reached the infield. "It fucking lets you know he's coming."

I chuckled, he did too, and I stood. I put my hand on his shoulder to say, no, he didn't need to. We shook hands, his grip was firm, and I thanked him, meaning it more than I heard my voice conveying. I'd expected to feel thankful, I'd expected to mean it when I said so, but how foolish I was to think my thanks could have been a simple thing to say.

"Say 'hi' to your old man," he said.

"I will," I said, both of us pretending, Ruth that he truly remembered him, and me that it would be a casual, uncomplicated thing to tell him.

The salesman reached us then, and before he could speak, I said I was just leaving. That I knew they had some place they needed to be.

I wished Ruth luck, and he said, "Yeah. I wish me luck too." His smile looked tired. And maybe what I described, what I've thought of as a shyness, was merely that; that he'd spent his energy on his morning and our talk, and they'd made him very tired.

It's just four miles, a little longer, from Sioux City to the farm, but I needed more time than that. Quickly back on the country roads, I began a slow, vaguely northerly route to nowhere in particular, except not home, not yet. As I drove, I felt my thoughts encompassing all that Ruth hadn't remembered. I was struck by the powerful need I'd felt for him to recall the day, the tour, my father and me. What had I been looking for? A validation, it seemed, but of what, and why?

I was thinking too of Ruth himself, the badly battered marvel of what was left of him. I saw him now as a kind of valiant hobo trudging through his days, carrying his history, and his reservoir of strength, and whatever else he hadn't lost, in a huge kit bag.

I slowed down even more, traveling the new June land. Looking up, I sensed, as I often did, that the bright sky was the world. I sometimes think, and for obvious reasons I was thinking it that day, of this landscape compared to the one I watched from the Pullman. The way I'd seen the mountains jutting up to claim every bit of the beauty in the world for themselves. And how the more I got used to being surprised by this, the more that everything I saw surprised me. Which means,

I guess, that I sensed even as a child that you could admire that land-scape, you could be humbled, made speechless, by it. But there was no way to feel invited *into* it. At least none I felt then or could imagine now. Here, I sense the land's dependence, sense it needing me. The ordered beauty of this landscape is the fields, and the fields aren't fields until you make them.

I drove, and as I did it came to me that I couldn't fathom not telling my father something of the day.

I was thinking I could say, *Let me tell you who I saw.*

I could say, *You'll be surprised to hear . . . You'll never guess.*

I could say, *Someone you played ball with asked me to say "hi." And someone else who loved to watch you pitch asked me to say the same.*

I had it in my mind that I could start with something like that and, less than hearing what he said in response, or tried to say, I would focus on his eyes and let them tell me where to take it next, then next, then after that. Or maybe they, along with the blunt notes of his words, would tell me to stop right there, not take it any further. Surely I could do that much without needing to get back anything from him that reassured me I'd been right not to take him with me.

"I talked to his eyes," Alice had said, the first time she met my father. "I just talked to them and they talked to me."

Her name is Alice Toller, we've been seeing each other just a short while, six months or so, and the day she said that, describing her and my father and their first, easy conversation, she spoke of it as something natural, obvious, nothing remarkable about it, and I realized I was in love with her. When she visits with him, when their eyes converse, she speaks simply of her day, what she's been reading, of some silly thing a customer where she works has said, and her voice becomes low and languid, but still and always with the lift of inclusion in it.

She's the daughter of a druggist in Sioux City, a slender, lively woman, and it's that, her wonderful vibrancy, that makes her so beautiful to me. She sometimes wears her long, blonde hair in braids, and she was wearing them the morning we met. I'd come to the pharmacy to pick up some medication for my grandfather. She was working that day, and when she handed me the pills, I blurted, "Heidi!" Something in her manner, so open and inviting, made me feel I had permission, and she laughed and said, *Well,* hidee *to you too,* and I laughed then as well and said, *I meant your braids,* and she said, *Ahh. But I'll warn you right off, I don't yodel, so don't ask,* and that was pretty much that. Her beauty, her ease, her sense of humor. I saw it, heard it, felt it all in an instant.

When I think of Alice and how quickly I've fallen in love with her, I sometimes remember what Horace Meadows said to me. It was the last night my father and I were with them all, though of course we didn't know that yet. Horace and I were alone in the Pullman kitchen, everyone else out somewhere in Green River (it was the night of Ruth's memory, I now suspect, which meant my father was there too and Ruth hadn't mentioned him), and he must have decided he could relax and have a drink or two while I ate a piece of an apple pie he'd just baked.

We talked with the warm familiarity, I would say, from the place of affection we had reached. We talked of this and that, of the power of Mother Nature, the strength of rain, the damage that rushing waters could do to railroad tracks, which a man would think were indestructible, and as I remember, he said it was his sense that we'd be on our way by the next afternoon. When Horace felt he could relax (and I'm pleased to think he could feel that way with me), he moved his hands in subtle sweeps as he talked, as if he'd freed them from a kind of required deportment, and I tried that night, as I always did, to glimpse his pink palms, which fascinated me, their skin looking newly grown and much too tender.

It seemed a change of subject when he said next that he wanted to repeat he was grateful for a suggestion I'd made during one of our talks, that since he'd had no luck meeting the right woman, he might find Mormon wives aplenty once we got to Utah. And then, out of nowhere, surely helped by the whiskey, he leaned forward and said the most astonishing thing to me. He said that the parable of love, the lesson of it, was that before a man lets it have him, he must do his blessed best to find out what might doom it, even as he knows it takes you up before you can.

I had no idea what to say to this, young as I was, and I know I don't quite have it, its intricate twists, the sudden turn it takes from "him" to "you" and moving toward a kind of helpless fate at the finish. But I'm confident I'm close to quoting him from memory, for I was entirely charmed by the mystery of what he said, and of certain words and phrases—parable, doom, blessed best—each one resonant on its own and sounding so particular to Horace and the moment. It was as if they'd never been spoken by anyone but him, and not until right then. I was taken too with his voice, without its usual melody, as if somehow imported, with the rhythm and the reverence of an oracle's about it.

I've wondered what it was, who it was, in Horace Meadows's past that led him to fashion his warning parable. And what I feel more sure of every day, as it fits my feelings for Alice, is that they're hurrying toward an absolutely lovely lifelong doom.

She asked me recently to take her to a show of French Impressionists at the museum in Omaha. She'd read that it was coming and thought we both should see it. We moved among the paintings, vast landscapes and intimate ones too, looking and feeling their beautifully muted allusions as we stood in front of them, and at one point, standing close to me, she said, "I wanted to see how you see it." I didn't need to ask her what she meant. She meant the land. How I see the land. I'd tried a few weeks before to describe for her how, working a field, I became alertly absent-minded—a contradictory phrase, I knew, but the one that best explained it. And how, following crop rows to their end, I sometimes felt myself moving straight into the sky, not *toward* it, *into* it, breathing it greedily, its blue infinity.

There's a ball room in Sioux City where touring orchestras play. Harry James and Glen Miller and, one week, Benny Goodman. She's a wonderful dancer, and I'm a fairly good one too. We move smoothly, our steps conventional. We hear the music as lush and full of sass.

A week or so ago, my grandfather teased me that Alice was saving me from a future as one of those miserly, odd-duck bachelor farmers.

I laughed, agreeing, and I do see how right he was. How, with all the ways I love what the work asks of me, I might have been unconsciously heading for that solitude with its fixed and routine seasons, until one day, maybe twenty years from now, I'd look around and ask myself how it had happened that the life I saw around me was the one I'd settled for.

I drove, replaying the day, my talk with Ruth, once more, and thinking now of the chances I'd had to speak of my father and how I'd turned away from them each time. When Hubert Hodge had asked what he was up to these days. When I'd said nothing to Ruth about why he hadn't come. When, as I was leaving, he'd said to say hello and I'd said I would, as though if I said *that*, it was all I'd need to say. And as I thought more about my cowardly avoidance, I began to think I knew something more of why I'd felt such a pull to see Ruth again. And what I'd hoped for in wishing he'd recalled us and those days.

I hadn't known how much I was wanting to remember who my father had been. To have him back, the man in full—not just his skills with a baseball, that least of all, but wanting his strength and his wit and his warmth returned to me—even if for a short while. And it had seemed I needed someone who'd known him only as that man. So I'd come to see Babe Ruth—not knowing how close he was to dying and that his memory had always been a sieve—thinking I couldn't bring my father with me; thinking, how could Ruth tell me who my father had been if he were distracted by seeing who he was now?

Pure selfishness then, running as deep as selfishness runs, and yet I got what I had come for, a piece of unearned luck, bless Hubert Hodge's soul and his faraway smile and the light rhapsody of his priceless *Goddamn.*

I turned south, toward the farm, remembering what I'd found when I got to my father that day. How he lay partially beneath the oblivious cow, looking up into her pale and blue-veined udder, in the spreading puddle of milk and wet straw. The left side of his face had begun its fall, his mouth down-slanting to a rictus, and as I crouched beside him he began to struggle, to use the strength he had, all of it, to turn his head, bits of straw clinging to his hair, toward a wide band of late-day sunlight where the barn's sliding doors hadn't been closed.

And as I drove I understood I should have seen right then that who he'd been was who he would be.

I'd needed no one else to tell me. *He'd* been telling me. For I'd watched my father's eyes. They were quick with life.

I dreamed, after reading that Ruth had died, that he was standing at the window of a hotel room, waving down to a crowd of boys who'd gathered below, hoping to get a glimpse of him. I was one of them, about the age I'd been, just shy of ten, when I'd lived those few enchanted days.

We were all waving back up to him and calling his name. There was a breeze of worship in our voices. Then he raised his window, his fisted hands reached out, and he opened them to release pieces of paper into the air. They floated down like confetti, and all of us started jumping up to try to snatch them, greedy to catch as many as we could for the sheer sport of it, not knowing he'd written his Palmer-perfect signature on every slip. He dropped still more, dozens and dozens of slips of paper falling, a summer snow of Babe Ruth's autographs. He stood at his window, still smiling, and I somehow understood that in his mind he was sending money, a kind of currency, floating down to us. I suspect his signature is worth far less than it was at the peak of his fame. But if that is so, if it's true in life, it was not true in my dream.

We began to scuffle for position, push and shove, but the contest was festive, and there, in the midst of the scrum, I saw my father. He was a child too, in tweed knickers and a wool newsboy cap, his face fair and soft and round, a cupid's, not the long, strong-boned face his was and mine has become. But I knew instantly that it was him, and he saw that I did, for he paused, caught my eye, and laughed, shouting through his laughter, "How many have you got?" And I shouted, "None yet!" He shouted back, "Me neither! I'll give you mine if I get any!" and then, next, as he was jumping up to try to snag one, "God, this is fun! Isn't this fun!?"

"Yes!" I called, exuberant now, and when I looked at him again I saw a boy who was my friend and a man who was my father. He was both in the dream, and I would say, too, in my life, and that laughing voice was his, was just as it had sounded.

ACKNOWLEDGMENTS

//

Measureless thanks to my agent, Henry Dunow, and my editor, James McCoy. How'd I get so lucky?

My gratitude for their more than generous help and support goes to Carol Bauer, and for her photos of the Denver neighborhood where a baseball park once stood; to Eric H. Bowen, for his willingness to answer endless questions about the history of train travel, and for his website, streamlinersschedules.com; to Lacey Fullerton at the Sioux City Public Library; to Todd Gilbert at the New York Transit Museum; to Edward B. Herwick III at the WGBH Curiosity Desk, for his story on the 1918 influenza pandemic; to Marcy Peterson and Barry Poe at the *Sioux City Journal*; and to Matt Rothenberg at the Baseball Hall of Fame.

These books were invaluable to me in writing mine: *Kyrie*, by Ellen Bryant Voigt; *One Summer: America, 1927*, by Bill Bryson; *Babe: The Legend Comes to Life*, by Robert S. Creamer; *Luckiest Man: The Life and Death of Lou Gehrig*, by Jonathan Eig; *The Given Day*, by Dennis Lehane; *Night Trains: The Pullman System in the Golden Age of Trains*, by Peter T. Maiken; *Pitching in a Pinch: Baseball from the Inside*, by Christy Mathewson; *They Came Like Swallows*, by William Maxwell; *The Big Bam: The Life and Times of Babe Ruth*, by Leigh Montville. Also, the websites Baseballhistorydaily.com and the Center for Negro League Baseball Research's cnlbr.org were extremely helpful.

Such family and friends! For asking how it was going at the uncannily right time and actually wanting to know: Sam Allis, Paul Astorino, Jack Beatty, Rebecca Boucher, Kate Canfield, Henri Cole, Joe Finder,

Craig Holt, Katie Hurlbut, Ben Miller, Zoe Miller, Leigh Montville, Kevin O'Hara, Lynne O'Hara, Michele Souda, Michael Thurston, Chris Walsh, John Wapner, Jay Wickersham, Joan Wickersham, and Laura Zigman. Too, my debt runs deep to the staff, faculty, and students at the Bennington Writing Seminars for making the life of literature the life one wants to live. Also to Dr. Steven Spector, for his knowledge of medical procedures as they would have been practiced in 1927.